THE COMPEN
MYTHICAL ARTIFACTS

Volume 1

The Compendium of Mythical Artifacts – Volume 1

This book is a work of fiction. Some characters, incidents, and dialogues are products of the author's imagination and are not to be construed as real. Any resemblance to actual events, locales, organizations, or persons, living or dead, is entirely coincidental.

Disclaimer: The information and content provided in this book are for general informational purposes only. While every effort has been made to ensure the accuracy and completeness of the information presented, the author makes no representations or warranties of any kind, express or implied, about the completeness, accuracy, reliability, suitability, or availability with respect to the book or the information contained herein. Any reliance you place on such information is strictly at your own risk.

The author disclaims any liability for any loss, damage, or injury caused by the use or misuse of the information presented in this book. It is advised to consult appropriate professionals or experts for specific advice related to individual situations or circumstances.

ISBN: (Paperback): 9789359801049

For inquiries or permissions requests, please contact:
author.nileshprabhu@gmail.com

Words from the Author

Dear Reader,

As you turn these pages, you are about to embark on a journey unlike any other – a voyage through time, cultures, and imaginations, visiting relics of tales that have shaped and been shaped by countless generations.

My fascination with mythical artifacts began when I was just a child, listening with wide-eyed wonder to stories of magical swords, enchanted amulets, and talismans that held the power to change fate. These weren't just objects; they were the heartbeats of legends, the symbols of cultures, and the dreams of civilizations that once were and continue to inspire.

This book is the culmination of months of research, passion, and a deep reverence for the power of storytelling. Each artifact presented here offers a window into the psyche of its origin culture and serves as a testament to humanity's age-old desire to understand, explain, and influence the world around us.

Whether you're a lover of mythology, a history enthusiast, or someone seeking to lose yourself in tales of wonders and mysteries, I hope this compendium serves as a bridge to those ancient worlds and sparks the same sense of wonder in you that I felt during my first encounter with these tales.

Thank you for allowing me to share this passion with you. May you find as much delight in these tales as I did in curating them for you.

So, turn the pages, immerse yourself in the stories, and let your imagination roam freely among the gods, heroes, and epic quests that have shaped our collective human imagination. May this compendium be a key that unlocks the doors to worlds both familiar and fantastical.

Preface

Throughout the passage of time, myths have been the bedrock of human civilization, forging connections, evoking emotions, and giving rise to countless cultural narratives. They serve as both mirrors and windows—reflecting societal values while opening vistas to worlds unknown. It's within these intricate narratives that artifacts emerge as powerful protagonists, intertwining fate with function, magic with might.

Every civilization, from the soaring empires of old to small isolated tribes, has its cherished tales of artifacts that boast abilities far surpassing ordinary confines. Whether they're seen as gifts from the gods, curses to be wary of, or tools for heroes on their epic quests, these items encapsulate the hopes, fears, and aspirations of the people who revered them.

In this compendium, we journey through a labyrinth of tales, uncovering the stories and secrets behind these fabled objects. Each entry seeks to illuminate not just the artifact itself but also the context in which it was conceived—the historical backdrop, the societal values, and the intricate web of myths that gave birth to it. While stalwarts like Excalibur or the Golden Fleece might be tales retold across generations, this collection also shines a light on the less-chronicled, yet equally enchanting artifacts that have been overshadowed with time.

Assembling this compendium has been a task of reverence and research. With every page, there's an endeavor to fuse ancient traditions with contemporary interpretations, offering readers a collage of insights that spans epochs. Myths may be tales of yore, but their resonance is timeless. In understanding these artifacts, we not only delve deep into the mythological realms but also uncover nuances of human nature, desire, and imagination.

It's my aspiration that as you navigate this compendium, you experience a blend of nostalgia and discovery, recognizing familiar tales while unearthing new stories, all the while appreciating the profound impact these mythical artifacts have had on the chronicles of human storytelling.

Table of Contents

Greek Mythology

9 Aegis
41 Armor of Achilles
46 Bag of Wind
68 Caduceus
73 Cap of Hermes
81 Club of Heracles
88 Crown of Immortality
129 Girdle of Aphrodite
132 Golden Fleece
166 Horn of Plenty
194 Mandrake
223 Pandora's Box
239 Ring of Gyges
252 Scythe of Cronos
259 Talaria

Hindu Mythology

16 Amrita
184 Kaumodaki
227 Pasha
255 Sudarshan Chakra

Norse Mythology

32 Andvaranaut
38 Apples of Idunn
63 Brisingamen
91 Draupnir
137 Gungnir
154 Heimdalr's Horn
158 Helskor boots
162 Hliðskjálf
175 Járngreipr
203 Megingjörð
207 Mjolnir

Asian Mythology

21 Amenonuhoko
77 Chintamani Stone
142 Hagoromo
150 Headband of Sun Wukong
171 Jade Books in Heaven
179 Kusanagi no Tsurugi
243 Ruyi Jingu Bang
268 Yasakani no Magatama
271 Yata no Kagami

Table of Contents

Celtic & British Mythology

52 Cauldron of Dagda

85 Cohuleen Druith

95 Dyrnwyn

100 Excalibur

111 Fairy Flag of Dunvegan

121 Fragarach

125 Gáe Bulg

146 Harp of Dagda

213 Nanteos Cup

264 The Boots of Seven Leagues

Egyptian Mythology

26 Ankh

57 Book of Thoth

107 Eye of Horus

Other Origins

116 Fountain of Youth

188 Lance of Longinus

198 Maui's Fishhook

217 Necronomicon

233 Philosopher's Stone

247 Sampo

Aegis

In the vast mosaic of Greek mythology, few artifacts capture the imagination quite like the Aegis. More than a mere shield or cloak, the Aegis embodies divine might, protection, and authority, primarily associated with Zeus, the sky and thunder god, and Athena, his wisdom-wielding daughter.

The Aegis finds its roots deep within the chronicles of ancient Greek lore. The myths often waver between it being a possession of Zeus or Athena, though both have been depicted with it. Its name derives from the Greek "aigis," meaning "goat skin." This etymology traces back to the legend of the sacred goat Amalthea, who nurtured the infant Zeus. Upon her death, her hide was said to have been used to create the Aegis, symbolizing protection and nurturing.

While the Aegis's representation varies, it is most famously depicted as a protective cloak or shield, ornate in design. The centerpiece, a Gorgon's head (often Medusa's), serves as both a deterrent and a symbol of power. Occasionally portrayed as serpents, Tassels fringe its borders, a testament to its intricate craftsmanship and the deadly nature it encapsulates.

The Aegis's primary power lies in its ability to invoke fear and reverence. Merely bearing it could sway the tide of battles, as enemies were often paralyzed by its daunting visage. Aligned with Zeus's control over natural phenomena, the Aegis, when brandished, could summon thunderstorms, encapsulating the tempestuous wrath of the gods.

The Sacred Goat Amalthea

One of the earliest tales regarding the Aegis's origin links it to Amalthea, the divine goat that nourished the infant Zeus while he was hidden from his father, Cronus.

Cronus, the ruler of the Titans and father to several Olympian gods, was foretold a prophecy that one of his children would overthrow him, much like he had done to his own father, Uranus. To prevent this, every time his wife Rhea gave birth, he would swallow the child whole.

When it was time for Zeus, the youngest, to be born, Rhea, desperate to save her child, devised a plan. Rhea gave birth to Zeus in secret on the island of Crete. To deceive Cronus, she handed him a stone wrapped in swaddling clothes, which he promptly swallowed, thinking it was his son. Meanwhile, the infant Zeus was hidden in a cave on Mount Ida, shielded from his father's prying eyes and wrath.

In this secluded and protected environment, Zeus was cared for by nymphs and fed by the she-goat Amalthea. Some versions of the myth present Amalthea as a nymph with a goat's form, while others describe her strictly as a divine goat. Regardless of the specifics, Amalthea's role was crucial: she nourished the young god, providing him with her milk, and ensuring he grew strong and resilient.

As Zeus grew and eventually fulfilled the prophecy by overthrowing Cronus and the Titans, he never forgot the protection and nurturing he received during his infancy. Upon Amalthea's death, her hide was used to craft the Aegis, a powerful shield or breastplate.

This transformation served multiple purposes: it was a commemoration of the goat that had played a pivotal role in Zeus's life, and it imbued the Aegis with symbolic meanings of protection and nurturing, reflective of Amalthea's role in Zeus's infancy.

Zeus, the Thunderbearer

Before looking into Zeus's relationship with the Aegis, it's important to understand his journey. After overthrowing his father, Cronus, and liberating his siblings, Zeus led the Olympian gods in the Titanomachy, the great war against the Titans. His victory solidified his position as the king of the gods and ruler of the sky, asserting his dominion over the heavens and celestial phenomena.

As with many rulers, both mortal and divine, symbols of authority and power are paramount. For Zeus, these symbols included his thunderbolts and the Aegis. While the thunderbolts were his weapons, instruments of punishment, and assertion, the Aegis was both a protective and offensive tool.

The Aegis, often described as a shield or protective cloak, bore the Gorgon's head (usually Medusa's), turning it into a formidable instrument. When Zeus brandished the Aegis, the very atmosphere would change: clouds would gather, thunder would roll, and lightning would pierce the skies. This was not just a display of his power but also a manifestation of his wrath or intent. In moments of cosmic upheaval or conflict, Zeus would wield the Aegis to rally the gods. Its sight was not only a beacon for divine unity but also a signal that their leader was ready for battle.

During events like the Gigantomachy (the battle against the Giants) or skirmishes against monsters, the Aegis served as both a standard and a deterrent.

Zeus's relationship with the Aegis wasn't exclusive. Athena, his favored daughter, also bore the Aegis in many myths. However, when Zeus wielded it, it was often in a context of universal or cosmic importance, emphasizing his role as the principal deity and protector of the divine order.

Athena and Medusa

Medusa was once a priestess in Athena's temple and was renowned for her beauty, particularly her striking hair. Legend has it that Poseidon, enamored by her beauty, pursued her. Medusa, trying to evade him, sought refuge in Athena's temple. However, Poseidon caught up with her, and they became entangled within the sacred temple's walls. Athena, viewing this act as a desecration of her temple and a violation of a priestess's vow of celibacy, transformed Medusa into a Gorgon. As a Gorgon, her once beautiful hair became a tangle of venomous snakes, and her gaze had the power to turn any onlooker to stone.

Perseus, a Greek hero, was tasked with bringing back the head of Medusa. This was not a simple heroic quest but rather a devious plan by King Polydectes, who hoped Perseus would fail and never return because he had his sights set on Perseus' mother, Danaë.

With the help of the gods, including Athena and Hermes, Perseus was equipped with divine tools to aid in his quest: winged sandals to fly, a cap to render him invisible, a sword, and a reflective shield. Athena, being a strategic and wise goddess, advised Perseus to use the reflective shield as a mirror to avoid looking directly at Medusa and being turned to stone. Using the Helm of Darkness to remain unseen, Perseus flew to the Gorgons' lair with the winged sandals. To avoid being turned into stone, he did not look directly at Medusa. Using the reflective surface of his shield as a tool, Perseus faced Medusa. When she opened her eyes, her petrifying gaze was reflected back onto herself, momentarily stunning her. Seizing this opportunity, Perseus approached and swiftly decapitated her with his sword.

After slaying Medusa, Perseus used her severed head as a weapon in various other confrontations due to its petrifying gaze. The most notable instance was when he saved Andromeda from the sea monster Cetus by turning the creature into stone using Medusa's gaze. However, after his adventures concluded, he gave the Gorgon's head to Athena.

In a blend of respect, remembrance, and power, Athena with the help of Hephaestus, affixed Medusa's head to the center of her Aegis. Some interpretations suggest this act was to commemorate the tragic tale of Medusa and to serve as a reminder of the consequences of desecrating sacred spaces. Others opine it was a strategic move, enhancing the Aegis's power. The head of Medusa on the Aegis exemplified ultimate protection, as enemies would be petrified by its mere sight.

The Aegis, when wielded by Athena, becomes more than just a tool—it's an extension of her essence. As the goddess of strategic warfare (as opposed to the more brutal, violent warfare represented by Ares), the Aegis's defensive and offensive capabilities reflect Athena's balanced approach to conflict. Athena's patronage extends to numerous heroes and cities in Greek mythology. Perhaps most famously, she is the patron goddess of Athens, having gifted the city with the olive tree. In various myths, when these heroes or cities faced threats, Athena often intervened, wielding the Aegis to protect or empower her proteges.

In Homer's Iliad, the Trojan War provides several instances where Athena's intervention, often accompanied by the Aegis, plays a pivotal role. One memorable moment is when she descends to the battlefield to aid Diomedes. With the Aegis and her guidance, Diomedes becomes a force of nature on the battlefield, even daring to wound gods opposing the Greek forces.

In another instance, to instigate conflict and prevent a truce between the Trojans and Achaeans, Athena descends to the battlefield. Concealed by the Aegis, she tricks the Trojan archer Pandarus into breaking the truce, reigniting the war's fury.

The Aegis, especially with the Gorgon's head, embodies both protection and terror. When Athena bore the Aegis into battle or in defense of a city, it acted as a deterrent, its fearsome visage instilling terror in enemies. Conversely, for allies, it was a symbol of divine protection and favor, an assurance that Athena was watching over them.

The enduring legacy of the Aegis is evident in our modern vernacular with phrases like "under someone's aegis," symbolizing protection or endorsement. Its influence permeates modern media, with the Aegis being featured in films, literature, and video games that draw inspiration from Greek mythology. Its portrayal, while evolving, continues to emphasize the themes of divine might and protection.

As a nexus of power, protection, and divine authority, the Aegis encapsulates the grandeur and might of the Greek pantheon. Its legacy, transcending millennia, remains a testament to the timeless allure of Greek mythology. In every strand of its lore, from its intricate design to its awe-inspiring powers, the Aegis serves as a beacon of the divine's direct influence on mortal affairs.

Sources/Further Reading:

Hesiod. Theogony.
Homer. The Iliad.
Graves, Robert. The Greek Myths.
Burkert, Walter. Greek Religion.

Amrita

In the vast expanse of Hindu mythology, few treasures are as coveted and revered as the Amrita, the Nectar of Immortality. A symbol not just of life without end but also of the supreme power and divine essence, the Amrita has inspired tales of ambition, deception, and cosmic struggle. Central to many pivotal narratives, it represents humanity's age-old quest for longevity and transcendence. More than just a mystical elixir, the Amrita encapsulates the spiritual aspirations of a culture, painting a vivid portrait of a world where gods, demons, and mortals intersect in their pursuit of the ultimate prize.

The Amrita symbolizes the quest for eternal life and ultimate knowledge. It highlights the eternal struggle between gods and demons, good and evil. The story of the Amrita reflects the concept of cosmic balance, as well as the notion that immortality and divine wisdom are reserved for the gods.

According to Hindu mythology, the Amrita was churned from the cosmic ocean during the churning of the ocean, known as the Samudra Manthan. This grand event was a joint effort between the gods (devas) and demons (asuras) to extract the nectar from the ocean depths.

The Churning of the Ocean (Samudra Manthan)

The story begins with the Devas (gods) being weakened, having been cursed with a short-lived existence. In search of a solution, they turned to Lord Vishnu, the preserver of the universe. He advised them to churn the Ocean of Milk to obtain the Amrita, the nectar of immortality. However, such a colossal task required the strength of their rivals, the Asuras (demons). The Devas approached the Asuras with a proposal: a joint venture to churn the ocean and share the resultant treasures. Recognizing the potential rewards, the Asuras agreed.

The Churning Tools:

Mount Mandara: Selected as the churning rod due to its vast size and stability.

Vasuki: The king of serpents offered himself as the churning rope. The Devas held onto his tail, and the Asuras took his head, pulling alternately causing the mountain to rotate and churn the ocean.

As the churning began, Mount Mandara started to sink into the oceanic floor. To prevent this, Lord Vishnu took the form of Kurma, the tortoise avatar, and supported the mountain on his back.

As the ocean churned, it began to release various treasures. The first to emerge was a deadly poison named Halahala. It threatened to destroy all creation. Lord Shiva consumed the poison to protect the universe, and though he held it in his throat without swallowing, it turned his throat blue, earning him the name Neelkanth. Other treasures eventually emerged including Kamadhenu, the divine cow that fulfills wishes; Kalpavriksha, the wish-fulfilling tree; Apsaras, celestial nymphs renowned for their beauty; Chandra, the Moon; and finally, Dhanvantari, the god of Ayurveda, bearing the pot of Amrita.

The appearance of the Amrita was unlike any other treasure birthed from the ocean. Radiating a divine luminescence, the nectar shimmered under the celestial light, casting ethereal reflections. Its allure was undeniable—its brilliance rivaling the sun, and its fragrance, a blend of heavenly aromas, pervaded the atmosphere, intoxicating and beckoning all those present.

As Dhanvantari emerged with the pot of Amrita, the Asuras, driven by greed, seized it. The Devas, in their weakened state, turned to Lord Vishnu for help. Taking the form of the enchantress Mohini, Vishnu charmed the Asuras and managed to distribute the nectar to the Devas. Once the Devas consumed the Amrita, they regained their strength. An enraged battle ensued between the Devas and Asuras. Empowered by the nectar, the Devas emerged victorious, driving the Asuras away.

Rahu and Ketu: The Shadowy Serpents of Eclipses

In the wake of the Amrita's appearance, a mad scramble ensued as both Devas and Asuras realized its value. To ensure the nectar did not fall into the hands of the Asuras, Vishnu took the form of the enchanting Mohini to distribute it amongst the Devas.

Rahu, an astute demon, saw through the subterfuge. Disguising himself as a Deva, he seated himself between the Sun and Moon deities during the distribution. As Mohini went about distributing the Amrita, Rahu received a portion of the elixir. However, before he could consume it fully, the Sun and Moon, recognizing his deceit, alerted Vishnu. Reacting swiftly, Vishnu in his Mohini form brandished his discus, the Sudarshana Chakra, beheading Rahu. But since the Amrita had already touched Rahu's lips, he became immortal. Thus, the two entities were formed: Rahu, the severed head, and Ketu, the headless torso.

Embittered by their betrayal, Rahu and Ketu held a grudge against the Sun and Moon, the informants of their subterfuge. This animosity manifests in the form of eclipses. Rahu, with his mouth, swallows the Sun or the Moon, causing an eclipse, but since he is just a head, they re-emerge from his severed neck, symbolizing the end of the eclipse.

In Vedic astrology, Rahu and Ketu are considered shadow planets or "chaya grahas." They do not have physical bodies like other planets but are mathematically calculated points in the sky. Representing the North and South lunar nodes, respectively, they are indicators of karmic influences and life lessons in an individual's birth chart. Rahu is often seen as the amplifier, intensifying the traits of any zodiac sign or house he is associated with, while Ketu is the spiritual force pushing one towards liberation and self-realization, often by creating detachment from material desires.

The Amrita is not just a potion for immortality; it symbolizes the profound aspirations of the soul. In a culture that views life as a cycle of birth, death, and rebirth, the Amrita captures the essence of breaking free from this cycle and achieving a state of eternal bliss. Vedas, Upanishads, and the Puranas frequently allude to the

Amrita. These mentions elevate it from a mere mythical object to a spiritual concept that seekers are encouraged to understand and internalize.

From classical dance performances to epic sagas recited during festivals, the tale of the Amrita and its significance has inspired countless artistic endeavors. Murals in ancient temples often depict the churning of the ocean, reflecting the cultural importance of this myth.

Hindu philosophers have often likened the churning of the ocean to the inner turmoil and challenges one faces in life. The emergence of the Amrita, after much strife, is likened to the attainment of wisdom and enlightenment after a period of spiritual struggle.

Modern storytellers, authors, and filmmakers continue to be inspired by the tale of the Amrita. It is used metaphorically to discuss the quest for meaning, purpose, and the eternal in an ever-changing world.

The Amrita's influence on Hindu culture and beliefs transcends time. It remains a potent symbol, encapsulating the essence of life's journey, spiritual aspirations, and the eternal quest for the divine. Through tales, teachings, and traditions, the Amrita's legacy continues, guiding and inspiring generations in their spiritual and philosophical pursuits.

Sources/Further Reading:

Mahabharata and Puranas (Hindu Epics and Mythological Texts).
Mithya: A Handbook of Hindu Mythology.
The Hindus: An Alternative History by Wendy Doniger.

Amenonuhoko

In the vast and intricate tapestry of Japanese mythology, the Amenonuhoko stands out as a beacon of creation and celestial might. Often described as the "heavenly jeweled spear," its very name evokes imagery of divine craftsmanship, merging the ethereal with the tangible. More than just a weapon or tool, the Amenonuhoko is enshrined in legend as the instrument that sculpted the very islands of Japan from the primordial seas. Its tale is one of gods, chaos, and the birth of a land that would come to be steeped in history and culture. Within its gleaming form lies not just the power of creation, but the weight of a nation's origin story—a symbol that embodies the harmonious dance of the cosmos and the earth, the eternal interplay between the celestial and the terrestrial.

Izanagi and Izanami's Celestial Dance

In the nascent stages of creation, the universe was an endless expanse of chaotic soup, an undifferentiated blend of potentiality, waiting for form and purpose. Amidst this cosmic murkiness, a divine mandate was decreed: the birth of solid land. Chosen for this monumental task were Izanagi and Izanami, the male and female divine beings, emanations of the primordial heavens. Their union represented the yin and yang, the complementary forces essential for creation. Together, they bore the responsibility of crafting something tangible from the intangible.

Suspended between the realms of potentiality and reality was the Ama-no-ukihashi, the "Bridge to Heaven." This ethereal bridge was a liminal space, a point of convergence between the heavenly and the yet-to-be-formed earthly realm. Here, the divine couple stood, poised at the precipice of creation.

In their hands, Izanagi and Izanami held the Amenonuhoko, the "heavenly jeweled spear," a divine artifact that glittered with cosmic energy. With deliberate intent, they thrust the spear into the oceanic abyss below. As they stirred the chaotic waters, matter began to coalesce, and structure began to emerge. Drawing the spear upwards, droplets fell from its tip, each one crystallizing upon contact with the void below. From these droplets, islands began to take shape, emerging from the sea in a testament to divine artistry. These were the first formations of what would become the Japanese archipelago.

The actions of Izanagi and Izanami on the Bridge to Heaven set the stage for further tales of love, loss, and rebirth, but their initial act of creation remains a foundational myth in Japanese cosmology. The islands birthed from their endeavors symbolize the transformative power of divine will, the transition from chaos to order, and the perpetual dance between the celestial and terrestrial realms.

Amaterasu, and the Legitimacy of the Imperial Throne

Amaterasu, often revered as "Amaterasu-Ōmikami," is not just any deity in the Japanese pantheon. As the sun goddess, she illuminates the world, bringing warmth, life, and sustenance. Her luminosity is not merely physical; it signifies purity, benevolence, and celestial authority over the earthly realm. A pivotal episode in Amaterasu's lore is her retreat into a cave following a feud with her boisterous brother, Susano-o. Her absence plunged the world into darkness and chaos. The significance here is profound: it underscores Amaterasu's indispensable role in maintaining cosmic balance.

As the narrative goes, Ninigi-no-Mikoto, Amaterasu's grandson, descended to the earthly realm from the celestial Takama-ga-hara. He was the father of Emperor Jimmu, the legendary first Emperor of Japan. This lineage inherently connected the mortal emperor to the divine sphere, granting him both authority and a sacred duty to uphold the cosmic balance on earth. When Amaterasu bestowed the Amenonuhoko upon Emperor Jimmu, it was more than a mere transfer of a celestial artifact.

This divine spear, already a symbol of creation and celestial might, became a representation of the sacred covenant between the heavens and the Japanese imperial line. The act of bequeathing emphasized Jimmu's role not just as a political leader but as a spiritual guardian of the land and its people. The Amenonuhoko, along with the other regalia like the Kusanagi sword and the Yasakani jewel, bolstered the legitimacy of the imperial throne. But more than mere symbols of power, they were reminders of the sacred duty bestowed upon the emperor: to rule with wisdom, justice, and in harmony with the divine will.

The narrative of Amaterasu and the divine lineage has been instrumental in Japanese history. It played a role in asserting the emperor's divine right to rule, especially during periods when the imperial institution sought to reaffirm its authority. Even in contemporary Japan, while the emperor's role is largely ceremonial, the narratives of the divine lineage continue to resonate, underscoring a deep connection to tradition and spirituality.

The term "heavenly jeweled spear" signifies not only the physical attributes of the artifact but also its spiritual and cosmic significance. The "heavenly" aspect alludes to its divine origin, while "jeweled" highlights its intrinsic value and celestial nature. As a spear, it carries connotations of authority, protection, and power.

The Amenonuhoko is part of the Imperial Regalia of Japan, along with the Yasakani no Magatama (curved jewel), Yata no Kagami (sacred mirror), and the Kusanagi no Tsurugi (grass-cutting sword). These artifacts are symbols of the imperial family's legitimacy and divine connection. While the locations of the Yasakani no Magatama, Yata no Kagami, and the Kusanagi no Tsurugi are known, the whereabouts of the Amenonuhoko are a mystery, adding an air of mystique.

The Amenonuhoko isn't just a mythical artifact; it is intertwined with Japan's cultural identity and history. It symbolizes the divine origins of the Japanese people and their connection to the land. The story of its creation underscores the deep respect and reverence for nature in Japanese culture. The Amenonuhoko's story has been told and retold through generations, finding its way into literature, art, and even modern pop culture.

The Amenonuhoko, the heavenly jeweled spear, is more than a mere artifact—it's a vessel of creation, authority, and cultural identity. Its mythical origin and its association with the creation of Japan and the divine lineage of its rulers elevate it to a position of profound significance in Japanese mythology and history.

Sources/Further Reading:

Kojiki (Records of Ancient Matters)
Nihon Shoki (Chronicles of Japan):
Japanese Gods & Myths by Juliet Piggott

Ankh

Carved into the stone reliefs of temples, painted onto the coffins of the pharaohs, and worn as amulets by the common folk, the Ankh has steadfastly stood the test of time, emerging from the heart of ancient Egypt to be its most enduring symbol.

The T-shaped design of the Ankh, culminating in an upward oval loop, distinguishes it from any other symbol of its era. Its form evokes intrigue: the teardrop loop, perhaps a nod to the sun or a protective womb, and the cross below, grounding it to the earth and the human experience. As a hieroglyphic sign, the Ankh was an integral part of Egypt's written language. Its presence in inscriptions was not mere adornment; it breathed life into the words, bestowing them with potency and vitality.

At its core, the Ankh symbolizes life. In various hieroglyphic inscriptions, it's used to denote the verb "to live". It's often seen in the hands of Egyptian deities, either being offered to the pharaohs as a symbol of life or held to the gods' noses, granting them the "breath of life".

In the complex pantheon of ancient Egyptian beliefs, the Ankh occupied a position of reverence and mystique. More than just a hieroglyph or a decorative element, it became a bridge between the mortal realm and the heavens, a conduit through which divine energy flowed.

Isis: Often regarded as the mother goddess, Isis embodies the ideals of healing, protection, and magic. In various depictions, she is seen holding the Ankh close to her lips, offering the "breath of life" to the deceased, ensuring their safe passage and resurrection in the afterlife.

Osiris: As the god of the afterlife and rebirth, Osiris's association with the Ankh is profound. After his infamous murder and resurrection, Osiris became a symbol of regeneration and eternal life. The Ankh in his grasp amplifies this promise of rebirth and continuation of the soul's journey.

Ra: The sun god Ra, one of the most revered in the Egyptian pantheon, represented the daily cycle of birth, death, and rebirth. The loop of the Ankh, believed to symbolize the sun rising on the horizon, resonates deeply with Ra's daily journey across the sky. The Ankh, when associated with Ra, celebrates not just the physical sun, but the cyclical nature of existence.

Isis and Osiris: A Tale of Love, Betrayal, and Resurrection

Osiris, Isis, Set, and Nephthys were siblings, born of the sky goddess Nut and the earth god Geb. Osiris and Isis, besides being siblings, were also husband and wife, and their reign was characterized by peace and prosperity over the lands of Egypt.

Set, the god of chaos, grew increasingly jealous of Osiris's popularity and successful reign. This envy turned to murderous rage, leading Set to plot against his brother. He hatched a devious plan, designing a beautifully adorned coffin tailored to fit Osiris perfectly.

During a grand feast, Set unveiled the coffin and promised it as a gift to anyone who could fit inside. As Osiris lay down in the coffin, Set and his accomplices quickly sealed it shut and threw it into the Nile. The coffin drifted to the city of Byblos, where a tree grew around it, encasing Osiris.

Upon learning of Osiris's disappearance, Isis, the goddess of magic and motherhood, was overcome with grief. But her sorrow quickly turned into determination. She set out on a quest to find her beloved, traveling far and wide. In Byblos, she learned of the tree that had grown around the coffin and persuaded the king of Byblos to give it to her. She retrieved Osiris's body, bringing it back to Egypt.

Set, upon discovering that Osiris's body had been recovered by Isis, was infuriated. In a fit of rage, he dismembered Osiris's body into fourteen pieces and scattered them across Egypt. Isis, undeterred by this gruesome act, once again set out, this time to gather the pieces of her husband. With the help of her sister Nephthys, she managed to find and piece together thirteen of the fourteen parts; only Osiris's phallus remained missing, having been consumed by a fish.

Using her profound magical abilities, Isis fashioned a golden phallus to replace the missing part. She then used her magic, along with rituals and incantations, to bring Osiris back to life. It is in some of these depictions that Isis is shown using the Ankh, placing it near Osiris's lips, symbolizing the breath of life.

Though Osiris could no longer rule the living, having journeyed to the underworld, his brief reanimation allowed him to conceive a child with Isis. This child, Horus, would grow up to challenge Set, seeking revenge for his father's death and ultimately establishing his own rule over Egypt.

The tale of Isis and Osiris isn't merely a story of love and betrayal; it serves as an allegory for the cycles of life, death, and rebirth. Osiris's resurrection and subsequent rule over the underworld symbolize the belief in life after death, a core tenet of ancient Egyptian spirituality. The use of the Ankh in this narrative underscores its significance as a symbol of life, restoration, and eternal existence.

Ra and the Tales of Creation

The city of Heliopolis had its version of creation where the sun god Ra (or Atum in some versions) emerged from the chaotic waters of Nun. He then created Shu (god of air) and Tefnut (goddess of moisture), who went on to give birth to the sky goddess Nut and the earth god Geb.

The sun's daily journey and its life-giving properties can be related to the Ankh, representing the vitality and essence of life. In Hermopolis, creation began with the Ogdoad, a group of eight deities representing the primordial elements. These included the concepts of water, boundlessness, darkness, and invisibility. These gods existed in the waters of Nun before the creation of the world. The emergence of the mound from the water, where the sun first rose, is reminiscent of the Ankh's symbolism, where water and the sun converge to bring forth life.

In Thebes, the god Amun was considered the primeval creator. Amun became synchronized with Ra to become Amun-Ra, a deity that combined the mysteries of creation and the power of the sun. Again, while the Ankh might not be explicitly mentioned in the creation tale, the concepts of life, light, and sustenance intrinsic to the Ankh are heavily featured. Given the Ankh's symbolism, it's easy to draw parallels between it and the core elements of these creation myths. In narratives where the gods bestow gifts upon humanity, the Ankh stands out as a divine gift representing life's essence. It embodies both the life-giving properties of the Nile and the sun—two paramount entities in ancient Egyptian daily existence.

Ritualistic Uses of the Ankh

In the rich fabric of ancient Egyptian rituals, the Ankh played a pivotal role as an instrument of divine intervention and protection. Revered not merely for its symbolic representation of life, the Ankh was believed to possess tangible powers, able to channel divine energies during ceremonies. A crucial component of the burial rites, the "Opening of the Mouth" ceremony was a ritualistic performance designed to reanimate the deceased in the afterlife.

Ancient Egyptians believed that death was but a doorway, and for the deceased to thrive in the beyond, they had to retain their earthly faculties. To ensure the deceased could eat, drink, see, hear, and speak in the afterlife, the "Opening of the Mouth" ceremony would symbolically and spiritually "re-open" these faculties, which were believed to be sealed by death.

Priests and close family members would partake in this ritual, invoking a series of chants and actions to restore these abilities to the mummified individual. Integral to this ceremony was the Ankh. Its touch was seen as a conduit of life. By touching the mummy or the deceased's statue with the Ankh, it was believed that the life-force inherent in the symbol would transfer to the deceased, ensuring they would not be mute, blind, or starving in the realm beyond.

The ceremony would often begin with purification rites, where the deceased was cleansed with sacred water. Following this, the Ankh, along with other sacred tools, would be used on various parts of the mummy. The mouth, in particular, would be touched to "open" it, allowing the deceased to speak and eat. Similarly, eyes, ears, and nostrils would be symbolically "opened" to grant sight, hearing, and the breath of life.

The Ankh: Life's Mystical Gateway

In a land like Egypt, where the ever-giving Nile flowed through arid deserts, contrasts were a fundamental aspect of existence. This interplay of opposites found its embodiment in the Ankh. Beyond representing life, the Ankh became a harmonizing symbol, melding life's contradictions and mysteries into a coherent whole.

The lower vertical section of the Ankh, resembling a physical key, could be said to represent the tangible, earthly existence. Here, life along the Nile—with its floods, harvests, and daily chores—echoed the cyclical rhythms of nature. This was a life governed by the sun, the seasons, and the river. The loop, ethereal and infinite, might be seen to symbolize the realm beyond mortal understanding—the afterlife, the realm of the gods, and the cycle of the soul. This is where the departed were believed to embark on a journey, laden with trials, judgements, and eventual rebirth or union with the divine.

Just as the Nile ebbed and flowed, so too did the Egyptian understanding of the soul's journey. The Ankh's design, with its continuous, looping head, might have been seen as embodying this cyclical worldview. Birth, death, rebirth—each was a step in the eternal dance of existence, with the Ankh serving as both guide and protector.

The beginnings of the Ankh remain enigmatic, much like the mysteries it symbolizes. Was it inspired by the rising sun, the knot of Isis, or perhaps a sandal strap, as some theories propose? Its true origin may forever remain a riddle, but this only adds to its allure, making it a true key to the unknown. The Ankh's resonance extends far beyond its physical form or hieroglyphic function. It speaks to the ancient Egyptian understanding of existence, both seen and unseen. Through its design and the belief it upholds, the Ankh invites us to contemplate life's greatest mysteries, serving as a timeless reminder of the intertwined nature of life and death, the known and the unknown.

Sources/Further Reading:

The Complete Gods and Goddesses of Ancient Egypt by Richard H. Wilkinson

The Oxford Encyclopedia of Ancient Egypt: by Donald B. Redford

The Theoi Project (www.theoi.com)

Andvaranaut

The Andvaranaut, often simply referred to as Andvari's ring, is a significant artifact within Norse mythology. This gold ring is best known for the curse it carries, which brings misfortune and doom to its possessors. Its story intertwines with that of gods, dwarves, and heroes, showcasing the often-tragic interplay of fate, greed, and vengeance in Norse tales.

While the specific physical appearance of the Andvaranaut isn't detailed extensively in the Norse sagas, it's generally depicted as a beautiful gold ring, irresistibly captivating to those who set their eyes on it. The allure of the ring isn't just its material value; it represents power, wealth, and desire.

Advari and his Ring

Nestled in the secretive crevices of the mountains lay a hidden realm where water and earth conspired in hushed whispers. In this realm, behind the veil of a cascading waterfall, dwelt the dwarf Andvari.

Unlike many of his kin who preferred the subterranean mazes of mountains, Andvari favored the world of waters. He possessed the unique ability to transform into a fish, allowing him to traverse his watery domain with ease.

Legends spoke of a vast treasure hoarded by Andvari, a collection that glittered with the wealth of ages. From goblets adorned with gemstones that captured the hues of the cosmos to armors that shimmered like starlight, this treasure was the envy of both mortal and immortal beings. Dwarves, with their innate affinity for metals and craftsmanship, often accumulated treasures, but few could rival the magnificence of Andvari's collection.

Amidst the mountains of gold and artifacts, one item held a particular allure: the Andvaranaut. This simple gold ring, devoid of the extravagant gemstones that adorned other pieces in the collection, possessed an enchantment that was both a blessing and a curse. The ring was imbued with the ability to produce gold, ensuring that Andvari's treasure would never diminish. Yet, it was not just its magical properties that made the Andvaranaut special. It was a testament to Andvari's prowess and the embodiment of his dominion over his territory.

To possess the ring was to claim authority over the treasure and, by extension, over a fragment of the world's wealth. In many myths worldwide, objects that offer endless wealth or sustenance often come with a hidden cost. The Andvaranaut's ability to produce endless gold can be seen as a reflection of nature's bounty but also a warning against unchecked greed. For while nature provides abundance, it requires respect and balance. The eventual curse attached to the ring further emphasizes this theme: that limitless desire can lead to one's downfall.

Loki and the Stolen Treasure

On a day seemingly like any other, Loki, the god of mischief, along with Odin and Hoenir, ventured into the mortal realm. Their wanderings brought them to a serene river where they spotted an otter basking in the sun. Loki, in a moment of misjudgment or perhaps typical recklessness, hurled a stone at the otter, killing it instantly. Imagining the otter's pelt would fetch a handsome price, the trio skinned it and continued on their journey.

In the evening, they sought shelter in the dwelling of Hreidmar, a sorcerer of considerable power. Unbeknownst to the gods, the otter they had slain was Hreidmar's son, Otr, who had the ability to transform into an otter. When Hreidmar discovered the pelt, he recognized it immediately and, in a fury, captured the gods. He demanded a ransom for their release: the otter's skin had to be filled with gold and covered entirely with it.

Loki, being the cause of their predicament, was sent to procure the gold. Aware of Andvari's legendary treasure, Loki decided to seize it to meet Hreidmar's demands. Using a net borrowed from the goddess Ran, Loki captured Andvari in his fish form. Threatened with death, Andvari reluctantly agreed to part with his hoard.

However, as Loki was about to leave, he noticed a single gold ring that Andvari clung to. Loki demanded it, but Andvari hesitated, for this was the Andvaranaut, the source of his wealth. Reluctantly, Andvari handed over the ring.

Bitter and enraged at the loss of his treasure and the means of replenishing it, Andvari unleashed a curse upon the Andvaranaut. He declared that the ring, and with it the entire hoard, would bring death and misfortune to whoever possessed it. The curse would ensure that the gold would be the doom of its owners, turning blessings into tragedies.

Loki returned with the cursed gold and the Andvaranaut to Hreidmar's dwelling. True to his word, Hreidmar released the gods once the otter's skin was filled and covered with the treasure.

The first taste of the curse came swiftly. Hreidmar, having received the gold and the Andvaranaut as blood compensation for Otr's death, soon faced the wrath of his remaining sons, Fafnir and Regin. Driven by greed and the allure of the treasure, especially the gold-producing ring, Fafnir took the life of his own father. It was clear: the treasure tainted the hearts of those around it, making kin turn on kin.

Overwhelmed by paranoia and an insatiable desire to guard his ill-gotten wealth, Fafnir underwent a grotesque transformation. From a dwarf, he became a fearsome dragon, the very embodiment of greed. He took to the wilderness, laying atop the treasure horde, with the cursed Andvaranaut close to him. His once close bond with Regin was severed, replaced by suspicion and hostility.

Into this tale of treachery stepped Sigurd, a descendant of the great Volsung lineage. With aspirations of heroism and urged by Regin, who had his own designs on the treasure, Sigurd sought to slay Fafnir. Using a sword reforged from his father's broken one, Sigurd succeeded in his quest and defeated the dragon.

Upon Regin's advice, Sigurd roasted Fafnir's heart with the intention of letting Regin consume it. However, when Sigurd tasted the dragon's blood from his thumb, he suddenly understood the language of birds.

Overhead, birds chattered, revealing truths unknown to Sigurd. They spoke of Regin's deceitful intentions: the older dwarf planned to betray and kill Sigurd to claim the treasure for himself. Forewarned, Sigurd acted first, beheading Regin and solidifying his claim on the cursed hoard, including the Andvaranaut.

The Lingering Shadow: Sigurd's Tragic Fate

After obtaining the cursed treasure, Sigurd's destiny led him to Brunhild, a Valkyrie and a warrior maiden. Initially, they fell deeply in love, and Sigurd gave her the ring Andvaranaut as a pledge of his love. However, the curse of the ring and the intricate weavings of fate would soon taint their love story.

On his travels, Sigurd came to the court of King Gunnar and his sister Gudrun. Through various manipulations and a potion that made Sigurd forget Brunhild, Gudrun's mother made Sigurd marry Gudrun. In a further twist, to win Brunhild for King Gunnar (as she had sworn to marry only the bravest of men), Sigurd was magically disguised as Gunnar, and he went through trials set by Brunhild to win her hand on Gunnar's behalf. Thus, Brunhild was tricked into marrying Gunnar, not knowing his true identity during the trials.

As time passed, the truth of the deceptions unraveled, and Brunhild realized she had been deceived by Sigurd and Gunnar. Feeling deeply wronged and betrayed, she sought vengeance. Fueled by the malign influence of the Andvaranaut and her feelings of betrayal, she demanded Sigurd's death.

Gunnar and his brother Hogni, although initially reluctant, eventually plotted to kill Sigurd, fearing Brunhild's wrath and the loss of her dowry. In some versions of the tale, it's Gunnar and Hogni's younger brother, Gutthorm, who is manipulated into delivering the fatal blow while Sigurd slept.

Gudrun, devastated by Sigurd's death and filled with rage, avenged him by killing her own children by Sigurd and serving them to Gunnar and Hogni. The Andvaranaut's curse had turned kin against kin. This gruesome act would set in motion a series of vengeful acts leading to the near extinction of the Volsung line.

Later, to avenge her brothers and Sigurd, Gudrun instigated a massive war between her new husband Atli (often identified with Attila the Hun), and her brothers. This war resulted in the deaths of Gunnar and Hogni and eventually Atli himself. The tale culminated in a maelstrom of bloodshed, treachery, and sorrow.

Beyond its literal significance in Norse sagas, the Andvaranaut can be viewed as a symbol of the dangers of unchecked greed and ambition. The curse it carries is not just of supernatural origin but also a reflection of human flaws. When one's desires become obsessions, ruin often follows. In this way, the ring and its curse parallel other cursed treasures in world literature, such as the One Ring in J.R.R. Tolkien's Middle-earth legendarium.

The tale of the Andvaranaut offers a glimpse into the expansive panorama of Norse mythology. Through its cursed existence, it connects various characters, fates, and sagas, serving as a testament to the rich narrative traditions of the Norse people and the timeless themes their stories addressed.

Sources/Further Reading:

"The Prose Edda" by Snorri Sturluson: This is a primary source for Norse myths and legends.
"The Volsunga Saga": This saga provides a detailed account of the tragic tale of the Volsung dynasty.
"Norse Mythology" by Neil Gaiman.
"The Norse Myths" by Kevin Crossley-Holland: A comprehensive collection of Norse myths with detailed notes and interpretations.

Apples of Idunn

Nestled within the complex matrix of Norse legends are the Apples of Idunn, fruits of unparalleled magic. They are not mere apples, but symbols of youth, vitality, and the gods' reliance on the natural world. Idunn, a goddess associated with youth and rejuvenation, is the keeper of these magical apples. It's her sacred duty to care for them and dispense them to the gods. With each consumption, the gods maintain their youthful vigor and vitality, keeping old age and decay at bay.

The gods of Norse mythology, unlike many other pantheons, aren't inherently immortal. They are long-lived and powerful, but they face eventual decline without the Apples of Idunn. Thus, these fruits are more than mere nourishment; they are the essence of their continued dominance and existence.

Loki's Mischief and the Theft of Youth

The tale begins not with the lure of the apples but with Loki's knack for landing himself in dire straits. One day, while on a journey, Loki, Odin, and Hoenir were ambushed by the giant Thiazi. Thiazi was no ordinary giant; he possessed the ability to transform into an eagle. In his eagle form, he captured Loki, intending to consume him. Cornered and desperate, Loki bargained for his life. He made a pledge to the giant: he would deliver the Apples of Idunn, ensuring Thiazi's own everlasting youth and strength.

Returning to Asgard, Loki hatched a plan. He approached Idunn with stories of fruits in a forest that rivaled her own apples in magical potency. Curious and unsuspecting, Idunn followed Loki out of the safety of Asgard's walls. This was her downfall. Thiazi, lying in wait, captured her and took her to his stronghold, securing the treasured apples alongside the goddess.

With Idunn's absence and the loss of her rejuvenating apples, a calamity befell Asgard. The gods, usually vigorous and youthful, started to age at an alarming rate. Their strength waned, their skin wrinkled, and their vitality faded. They were shadows of their former selves. Realizing the sudden and unexplained aging, they convened and quickly deduced that Idunn's absence was the cause. And the last to be seen with her was Loki.

The gods, now weak but still formidable, cornered Loki. Realizing the depth of his treachery, they threatened him with tortures unimaginable. To save himself, Loki promised to retrieve Idunn and her apples. With the help of Freyja's falcon cloak, which allowed its wearer to transform into a falcon, Loki flew to Thiazi's stronghold.

Finding Idunn alone, Loki used his transformative powers to turn her into a nut (a form that would be easy for him to carry) and began his journey back to Asgard.

But the quest was far from over. Thiazi returned and, finding his prize gone, transformed into his eagle form, pursuing Loki with furious speed. A chase of epic proportions began, spanning the skies, with Thiazi's massive wings causing storms as he flew.

Asgard's walls were in sight when the gods, seeing the approaching falcon and the menacing eagle behind it, set a trap. They lit a vast fire at the perimeter of Asgard's walls. Loki, using the last of his strength, soared over it. Thiazi, in hot pursuit, was unable to stop in time and was engulfed by the flames. His wings burned, and the mighty giant fell, meeting his doom at the hands of the gods.

With Idunn and her apples restored to Asgard, the gods' youth and vigor returned. They were once again the powerful deities of lore, their strength undiminished. While they celebrated their rejuvenation, the tale served as a poignant reminder of their vulnerabilities and their reliance on the natural world.

The Apples of Idunn, like many mythical objects, are teeming with symbolic meanings. They represent the cyclical nature of life, death, and rebirth. Their rejuvenating properties might also symbolize the periodic renewal of nature, as seen in the changing of seasons.

The dependence of the powerful Norse gods on Idunn's apples reflects the vulnerability of even the mightiest beings. It serves as a reminder of the delicate balance of life and the inevitability of aging, making the gods more relatable in their imperfections and dependencies.

The Apples of Idunn, with their promise of youth, offer a tantalizing glimpse into the values, beliefs, and fears of the Norse people. These aren't just tales of adventures and deities, but stories reflecting human desires for vitality, longevity, and the quest for immortality. Through Idunn and her treasured apples, the Norse myths encapsulate the universal hope to ward off the ravages of time and remain forever young.

Sources/Further Reading:

"The Prose Edda" by Snorri Sturluson: This is a primary source for Norse myths and legends
"The Norse Myths" by Kevin Crossley-Holland: A comprehensive collection of Norse myths with detailed notes and interpretations.
"The Gospel of Loki" by Joanne M. Harris

Armor of Achilles

Fashioned by the gods and tailored for one of the greatest Greek warriors, the Armor of Achilles is emblematic of divine intervention in the mortal realm. This isn't just a suit of armor; it represents the pinnacle of divine craftsmanship, embodying both protection and prestige.

The Divine Creation

Hephaestus, the son of Zeus and Hera, was the only physically imperfect god among the Olympians, having been born with a limp. But what he lacked in physical strength, he more than compensated for with his craft. His forge was believed to be beneath a volcano, and there, with the assistance of the Cyclopes, he crafted wonders that no mortal or god could rival.

Thetis, a sea-nymph of incredible beauty and significance, had always been protective of her son, Achilles. Witnessing the difficult predicament he found himself in following Patroclus' death and knowing his fate was interlinked with Troy's fall, she felt compelled to assist him. Her journey to Hephaestus' forge was one of a desperate mother seeking the best protection possible for her son.

The breastplate was conceived not merely as protection but as an emblem of Achilles' heroism. Starting with the finest celestial metals, Hephaestus began the meticulous process. He pounded and shaped, ensuring that this breastplate would hug Achilles' form, amplifying both his mobility and protection.

Upon the polished metal surface, Hephaestus began etching designs. Each design had a tale, a purpose. There were depictions of legendary battles, showcasing the bravery and valor of heroes of old. Perhaps there were scenes from Achilles' own life, chronicling his journey from his training with Chiron the centaur to his indomitable feats in the Trojan War.

But Hephaestus, with his wisdom and foresight, might have also incorporated symbols of divine significance. Patterns that invoked the blessings of the gods, ensuring that Achilles would have their favor as he stepped onto the battlefield.

The shield, undoubtedly the most iconic part of the armor, was Hephaestus' masterpiece. It was not just an item of defense but a work of divine art. The crafting of the shield wasn't just Hephaestus hammering away; it was him weaving the narrative of life, death, and everything in between. The armor as a whole was forged with such brilliance that it shone with an ethereal light, reflecting the divine essence from which it was made.

The Shield is described in great detail in the "Iliad." On it were depicted:

Scenes of cities at peace and cities at war.

Scenes of farming and agriculture.

The celestial bodies: the sun, the moon, and the constellations.

Scenes of young men and women dancing.

A vast expanse of the ocean.

The armor crafted by Hephaestus wasn't just metal and design; it was a microcosm of the world. As Achilles put on the armor, he wasn't simply armoring himself for battle, but embodying the entirety of the universe. This wasn't just protection against swords and spears; it was the weight of life, nature, gods, and mankind.

The renewed vigor and wrath of Achilles

When Achilles stepped onto the battlefield donning his new armor, it was not merely the return of a warrior but the rebirth of a legend. The hiatus, the mourning for Patroclus, and the divine intervention of the new armor converged, transforming Achilles from a brooding hero into an avenging force of nature. The gleaming armor, meticulously crafted by Hephaestus, mirrored the brilliance of the sun. As Achilles emerged, it was as if a new dawn broke on the battlefield. To the Trojans, this dawn was not hopeful but foreboding. The radiant armor symbolized the raw, unfettered power and wrath of Achilles, now magnified. The very sight of this luminous presence sent shivers down the spines of Trojan warriors, foreshadowing the onslaught to come.

With each step, with each swing of his spear, Achilles was a tempest. The armor didn't just protect him; it magnified his presence, making him seem larger than life. Trojans fell before him, not just from the might of his arm but also the sheer terror his visage invoked. The battlefield became a dance floor where Achilles moved with grim grace, every step and thrust orchestrated by his thirst for vengeance.

The climax of Achilles' wrathful return was his encounter with Hector. The air grew thick with tension as the two great warriors, each a champion of their people, locked eyes. Hector, the noble

Trojan prince, stood his ground, aware of the significance of this duel. It wasn't just a personal battle but a clash of ideals, honor, and destiny.

The duel was epic in every sense. Every move, every parry and thrust was laden with emotion — Achilles' burning desire for vengeance and Hector's determination to defend his city's honor. The divine armor of Achilles played its part, not just as protection but as a testament to the gravity of this confrontation.

Despite Hector's valor, the outcome seemed ordained by the gods. The culmination of Achilles' wrath, symbolized by his brilliant armor, was too potent. With Hector's fall, the tragic trajectory of the Trojan War continued its march towards a sorrowful climax.

Achilles' heel

The legend of Achilles' heel has its roots in his infancy. When Achilles was a baby, his mother, Thetis, wanting to make her son immortal, dipped him in the River Styx. The waters of this river had the power to confer invincibility. However, Thetis held Achilles by his heel, which meant that this part of him never touched the water, leaving it vulnerable.

It's ironic that while Thetis, a protective mother, sought to shield her son from all harm, her very act of protection became Achilles' singular point of vulnerability. Similarly, while Hephaestus's armor, including the magnificent breastplate and shield, was meant to protect Achilles during battle, no armor could protect him from the fate tied to his heel.

The entire life of Achilles seems orchestrated by fate. Even his name is a poignant reminder of his destiny. In Greek, "Achilles" can be broken down into "Ach" (pain) and "Laos" (people or nation), effectively translating to "he who brings pain to his people." This preordained tragic trajectory of his life culminates with his heel, his most vulnerable point. While he had armor crafted by gods and skills unmatched by mortals, it was a mere arrow to the heel, directed by Paris and guided by Apollo, that brought down the mighty warrior.

Achilles' heel becomes a profound symbol of the human condition. No matter how great, how powerful, or how god-like one might be, everyone has a vulnerability, a flaw. Achilles, for all his divine armor and heroic prowess, was still mortal. His heel was a constant reminder of that mortality.

Hephaestus's crafting of the Armor for Achilles is a symbolic intertwining of art, warfare, and fate. It wasn't just a protective piece but a narrative of Achilles' life, his destiny, and the very essence of heroism and mortality in ancient Greek culture. The care and detail that went into its creation solidify its place as a divine artifact, merging the world of gods and men.

Sources/Further Reading:

"The Iliad" by Homer: For an immersive experience of the events, emotions, and grandeur of the Trojan War.
"Hephaestus: The God of Fire" by Carol Dougherty.
"Greek Armour: From the Bronze Age to the Hellenistic Period" by Evgenii Anatolevich Chernenko
"Arms and Armor of the Greeks" by Anthony M. Snodgrass

Bag of Wind

In the ever-shifting realm of gods and mortals, gifts bestowed by divine entities are not always straightforward in their intention or outcome. Such was the experience of the illustrious Greek hero, Odysseus, as he navigated the treacherous waters of fate on his journey back to Ithaca.

The gods, in their capricious nature, often granted favors that came with their own sets of trials. Among the many boons and banes encountered by Odysseus, the Bag of Wind, a gift meant to expedite his journey home, emerges as a poignant representation of the fragile balance between divine generosity and human frailty.

Bestowed with benevolent intent, it ultimately unraveled not due to any divine trickery, but because of human flaws — a stark reminder that even the most gracious divine interventions can be undone by human curiosity and impulsiveness.

The Folly of Odysseus

Odysseus, often hailed as the "man of twists and turns", stands as one of the most iconic figures in Greek mythology. King of Ithaca and a central character in Homer's epics, the "Iliad" and the "Odyssey," he is best known for his intellect, cunning, and eloquence, rather than mere physical prowess.

A hero of the Trojan War, Odysseus is credited with conceiving the idea of the famous Trojan Horse, which led to the downfall of Troy. However, it is his ten-year-long journey back home after the war, as chronicled in the "Odyssey," that truly defines his character. Facing tempests, monsters, enchantresses, and the gods' whims, his voyage becomes a testament to human resilience, wisdom, and the enduring spirit.

The story of the Bag of Wind is one such story mentioned in "The Odyssey" by Homer. After navigating treacherous seas and confronting manifold challenges, Odysseus and his beleaguered crew find themselves on the shores of Aeolia, an island unlike any other. Suspended between the realms of earth and sky, Aeolia floated, embodying the transient and capricious nature of the winds it harbored.

Guarding this ethereal realm was Aeolus, not just as its ruler but as the very embodiment of the winds' majesty and whimsy. With a beard as white as sea foam and eyes that sparkled like the horizon, Aeolus was a figure of both authority and mystery. He possessed the unique power to command the winds, a responsibility bestowed upon him by the Olympian gods.

When Odysseus arrived at his doorstep, Aeolus, already aware of the hero's legendary status and his ordeals, felt a wave of compassion. Here was a man, favored by some gods and scorned by others, desperate to reunite with his homeland and family.

To assist the weary wanderer, Aeolus employed his divine skills, harnessing the winds' vast energy. With incantations and rituals, he imprisoned the boisterous North, South, and East winds into a resilient leather bag, ensuring they wouldn't derail Odysseus's journey. These captured winds, usually wild and free, swirled and raged within their confines, but the bag, sealed with a white cord, held firm.

But Aeolus knew that the ship needed propulsion. So, he let the gentle West Wind remain free, ensuring it would caress the sails of Odysseus's ship, guiding it smoothly towards the sun-kissed shores of Ithaca.

Handing the bag to Odysseus, Aeolus's eyes bore into the hero's with a stern yet compassionate gaze. He warned Odysseus of the bag's contents and the necessity to keep it sealed until they reached Ithaca. The bag, though a gift, was also a test — a testament to the discipline and trust required in the face of tantalizing mysteries.

Sailing on the open seas, with the West Wind gently pushing their ship towards Ithaca, the journey, for once, seemed without peril. Odysseus, bearing the weight of leadership and the strain of his many confrontations with fate, succumbed to exhaustion. As he slumbered, the weight of his responsibilities rested, if only for a while, allowing him a much-needed respite.

But a ship is a small world, and in the confines of its wooden walls, whispers grow louder and doubts turn into certainties. The bag, with its rhythmic pulsations and mysterious contents, became a focal point of discussion among the crew. They whispered tales of its possible contents, with every speculation more extravagant than the last. In the minds of the already weary and homesick crew, the sealed bag became a metaphor for the secrets and treasures their leader might be hoarding.

Human curiosity is a powerful force, especially when coupled with the allure of untold riches. As the silhouette of Ithaca began to materialize on the horizon, the proximity of home further inflamed their desires. The idea that they might soon be returning home, but without their fair share of what they believed to be hidden treasure, became unbearable.

In a moment of collective folly, fuelled by suspicion and the dreams of wealth, the crew decided to unveil the bag's mysteries. Expecting a cascade of gold and jewels, they instead unleashed the tumultuous winds trapped within. As the leather confines of the bag split open, the pent-up winds exploded with a force that seemed to shake the very foundations of the world. The once serene waters became a raging theater of monstrous waves and roaring whirlwinds. It was as if the anger and might of all the gods were unleashed in that one fateful moment. The ship, which moments before was caressed by gentle breezes, was now tossed about like a mere plaything.

For the crew, the sight of Ithaca on the horizon had been a beacon of hope and safety. Its proximity had promised the end of their arduous journey and a return to familiar comforts. But as the winds howled and raged, that tantalizing glimpse of home was rapidly obscured, replaced by a horizon filled with threats and uncertainty. The tragedy was not just in being driven away, but in knowing how close they had come to their goal.

Awakened from his slumber by the ship's violent motions and the crew's panicked shouts, Odysseus beheld the calamity brought about by mistrust and greed. The weight of leadership bore down on him heavier than ever. The knowledge that they were once so close to Ithaca and were now being driven inexorably away was a blow more crushing than any physical threat he had faced.

When the tempest subsided, the ship found its way back to the floating island of Aeolia. The ship, battered and weary from the tempest, finally dropped anchor at the familiar shores of Aeolia. But this was not the triumphant return one might imagine. Instead, it was marked by desperation, a deep sense of defeat, and the daunting knowledge of lost time.

Ascending to Aeolus's dwelling, Odysseus took on the role not of a heroic leader but of a humble supplicant. Gone was the pride of the warrior; in its place was a man brought low by circumstance, pleading for mercy. With earnestness in his voice and the weight of responsibility for his men on his shoulders, he narrated their tragic folly and sought Aeolus's benevolence once more.

But Aeolus's reception was starkly different this time. His face, previously welcoming, was now a mask of contemplation and concern. In the eyes of Aeolus, the very fact that Odysseus had returned under such dire circumstances was an ill omen. For the master of the winds, events did not unfold randomly. The universe had an order, governed by the will of the gods.

To him, Odysseus's second arrival was not a mere stroke of bad luck; it was a clear sign that the gods, for some reason, harbored disfavor towards the Ithacan king. And in the realm of mortals and gods, one does not simply overlook such divine indications.

It was not personal animosity or disdain that drove Aeolus's refusal; it was caution, respect for the divine, and perhaps even fear. To assist Odysseus again, in light of such evident disfavor, would be to go against the very forces that had once blessed Aeolus with his power over the winds.

With a heavy heart and an apologetic tone, Aeolus expressed his inability to help. He made it clear that further intervention on his part might not only jeopardize his standing with the gods but could also exacerbate Odysseus's own cursed journey.

Odysseus and his crew departed Aeolia with heavier hearts than before, devoid of the hope that had briefly flared during their return to the island. The winds that once had the potential to guide them home now whispered of prolonged adventures and trials.

The opening of the Bag of Wind is not just a tale of misjudgment, but a reflection on human nature. It underscores the dangers of unchecked curiosity, the perils of suspicion, and the tragic consequences of mistrust, even amongst comrades. Odysseus, in his journey, faced monsters, gods, and nature's fury, but this episode reminds us that sometimes, the most profound challenges arise from within, from the very human traits that define us.

The Bag of Wind, in many ways, symbolizes the unpredictable nature of life, where both external factors and human choices shape destiny. While the divine might provide aid, human nature – with its flaws of greed, suspicion, and impulsiveness – often plays a pivotal role in determining outcomes. The incident serves as a lesson about the importance of trust, the dangers of assumptions, and the unintended consequences of unchecked curiosity.

Odysseus' journey is replete with tales that reflect the complexities of human nature and the interplay between mortals and the divine. The Bag of Wind stands as a testament to the delicate balance between divine intervention and human agency. While the gods may set the stage, it is human action and choice that often determine the course of the narrative.

Sources/Further Reading:

"The Odyssey" by Homer: Dive deep into the adventures of Odysseus and get an in-depth understanding of his trials, including the incident of the Bag of Wind.

"The World of Odysseus" by M. I. Finley: This provides a broader understanding of the world in which Odysseus operated, offering insights into the customs, values, and society of the time.

Cauldron of Dagda

The Cauldron of Dagda is an artifact steeped in Celtic mythology. Rooted in the lore of the ancient Irish gods, this mystical cauldron is one of the four treasured possessions of the Tuatha Dé Danann, the pantheon of pre-Christian gods and goddesses of Ireland. The Tuatha Dé Danann, the supernatural race in Irish mythology, are associated with four legendary treasures, each from a different city. These treasures are the Stone of Fal, the Spear of Lugh, the Sword of Nuada, and, of course, the Cauldron of Dagda.

Each of these artifacts was not only a physical entity but also a symbolic representation of the powers and responsibilities of the gods who wielded them.

The Cauldron of Dagda, often referred to as the "Undry," is an emblem of abundance, regeneration, and divine sustenance. Unlike any ordinary vessel, this cauldron possessed unparalleled powers. Legend has it that no company ever went away from it unsatisfied, emphasizing its boundless ability to provide.

Before diving into the cauldron's lore, it's pivotal to understand its owner. Dagda, also known as Eochaid Ollathair or the "All-Father," is a prominent figure in the Irish pantheon. Often described as a god of druidry, agriculture, and tribal prosperity, he is also renowned for his enormous appetite and his exceptional harp which, like the cauldron, possesses magical properties.

The Cauldron of Dagda, often described as never running empty and capable of resurrecting the dead, was less about its physical manifestation and more about the ideas it embodied.

The Cauldron of Dagda: An Artifact of Endless Sustenance

In the shimmering city of Murias, one of the four cities from which the Tuatha Dé Danann hailed, the finest craftsmen labored day and night, their skills gifted by the gods themselves. Among these craftsmen was Credne, the celestial artificer, whose latest commission was from none other than the mighty Dagda.

With the combined might of elemental magic and celestial craftsmanship, Credne forged a cauldron, large and ornate but with an unassuming nature. Unlike the opulent goblets and dishes of the city, this cauldron was simple, but its simplicity concealed its unparalleled magic.

As Dagda received the cauldron, unsure of its powers, a time of famine befell a part of their lands. As crops failed and rivers ran dry, the people's despair grew. Dagda, in his infinite wisdom, called upon a feast, placing the cauldron at the center of the grand hall.

With a deep breath, Dagda stepped forward, ladle in hand. As it pierced the surface of the cauldron, the hall fell silent. To everyone's astonishment, the ladle emerged, brimming with a thick, hearty stew. Its rich aroma — a blend of succulent meats, fresh herbs, and aromatic spices — wafted through the hall, reminding many of better times.

The first bowl was placed in front of an elderly woman, her face etched with lines of hardship. With trembling hands, she took a sip, and her eyes widened in delight. The magic of the cauldron wasn't just in the endless food it provided, but in the taste — every bite was a reminder of the land's potential bounty, of harvest festivals, and of the promises of the gods.

Word spread quickly, and soon, the grand hall was filled with the sounds of joyous laughter and clinking bowls. Tales of past glories and hopes for the future were shared, the cauldron's magic rekindling the spirit of unity among the Tuatha Dé Danann.

Children ran around with rosy cheeks, their laughter echoing in the corridors. Warriors, once weakened by hunger, felt a renewed vigor, raising their cups in honor of Dagda and his mysterious cauldron.

As the night deepened, the once despairing community lay in a contented slumber, the cauldron's magic having not just filled their bellies, but also their hearts with hope. The famine was far from over, but for one night, the Tuatha Dé Danann remembered the joys of fellowship and feasting, all thanks to Dagda's wondrous cauldron.

Resurrection and Cycle of Life

In some versions, the cauldron had powers not just to provide endless food but also to bring warriors back to life. However, the resurrected would be mute – alive, but perhaps not in their full essence. This duality captures the cyclical nature of life and death, a theme recurrent in many mythologies.

Amidst the verdant valleys of the Tuatha Dé Danann realm, a devastating battle raged. The rival faction, emboldened by the land's weakened state, launched a fierce attack. Dagda's warriors, though renowned for their valor, were met with overwhelming force, and many met their untimely end on that fateful day.

The battleground was a tragic sight, with fallen warriors lying amidst the remnants of what was once a pristine meadow. The songs of old, which once spoke of triumphs and heroism, now seemed distant echoes. Amongst the fallen was Aedh, Dagda's closest companion, his still form a stark reminder of the battle's ferocity.

Dagda, with tears blurring his vision, ordered the bodies of his fallen brethren to be laid in a sacred circle around the Cauldron of Abundance. While the cauldron had previously been a beacon of sustenance and hope, it now became the epicenter of Dagda's desperate plea to the cosmos.

Whispers of Dagda's intent spread like wildfire among the survivors. Some called it madness, while others clung to the hope of seeing their comrades once more. But all gathered around the cauldron, their collective grief and hope forming an intangible aura of anticipation.

With a deep breath, Dagda began an ancient chant, his voice imbued with the weight of his grief and the power of his position as a leader. The night around them seemed to grow even darker, the very stars in the sky dimming in reverence to the ritual unfolding below.

The cauldron, ever enigmatic, began to emit a soft, ethereal glow. This gentle light danced and twirled, enveloping each fallen warrior in a luminescent embrace. Time seemed to stand still, the night stretching endlessly, as the magic worked its course.

As dawn's first light broke over the horizon, a collective gasp arose from the gathered crowd. The fallen warriors, once lifeless, began to move. Limbs stretched, chests heaved, and eyes slowly opened. But, as they rose, it became evident that they were forever changed. Their eyes, though alive, held a distant, introspective gaze, and their lips, once boisterous in laughter and song, remained sealed. The price of their return was their voice, the silent mark of the cauldron's resurrection.

While joy and relief permeated the air at the return of the lost, a somber realization also took hold. The cauldron, in its infinite power, could defy the natural order, but not without consequence.

These warriors, returned from the brink, would forever bear the weight of their second chance, a silent testament to the cauldron's might and the fragile balance of life and death.

The cauldron as a symbol isn't unique to Celtic tradition. It resonates with other vessels of abundance and rebirth in different cultures. For instance, in Welsh mythology, there's the Pair Dadeni, or the Cauldron of Rebirth, associated with Bran the Blessed.

With the decline of the Tuatha Dé Danann's influence and their retreat to the sídhe mounds, the location of the cauldron became one of the greatest mysteries. Some say it was buried deep within the earth, its magic seeping into the land making Ireland the lush, fertile land it is. Others believe it was taken away by Dagda to the otherworld, awaiting a time when the world would need it again.

Beyond its ability to provide unlimited sustenance, the Cauldron of Dagda also held spiritual connotations. In various mythologies worldwide, the cauldron or vessel symbolizes the womb of rebirth and regeneration. The ever-flowing nourishment from Dagda's cauldron can be seen as a metaphor for the endless cycle of life, death, and rebirth. Its parallels with the Grail of Christian lore, which provides spiritual sustenance, and other magical cauldrons in Welsh mythology, such as the Cauldron of Dyrnwch the Giant and Bran the Blessed's cauldron that can resurrect the dead, amplify the universal significance of such symbols across cultures.

Sources/Further Reading:

"Celtic Myths and Legends" by Peter Berresford Ellis
"The Encyclopedia of Celtic Mythology and Folklore" by Patricia Monaghan

Book of Thoth

Deep within the annals of ancient Egyptian lore lies the mention of a tome so powerful, so mysterious, that it's said to grant its reader the knowledge of the gods. This is the Book of Thoth, a compendium of divine wisdom, allegedly penned by Thoth, the deity of wisdom, magic, writing, and the moon.

In the pantheon of Egyptian gods, Thoth held a singularly unique position. Often depicted with the head of an ibis, a sacred bird associated with wisdom, Thoth was more than just a deity; he was the embodiment of knowledge, wisdom, and understanding. In some traditions, Thoth was also portrayed with the head of a baboon, another animal held sacred to him.

Thoth's domain encompassed various realms of knowledge. As the divine scribe, he was said to have invented writing, giving humanity the gift of hieroglyphics. Every major event, decree, or significant moment was penned by Thoth, making him the chronicler of time and history.

Beyond writing, Thoth was revered as the god of the moon, measuring time, mathematics, and more. His association with the moon further solidified his image as a deity of wisdom and knowledge, with the moon's cycles representing the ebb and flow of understanding.

In his eternal pursuit of knowledge, Thoth encapsulated his wisdom into a tome of unparalleled potency: The Book of Thoth. This book was said to contain spells, incantations, and knowledge that granted its possessor powers that rivaled the gods. Within its pages, one could find the secrets to understanding the language of animals, the ability to perceive and communicate with deities, and incantations that could manipulate the very fabric of reality.

Guarded Secrets: The Book's Hidden Abode

The book's power was so immense that it was said to be a distillation of the universe's secrets, a tangible manifestation of the cosmos's mysteries. Recognizing the dangers of such knowledge falling into mortal hands, it was decided that the Book of Thoth should be concealed from humanity. The location chosen for its safekeeping was near Coptos, at the bottom of the Nile, a river deeply intertwined with Egyptian life and mythology.

But merely placing it at the river's bottom wasn't deemed sufficient. The book was encased within a series of enchanted boxes — each box within another, made from different materials like bone, ebony, silver, and gold. This nesting of containers served as layers of protection, both physical and magical.

To further ensure its safety, the outermost box was guarded by serpents, creatures seen as the protectors of sacred knowledge and treasures. These weren't ordinary serpents but magical entities that would fiercely guard the book against any intruders.

Setna's Quest for the Book

In the golden age of Pharaonic Egypt, amidst its sprawling temples and the mystique of its gods, there was a prince who stood out not for his royal lineage, but for his insatiable thirst for knowledge. Prince Setna, the accomplished son of the mighty Pharaoh Ramesses II, was more than just a royal heir. He was a scholar, a magician, an ardent seeker of truths hidden away in the dusty scrolls of the great Egyptian libraries. His reputation extended beyond the palace walls, with tales of his wisdom echoing throughout the land. Yet, for all his learning, Setna was about to embark on an adventure that would test the very essence of his intellect and spirit.

Prince Setna had always heard whispers of the Book of Thoth's existence. The legends spoke of its unparalleled wisdom, a book that held the universe's very secrets. Such an artifact was irresistible to Setna, who, despite his vast knowledge, yearned for more.

Guided by arcane signs and ancient texts, Setna journeyed to the depths of the Nile near Coptos. There, he encountered the resting place of the book, shrouded in enchantments.

Setna, being a learned individual and skilled in the magical arts, employed his knowledge to counteract and dispel the enchantments guarding the book. He used specific spells, incantations, and rituals to pacify the creatures or make himself invisible to them.

Upon accessing the innermost chamber and the book, Setna's trials were far from over. Confronted by the spirits of Naneferkaptah and his family, Setna was regaled with the tragic tale of how the book brought about their downfall. The sight of a family of spirits guarding the book was disconcerting, but it was Naneferkaptah's words that truly chilled Setna's bones. The former priest, in spectral form, narrated his tale: his own obsession with the Book of Thoth, the perilous journey to retrieve it, and the tragic consequences that followed.

Naneferkaptah spoke of the challenges he faced to acquire the book - battling the serpent guardians, breaking the layers of protective casings, and finally, the overwhelming power he felt upon reading the book. However, for every action, there was a price. His quest for the forbidden led to the successive deaths of his son, wife, and eventually, his own. Each death was a direct result of the book's curse, exacting its toll on those who dared defy the boundaries set by the gods. This psychological barrier – the weight of Naneferkaptah's story and the implications of taking the book – was perhaps the most challenging barrier Setna faced.

But even as Setna listened to the mournful tale, the allure of the Book of Thoth was powerful. Believing he could control its power, Setna took the book, invoking the wrath of the spirits and the curse attached to it. The weight of Naneferkaptah's tragic story failed to deter Setna, as the glint of the Book of Thoth shone brighter than any warning. Almost immediately, the still air of the tomb grew cold, and the mournful wails of the spirits echoed in protest.

However, blinded by ambition, Setna brushed aside these ominous signs and left, eager to unlock the book's secrets.

Outside the tomb, the world was no longer as Setna remembered. The path back to the palace was fraught with illusions, and traps set by the spirits to reclaim the stolen treasure. The land seemed unfamiliar, with the very sands of Egypt shifting beneath his feet, turning the once-familiar terrain treacherous.

During his journey, he met Taboubu, a woman of unparalleled beauty, who invited him for a game of senet. But this was no ordinary game. With every move on the board, the stakes grew higher. As Setna lost, he found himself agreeing to more perilous terms, each more dangerous than the last. By the game's end, Setna realized he was ensnared in a deadly trap, one of his own making. Taboubu's laughter echoed in his ears as the world around him crumbled, showing her to be a mirage, a manifestation of the book's curse.

Desperate and disoriented, Setna continued his journey. The once glorious landscapes of Egypt now turned nightmarish, filled with distorted visions of his loved ones condemning him and phantasmal creatures threatening to pull him into the sands.

Setna's brother, Anherru, seeing Setna's tormented state, realized the grave error his sibling had committed. He pleaded with Setna to return the book, emphasizing the price of meddling with divine artifacts. His words, combined with the torturous trials, finally pierced Setna's hubris.

Together, the brothers retraced their steps, braving the illusions and supernatural barriers, to return to the tomb. Naneferkaptah's spirit awaited, not with anger, but with the solemnity of one who had suffered similarly. With a heavy heart, Setna placed the Book of Thoth back, uttering a heartfelt apology.

In a moment of profound silence, the spirits forgave him. The tomb's atmosphere lightened, and the path back to the palace became clear.

As Setna emerged into the daylight, he felt as though a heavy weight had been lifted. He realized that some knowledge, however tantalizing, is best left untouched. With newfound respect for boundaries, Setna returned to his scholarly pursuits, forever changed by his perilous quest.

The Tale of Prince Setna serves as a cautionary tale about the allure of forbidden knowledge, the consequences of hubris, and the understanding that some powers, no matter how tempting, are best left untouched. It underscores the ancient Egyptian beliefs about the balance of ma'at (cosmic order) and the delicate equilibrium between humanity's ambitions and the divine order.

The idea of a book containing ultimate knowledge is not unique to Egyptian culture. The concept of a powerful, forbidden, or sacred book appears in various other cultures and mythologies. However, the Book of Thoth, due to its ancient origins, might have influenced or paralleled other such concepts.

The Book of Thoth has made its way into modern esoteric traditions and popular culture. Aleister Crowley, an English occultist, wrote "The Book of Thoth" in the 20th century, which is an interpretation of the Tarot, linking it to Egyptian concepts.

The Book of Thoth symbolizes humanity's eternal quest for knowledge, the allure of the forbidden, and the fine line between enlightenment and hubris. Its legend serves as a reminder that some knowledge, while tempting, might be beyond human comprehension or control.

Sources/ Further Reading:

"The Tale of Setna and the Mummies" - An ancient Egyptian story.
"The Egyptian Book of the Dead" - A comprehensive text on ancient Egyptian afterlife beliefs, mentioning Thoth's role as a divine scribe.
"The Hermetica" - Texts attributed to Thoth-Hermes, providing insights into the philosophical and mystical ideas linked to Thoth.

Brisingamen

In the vast labyrinth of Norse mythology, where gods and giants clash and heroes venture into realms unknown, certain artifacts stand out for their sheer magnificence and the tales they inspire. The Brísingamen, a necklace of unparalleled beauty, is one such artifact. Glimmering with an inner light, it is said to be crafted from the finest gold, interwoven with gems that capture the very essence of the dawn, or, as some tales suggest, made of amber that has captured the golden radiance of the setting sun.

Freyja, the vivacious Norse goddess of love, fertility, and beauty, was its proud possessor. Her already formidable allure was heightened manifold by the Brísingamen, making her irresistible to both gods and mortals. But this necklace was not simply a passive ornament; it was an emblem of Freyja's power, her desires, and the lengths she would go to fulfill them. The story of how this necklace came to be around the goddess's neck is one filled with passion, negotiation, and a hint of deception, reflecting the intricate dance of desire and sacrifice that even gods must engage in.

The Price of Desire

On a day when the borders between realms seemed especially thin, Freyja, often moved by her whims and passions, ventured beyond the golden halls of Asgard. Her wanderings led her deep into the labyrinthine caverns of Svartálfar, the land of the dwarves. It was here, amidst the dimly lit tunnels and echoing chambers, that a soft, mesmerizing glow caught her eye.

Drawn to it like a moth to flame, she found herself in the workshop of four dwarven craftsmen, known as the Brísings. These were no ordinary dwarves but master smiths, famed throughout the realms for their unparalleled skill. They had combined their expertise to forge an artifact that was their magnum opus - the Brísingamen.

The necklace lay displayed upon a stone pedestal, its golden links intertwined with precious gems that shimmered in colors Freyja had never seen before. Each gem seemed to pulse with an inner light, reflecting the very essence of the cosmos. The gold seemed alive, moving and swirling as if liquid, yet holding firm in its form.

Freyja, who had witnessed countless treasures and owned many herself, was left breathless. The sheer beauty of the Brísingamen resonated with her very being. She recognized its power, not just as an adornment but as a symbol of influence and prestige. It was clear that owning such a necklace would amplify her own powers, making her allure even more irresistible.

Without hesitation, she expressed her desire to have it. Yet the Brísings, aware of the value of their creation, were not easily swayed by mere gold or silver.

The dwarves, captivated by Freyja's allure, had their own terms for parting with the necklace. They each desired her company—one night for each of them. Freyja, understanding the depth of their desire and reflecting upon her own for the Brísingamen, conceded to their terms. After four nights, with the weight of her choices resting heavily upon her, the treasured necklace was hers.

Freyja, even without the Brísingamen, was a figure of immense significance in Norse mythology. As a goddess of love, beauty, fertility, and war, her influence spanned the breadth of both human emotions and the turbulent world of the gods. When she wore the Brísingamen, these attributes were not just enhanced—they transcended to a level of divine prowess that was unparalleled.

The Brísingamen's radiance wasn't solely an indication of its beauty, but a manifestation of its latent power. With this necklace, Freyja could tap into the primal forces of creation and destruction. It allowed her to bless the land, ensuring fertility and bountiful harvests, or curse it, bringing drought and famine. This was particularly significant given the harsh and unpredictable climate of the Norse lands, where a good harvest was a direct difference between life and death.

The Norse believed in the concept of fate, often personified by the Norns – goddesses who wove the destinies of both gods and mortals. With the Brísingamen, Freyja could, to an extent, intervene in this fabric. While she couldn't rewrite destinies wholesale, she could influence them, nudging events or granting favor to those she deemed worthy.

Given her dominion over love, the necklace also amplified Freyja's ability to sow affection or discord. Tales spoke of battles instigated by feuds of the heart or wars halted by sudden truces, all whispered to be the influence of Freyja and her prized necklace.

Understanding its power, Freyja was also fiercely protective of the Brísingamen. The necklace wasn't just a tool; it became an intrinsic part of her identity. In the hands of another, it could be a weapon of unimaginable consequence.

Loki's Mischief

Loki, ever the instigator of chaos, was well aware of the Brísingamen's power and the heightened status it bestowed upon Freyja. Whether motivated by envy, mischief, or a deeper agenda, the necklace's allure was too much for Loki to resist.

Using his gift of shape-shifting, Loki transformed into a fly, allowing him to discreetly enter Freyja's chambers. As the goddess lay in deep slumber, the shimmering glow of the Brísingamen around her neck was irresistible. Ever so gently, using his guile and dexterity, Loki reverted to his original form just long enough to unclasp the necklace and make his escape.

Awakening to find her cherished necklace missing, Freyja's grief was profound. But more than sorrow, it was a fiery rage that consumed her. Her suspicions immediately fell upon Loki, who had a history of thievery and mischief. Seeking justice, she approached Odin.

Odin, understanding the potential disaster that could arise if the Brísingamen remained in Loki's hands, ordered him to return it. However, he wanted Loki to understand the gravity of his actions and decided to teach him a lesson.

Odin alerted Heimdall, the ever-vigilant guardian of the Bifröst bridge, about Loki's theft. Heimdall, gifted with extraordinarily keen senses, could hear the grass grow and see for hundreds of miles. It didn't take long for him to spot Loki.

As Loki tried to escape, he transformed into a hawk. Heimdall responded by turning into an eagle, setting off a high-paced aerial chase. The skies of Asgard echoed with the flapping of wings and the screeches of the two adversaries.

The chase culminated near the borders of Asgard. Loki, sensing his imminent capture, tried one last trick, transforming again to slip away. But Heimdall was prepared. In a final, decisive confrontation, Heimdall managed to capture Loki and retrieve the stolen necklace.

Brought before Odin and a furious Freyja, Loki faced the combined wrath of the gods. Odin decreed a fitting punishment, ensuring Loki would think twice before crossing Freyja again. The necklace was returned to its rightful owner, its gleam a bit brighter, perhaps, as it bore witness to loyalty, cunning, and the relentless pursuit of justice in the realms of the gods.

The Brísingamen is more than just a physical adornment. It represents the dual nature of desire: the lengths one might go to obtain what they covet, and the potential consequences of such pursuits. Freyja, as a goddess of love and fertility, wearing a necklace that symbolizes intense desire, adds layers of meaning to her character and the myths surrounding her.

The Brísingamen, with its gleaming allure, is a symbol of both beauty and power in Norse mythology. Its intricate ties with Freyja, a goddess who embodies love, beauty, and fertility, underscores the intertwined nature of beauty, desire, and strength.

Sources/Further Reading:

"The Prose Edda" by Snorri Sturluson
"Norse Mythology: A Guide to Gods, Heroes, Rituals, and Beliefs" by John Lindow
Norse Mythology for Smart People by Daniel McCoy

Caduceus

The Caduceus, often mistaken for the Rod of Asclepius, is a symbol that has been associated with Hermes (Mercury in Roman mythology), commerce, and negotiation. It is represented by a staff entwined with two serpents, usually topped with wings.

The Caduceus is a captivating artifact, merging both mythological significance and modern misconceptions. Its origins trace back to ancient Greece, acting as the herald's staff for the god Hermes, the messenger of the gods, protector of merchants, and bringer of dreams. Over time, its symbolic associations expanded, even mistakenly linking it to medicine in modern contexts.

Hermes was no ordinary deity. As the son of Zeus and Maia, his influence spanned various domains. As the swift-footed messenger of the Olympian gods, he bridged the divine and mortal realms, carrying tidings and guiding souls. But his roles didn't stop there. Hermes was also revered as the patron of travelers and merchants, guiding them through perilous journeys and ensuring fair trade. In the realm of dreams, he was the silent visitor, ushering in visions and nighttime revelations.

Hermes, known for his swiftness and cunning, was a multifaceted deity. While primarily recognized as the messenger of the gods, his role extended to being the protector of travelers, thieves, and merchants. His position as a guide for souls to the underworld further emphasized his intermediary nature, a bridge between realms, both divine and mortal.

Hermes also played the role of Psychopompos, the guide of souls to the afterlife. In this capacity, the Caduceus helped him navigate between the mortal realm and the Underworld. The staff, with its intertwined snakes, might represent the delicate balance between life and death. Hermes, with the Caduceus in hand, ensured the souls' safe passage across the River Styx to Hades.

The Origin of the Caduceus: The Serpents' Dance

In the verdant valleys of Arcadia, where the boundaries between the mortal realm and the world of gods often blurred, a unique event transpired. One day, as Hermes, the swift-footed messenger of the gods, traversed the land, he chanced upon two serpents embroiled in fierce combat. Their bodies were entangled, their fangs bared, each striving for dominance over the other.

Recognizing the inherent danger and perhaps sensing a deeper cosmic significance in their struggle, Hermes approached the battling creatures. With a gentle but firm motion, he placed his staff between the two, urging them apart. The serpents, sensing the divine aura of Hermes and the power of his staff, ceased their conflict.

Rather than slithering away, something miraculous occurred. Drawn to the staff, the snakes began to wind around it, their once aggressive motions transforming into a dance of unity and balance. They coiled around the staff in perfect symmetry, their previous animosity replaced by a newfound harmony.

This transformational act was rich in symbolism. The two snakes could be interpreted as representations of opposing forces in nature: life and death, light and darkness, chaos and order. By intervening, Hermes brought these dualities into equilibrium, underlining his role as a mediator and messenger between realms and forces.

The sight of the harmoniously entwined serpents upon his staff imbued it with a powerful aura, marking it as an object of significance. Hermes would carry this emblem, not just as a symbol of his divine office, but as a constant reminder of the balance and reconciliation he had brought about. It became a representation of duality in unity, showcasing how opposing forces when guided by divine intervention, can achieve harmony.

Over time, the tale of the Caduceus spread throughout Greece, with poets and bards singing of the day when Hermes turned conflict into concord, making it an enduring symbol of equilibrium in a world often marked by contrasts.

The All-Seeing Guardian: Argus Panoptes

In the intricate web of Greek myths, Argus stands out as a unique sentinel. Argus, often referred to as Argus Panoptes (meaning "all-seeing"), was a giant with a hundred eyes. His epithet, "Panoptes", was not mere embellishment; it testified to his ability to see everything. With a hundred vigilant eyes scattered over his body, Argus could sleep with some eyes while others remained alert, making him the perfect watchman.

Io was once a beautiful priestess of Hera, but she caught the eye of the ever-roving Zeus. To protect her from his wife Hera's wrath, Zeus transformed Io into a white heifer. However, Hera, fully aware of her husband's antics, pretended to be charmed by the heifer and asked to keep it as a gift. Once Zeus reluctantly handed Io over, Hera assigned Argus to be her eternal jailer, ensuring that Zeus couldn't revert the transformation unnoticed.

Zeus, desperate to free Io and assuage his guilt, turned to his son Hermes for assistance. Renowned for his cunning and wit, Hermes was the ideal candidate to outsmart Argus.

Assuming the guise of a shepherd, Hermes ventured near Argus. Strumming his lyre, he began playing gentle, hypnotic tunes. As he played, he regaled Argus with stories, one for each of Argus's eyes, perhaps even inventing the art of storytelling during this mission. The combination of the lyre's sweet music and Hermes' droning tales made Argus drowsy. But even then, with most of his eyes closing, some eyes remained watchful.

It's at this crucial juncture that the Caduceus came into play. Enhancing the staff's innate magical properties, Hermes used it to amplify the soporific effects of his stories, sending all of Argus's hundred eyes into slumber.

Once Argus was deep in sleep, Hermes, using his divine might and the Caduceus as a weapon, struck down the giant, liberating Io from her vigilant jailer.

Caduceus vs. Rod of Asclepius

Over time, a point of contention has arisen surrounding the Caduceus, particularly in its modern representation. The Caduceus, often associated with Hermes and its original meanings of commerce and negotiation, has been mistakenly used as a symbol for medicine. The true medical symbol from ancient times is the Rod of Asclepius, which features a single serpent wrapped around a staff, without wings.

This confusion primarily stems from the early 20th century when the U.S. military adopted the Caduceus as the insignia for its Medical Corps. The mistaken association persisted, leading to the Caduceus's widespread, albeit inaccurate, use as a medical symbol.

Today, due to historical mix-ups and similarities in design, the Caduceus often finds itself erroneously adorning medical institutions, representing healing and healthcare – a departure from its original mythological intent.

Sources/ Further Reading:

"The Iliad" and "The Odyssey" by Homer
"The Greek Myths" by Robert Graves
"Hermes the Thief: The Evolution of a Myth" by Norman O. Brown

Cap of Hermes

A less highlighted but equally intriguing artifact from Greek mythology is the Cap of Hermes, also known as the Petasos. Often overshadowed by the Caduceus, Hermes's staff, this winged cap is emblematic of the swift nature of the god it belonged to. Hermes, recognized as the divine messenger of the gods and the patron of travelers and boundaries, wore this unique cap on his many journeys and exploits.

Historically, the Petasos was a type of hat worn by the ancient Greeks, especially those in rural areas. It typically had a wide brim, serving to protect the wearer from the sun and rain. For Hermes, however, this was no ordinary hat. Adorned with wings, it symbolized the swiftness and freedom with which the god moved between realms - mortal and divine, land and sky, and even the underworld.

While the Cap of Hermes is a recognizable element of Hermes's iconography, it is not as prominently featured in specific myths as, say, the Caduceus or Hermes's winged sandals. However, it does play a subtle but continuous role in many of the tales involving Hermes, emphasizing his swift nature and role as a messenger god.

The Cunning Caper of the Cattle

It was mere days after Hermes's birth to Maia that his insatiable curiosity and penchant for mischief first revealed itself. Nestled in a cave on Mount Cyllene, the infant god was restless. While the world outside was vast and full of wonders, Hermes felt a particular pull towards the radiant cattle of Apollo, his elder half-brother, grazing in the fields of Pieria.

Deciding on an audacious scheme, Hermes ventured forth. The Petasos, though seemingly simple in design, was an embodiment of Hermes's cleverness. Placing it upon his head, granted him swiftness, not just in movement but in thought as well. Every step he took, every decision he made, was calculated to conceal his identity. He craftily drove the cattle backward and created shoes for them from intertwined branches to further confuse any trackers.

However, his wit wasn't only reserved for the cattle. Before returning to his cave, he stumbled upon a tortoise, its hard shell inspiring him. Swiftly, using the strings from the cattle he had stolen, he crafted the first lyre. His fingers danced on the strings, pulling melodies into the evening air. This instrument would later play a crucial role in reconciling with Apollo.

Apollo, using his divine powers of prophecy and perception, soon discerned the thief but was perplexed by the confusing trail Hermes had left behind. When he finally confronted Hermes, the young god played innocent, the Petasos on his head concealing any mischievous glint in his eye.

A confrontation between the two seemed imminent, but Hermes, ever the charmer, began to strum his newly crafted lyre. The notes, so pure and mesmerizing, captivated Apollo, the god of music. The melody told stories of playful mischief, brotherhood, and the vast web of existence. By the song's end, Apollo's anger had melted away. In exchange for the enchanting lyre, Apollo allowed Hermes to keep the cattle.

The Petasos, meanwhile, remained with Hermes throughout, a silent witness to the young god's first adventure. It was not just a cap, but a testament to Hermes's quick thinking and unparalleled cunning, characteristics that would define many of his future exploits.

Hermes and the Secret of the Petasos

In ancient times, a challenge arose among the gods of Olympus: Who could traverse the world and return with the most unique treasure? As the gods set forth on their quests, Hermes knew that speed would be his advantage.

While his winged sandals would carry him swiftly across land and sea, Hermes realized that thoughts and dreams travel even faster than the wind. With this insight, he used the Petasos, a cap designed not just to protect him from the elements, but to capture the fleeting thoughts and dreams of mortals and immortals alike.

On his journey, Hermes encountered tales of love, ambition, hope, and despair. The Petasos, brushing against the minds of those it neared, gathered these stories. In the Far East, it captured the dreams of a young poet longing for his distant love. In the frozen North, the ambitions of a warrior dreaming of honor and glory whispered to the cap. From Africa, tales of vast landscapes and the rhythm of life pulsed into the Petasos. Returning to Olympus, while the other gods presented physical treasures — golden apples, pearls from the deepest oceans, and rare gems from the heart of mountains — Hermes offered stories, dreams, and the essence of humanity's spirit, all collected within the folds of his winged cap.

The gods were entranced. Physical treasures, they had seen aplenty, but the raw, unfiltered essence of mortal life was a rarity even for them. Hermes's treasure was declared the most unique, and the true power of the Petasos was acknowledged. From then on, the cap was not just a symbol of Hermes's swiftness but also a reservoir of dreams, stories, and the very spirit of life.

In artistic depictions, Hermes is often illustrated with his three primary attributes: The Caduceus, winged sandals (Talaria), and the Petasos. Each represents different facets of his nature, but the Petasos, in particular, underscores his unbounded nature, able to travel wherever and whenever he pleases. While it might not be the most famous artifact associated with Hermes, the Petasos is a testament to the intricate nature of myths and their capacity to embed multifaceted symbols into narratives. The Cap of Hermes, more than just an accessory, encapsulates the very essence of the god it adorned.

Sources/Further Reading:

"The Iliad" and "The Odyssey" by Homer
"Theogony" by Hesiod

Chintamani Stone

Deeply embedded in Eastern mythology, particularly within Hindu and Buddhist traditions, the Chintamani Stone is often referred to as the "Wish-Fulfilling Gem." It is said to possess unparalleled spiritual, cosmic, and transformative powers, making it a highly sought-after artifact in myths and legends.

The Chintamani Stone's roots can be traced back to ancient Hindu lore where it was often associated with the gods, symbolizing the divine power of fulfillment. However, its prominence is most notable within Buddhist teachings, where it's often connected to the Bodhisattvas, like Avalokiteshvara and Ksitigarbha. In these contexts, the stone represents the Bodhisattvas' vow to help sentient beings achieve enlightenment and liberate them from suffering.

The Chintamani Stone is typically depicted as a luminous blue gem, sometimes with a fiery intensity, shining from within. Though its size can vary across tales, its mystical abilities remain consistent. It's believed that merely possessing the stone can grant one's desires, bringing forth both material and spiritual benefits. In addition, its presence can induce enlightenment, transform the mind, and lead one to higher realms of existence.

Gift from the Sky

In the depths of space, the Sirius star system stands out, not just for its brightness but for its mystical connections to various ancient civilizations. Located in the Canis Major constellation, Sirius has been referenced by various cultures, from the ancient Egyptians to the Dogon tribe of Mali, all of whom attributed great significance to it. Within this cosmic context, the legend of the Chintamani Stone emerges as a bridge between Earth and the universe.

It is said that eons ago, as galaxies danced and stars collided, the Chintamani Stone was forged in the fiery heart of Sirius. Imbued with powerful energies, the stone encapsulated the wisdom of the cosmos, a literal fragment of the universe's soul. The legend recounts a moment, a cosmic event, when the stone, radiating celestial energy, began its descent towards Earth.

As it entered our atmosphere, it didn't crash like a typical meteorite. Instead, it is believed to have fragmented, scattering pieces across the globe. Each fragment, though separated, retained the essence and power of the original stone.

The places where these fragments landed became points of immense energy, sometimes referred to as 'Earth's chakras' or 'power vortexes.' These locations, over time, often emerged as significant spiritual hubs or places of mysterious occurrences, drawing seekers, sages, and mystics.

Those who stumbled upon or sought out these fragments often spoke of profound experiences: heightened intuition, visions of other realms, and deepened spiritual insights. Some legends speak of entire ancient civilizations that were built around the discovery of such a fragment, with its energy influencing their spiritual practices, technological advancements, and understanding of the cosmos.

Over time, as knowledge of the stone's origin and power spread, secret orders and societies arose, dedicating themselves to finding these fragments, understanding their power, and guarding them against those who might misuse them. They believed that the Chintamani Stone fragments were not mere objects but keys to unlocking the deeper mysteries of existence.

The Protector's Vow: Ksitigarbha and the Chintamani Stone

The underworld, a realm of wandering souls and unquenched desires, was often painted with imagery of desolation and eternal suffering. Within this realm, the story unfolds around Ksitigarbha, a Bodhisattva of immeasurable compassion, whose very name translates to "Earth Treasury" or "Womb of the Earth." His was a mission unlike any other: to be a beacon of hope and salvation in the depths of spiritual darkness.

Ksitigarbha, seeing the pain of souls trapped in cycles of karma and reincarnation, made a profound vow. He swore not to achieve complete Buddhahood until every corner of hell was emptied, a testament to his boundless compassion. But in his mission, he needed aid, something that could pierce through the dense layers of anguish and attachment binding these souls. This is where the Chintamani Stone enters the narrative.

Upon possessing the Chintamani Stone, it's said that its celestial radiance merged with Ksitigarbha's own inner light. This gem, with its cosmic origin, resonated with energies that could break the chains of karmic cycles. It wasn't just a tool but an extension of the Bodhisattva's own will, amplifying his powers and aiding his monumental task.

With the stone, Ksitigarbha would approach the souls, its glow casting a protective circle. He would communicate with them, and hear their tales of regret, pain, and unfulfilled desires. Using the Chintamani Stone, he illuminated their paths, making them recognize their past actions and guiding them toward liberation. The stone, in essence, acted as a mirror, making souls self-aware, aiding their journey from the depths of despair to the possibility of rebirth or even enlightenment.

Temples dedicated to Ksitigarbha often depicted him holding the radiant Chintamani Stone. Over time, tales of his deeds spread across lands, turning him into a symbol of hope for those grieving for their departed loved ones. Parents prayed to him, invoking the power of the Chintamani Stone, hoping their lost children would find solace and guidance in the afterlife.

The intertwining stories of Ksitigarbha and the Chintamani Stone reflect the profound belief in redemption, salvation, and the transformative power of compassion. They highlight the journey from darkness to light, the transformative potential every soul possesses, and the unyielding belief that even in the bleakest corners, there exists a guiding light, a path to salvation.

The legend of the Chintamani Stone has transcended its religious origins, making its way into popular culture. It's been a subject of interest in various novels, films, and video games, often portrayed as an artifact of immense power. Whether it's granting wishes, providing immense knowledge, or offering spiritual enlightenment, the Chintamani Stone remains a symbol of the infinite potential that lies within and beyond the human realm. Spanning across religious scriptures, ancient myths, and modern tales, the Chintamani Stone embodies humanity's eternal quest for enlightenment, fulfillment, and connection to the cosmos.

Sources/Further Reading:

"Ksitigarbha Bodhisattva Pūrvapraṇidhāna Sūtra"
"The Encyclopedia of Tibetan Symbols and Motifs" by Robert Beer
Buddhanet: An extensive online database on Buddhism.

Club of Heracles

One of the most iconic symbols associated with Heracles, the greatest of the Greek heroes, is his massive club. Often depicted as a crude wooden weapon, it signifies Heracles' raw power and primal strength. Paired with the Nemean Lion's pelt, these two items became the signature weapons of the hero and were as integral to his identity as his legendary labors.

The Club of Heracles doesn't have an elaborate origin story as some other mythical artifacts might. Instead, its significance lies in its simplicity. While many heroes in Greek mythology wielded weapons forged by gods or magical entities, Heracles' weapon of choice was often a massive club, likely hewn from a tree by the hero himself. This choice reflects his direct and brute-force approach to challenges.

The First Labor: Battle with the Nemean Lion

The Nemean Lion was not a mere beast; it was a monstrous creature, born from the union of Typhon and Echidna - two formidable entities in their own right. It was said to have terrorized the region of Nemea, its hide so thick that no metal or stone could pierce it. Legends whispered of its supernatural birth, suggesting that it was sent by Hera, a constant adversary of Heracles, to challenge and, possibly, destroy the hero.

Eurystheus, the king of Tiryns, who was overseeing Heracles' Twelve Labors due to a complicated curse and penance, knew that sending the hero against the Nemean Lion was no mere test of strength. It was a test of wits and resilience. The lion was not a foe that could be vanquished by traditional means, and Eurystheus hoped this task would be Heracles' undoing.

As Heracles ventured into Nemea, he quickly realized that conventional weapons were useless. His arrows bounced off, and swords bent upon contact with the lion's hide. The lion, sensing an advantage, became bolder in its attacks, pushing Heracles on the defensive.

But Heracles, ever the warrior, adapted. Realizing he couldn't pierce the hide, he opted for brute force. Using his massive club, he landed a stunning blow on the lion, disorienting it. Yet, even in its stunned state, the lion's hide was impenetrable.

Remembering his strength and training as a wrestler, Heracles grappled with the lion, attempting to strangle it. It was a perilous gamble, with each passing moment a battle of endurance between the two titans. But Heracles' sheer determination and might prevailed. As the lion's strength ebbed away, the landscape of Nemea echoed with the roars of their tumultuous struggle.

With the lion dead, Heracles faced another challenge: how to skin the creature when its hide couldn't be pierced by blades. Ingeniously, Heracles used one of the lion's own claws, sharp enough to cut through its magical hide. Draping the hide over him, it became a formidable piece of armor, offering him both protection and an imposing visage.

From this labor onward, the image of Heracles wearing the Nemean Lion's hide and wielding his club became iconic, a symbol of both his physical prowess and his ability to overcome seemingly insurmountable odds.

Confrontation with Death: The Rescuing of Alcestis

Admetus, King of Pherae, was granted a favor by the god Apollo — when his time came to die, he could avoid death if someone willingly sacrificed their life for him. When the day arrived, none volunteered, not even his elderly parents. Only his loving wife, Alcestis, chose to give her life for him, an ultimate gesture of love. She surrendered herself to Thanatos - the god of death, ensuring Admetus would live.

Heracles, while traveling, arrived at the court of Admetus on that fateful day. Admetus, in his grief, hid the reason for the mourning but offered Heracles hospitality, not wanting to deny the sacred laws of guest-friendship. Heracles, unaware of the tragedy, indulged in merriment. Once he learned of Alcestis's sacrifice, chagrined at his own behavior, he decided to right the wrong.

To repay Admetus and atone for his unintended slight, Heracles staked out the entrance to the Underworld. Upon encountering Thanatos, the son of Zeus, armed with his iconic club, lunged with fierce determination. His club landed on Death with resounding blows, forcing him to relinquish his claim on Alcestis. Indeed, Heracles was the hero who beat death with a club.

Heracles emerged from the Underworld's shadow, leading a veiled Alcestis by the hand. He presented her to an astonished Admetus, initially concealing her identity to test Admetus's resolve and to ensure he would not seek another wife. Once assured of Admetus's loyalty, he revealed Alcestis, restored to life and love.

Heracles's clash with Thanatos showcased his courage and the symbolic might of his club. More than a tale of strength, this story signifies the boundless limits of love, hope, and the idea that with champions like Heracles, even death can be overcome, if only momentarily.

The club, in many ways, is a manifestation of Heracles' nature: straightforward, powerful, and unforgiving. While it may not possess the enchantments of Excalibur or the history of the Spear of Destiny, the Club of Heracles stands out in its simplicity. It is a testament to the raw, untamed might of the greatest Greek hero, a symbol that power and success don't always come from intricate magics or divine blessings, but often from sheer determination, strength, and will.

Sources/Further Reading:

"The Greek Myths" by Robert Graves:
"The Complete World of Greek Mythology" by Richard Buxton
"The Library of Greek Mythology" by Apollodorus

Cohuleen Druith

The Cohuleen Druith is a magical, otherworldly item from the folklore of the Celtic Druids. Evocative of the deep, vast ocean and its untapped mysteries, this artifact, often envisioned as an ornate cap or hood, carries with it enchantments of old. When donned, the Cohuleen Druith bestows upon its wearer a profound gift: the ability to navigate the ocean's depths, breathe amidst the swirling currents, dancing with aquatic creatures, and uncovering secrets of the submerged world, all without the fear of the water's crushing embrace.

The origins of the Cohuleen Druith intertwine with the spiritual and mystical practices of the Druids. These ancient Celtic priests, scholars, and magicians held a deep veneration for the natural world, from the sprawling forests to the towering mountains and, of course, the expansive sea. The ocean, with its dual nature of beauty and peril, was especially significant in Celtic traditions, seen as both a source of sustenance and a gateway to otherworldly realms. The Cohuleen Druith emerged from this intersection of reverence and curiosity, embodying the Druids' aspiration to merge with nature in its most enigmatic form.

While descriptions vary across tales, the Cohuleen Druith is often imagined as a beautifully crafted piece, radiating with hues of the fiery horizon — deep crimson, burgundy, and rose-red. Its design may be adorned with patterns reminiscent of coral reefs or the mesmerizing dance of underwater flames. It might also be studded with rubies and garnets that gleam like the molten heart of a volcanic sea bed. Yet, beyond its aesthetic allure, it's the cap's inherent magic that truly captivates. A weave of ancient spells, chants of sea spirits, and the essence of the ocean itself might be infused into its very fabric, granting it its legendary properties.

The Tale of the Merrow and the Cohuleen Druith

In the depths of the Irish seas, beyond the reach of human eyes, lay the realm of the Merrow. These beings, with their long, flowing hair and entrancing voices, were the keepers of the sea's mysteries. Graceful and alluring, the Merrow swam amidst ancient shipwrecks, hidden caves, and coral palaces.

At the heart of their existence was the Cohuleen Druith, a cap of brilliant red hue that held more than just beauty. This magical artifact, interwoven with the enchantments of old and the blessings of sea deities, granted the Merrow the ability to dwell beneath the waves, dancing with dolphins and conversing with ancient sea turtles.

One day, a young Merrow maiden named Aine, known for her curiosity, ventured close to the shore. She was mesmerized by the world above: the golden sands, the singing birds, and the scent of blooming flowers. Engrossed in this new wonderland, she left her Cohuleen Druith on a rock and wandered further inland.

A fisherman named Sean, walking along the beach, stumbled upon the abandoned Cohuleen Druith. Picking it up and admiring its craftsmanship, he pocketed the magical cap, unaware of its powers and significance. When the sun began to set, Aine realized her mistake. Without her Cohuleen Druith, the sea — her home, was beyond her reach. She was stranded in a world she didn't belong to. Distraught, she searched for her lost cap but to no avail.

Sean, captivated by Aine's beauty and the sadness in her eyes, approached her. Through shared tales and moonlit conversations, Aine told him of her world beneath the waves and the magic of the Cohuleen Druith. Realizing what he had unknowingly taken, Sean returned the cap to the grateful Merrow.

But the story doesn't end there. Over time, the two fell deeply in love. Aine, torn between her newfound love and her longing for the deep, made a choice. Using the magic of the Cohuleen Druith, she granted Sean the ability to visit her underwater realm without having to stay there forever. Thus, the two lovers could traverse both worlds, forever bonded by the magic of the sea and the Cohuleen Druith.

The Cohuleen Druith is not just a magical accessory; it's a symbol. It speaks of the thin boundary between our known world and the uncharted, of the human longing to explore the unknown, and of the potential consequences of straying too far from one's natural realm. The tales of the Merrow, intertwined with the Cohuleen Druith, often carry a warning: the allure of the unknown is powerful, but every realm has its rules, and those who do not respect them might pay a price.

Sources/Further Reading:

"Fairy and Folk Tales of the Irish Peasantry" by W.B. Yeats
"The Celtic Twilight" by W.B. Yeats
"The Myths, Legends, and Lore of Ireland" by Amy Hackney Blackwell

Crown of Immortality

The Crown of Immortality, often depicted as a circlet of radiant, intertwined laurel leaves, is a timeless symbol deeply rooted in ancient mythologies. It stands as a testament to humanity's enduring aspiration for eternal life and triumph over mortality. Deeply rooted in ancient mythologies, this emblematic artifact symbolizes resurrection and the victory of life over death. Its form, whether simple or ornate, captures the essence of timelessness and the profound human desire for existence beyond the confines of the mortal coil. Representing eternal life and resurrection, it's an emblem of triumph over death, underscoring the enduring human desire for life beyond the mortal coil. The concept of an artifact bestowing eternal life is prevalent in many cultures, but the Crown stands out as an elegant, poetic representation of this aspiration.

The origins of the Crown of Immortality can be traced back to ancient civilizations that held nature in reverence. The laurel tree, in particular, was associated with the god Apollo in Greek mythology. The leaves of the laurel, evergreen and robust, became symbols of victory and were used to crown victors in the Pythian Games, which were held in Apollo's honor.

The Tale of Daphne and the Eternal Laurel

In the verdant woods of ancient Greece, the chase between a god and a nymph became the stuff of legends. Daphne, a nymph known not just for her beauty but also for her desire to remain untouched and free, spent her days basking in nature's glory. But like many of great beauty, she wasn't free from the eyes of admirers, the most formidable of whom was Apollo, the god of sun and music.

Their story began when Apollo mocked Eros, the god of love, belittling his archery skills. In retribution, Eros shot two arrows: one of gold that made Apollo fall deeply in love with Daphne and one of lead that made Daphne repel Apollo's advances. As Apollo, struck by the gold-tipped arrow, pursued Daphne with fervor, she, under the influence of the leaden arrow, sought only to escape.

Desperate to evade Apollo's relentless chase, Daphne made a heart-wrenching plea to her father, Peneus. She wished to remain untainted, even if it meant forsaking her beautiful form. Peneus, moved by his daughter's plea, transformed her into a laurel tree, her graceful limbs becoming branches and her flowing hair turning to leaves.

Apollo arrived at the scene only to find the object of his affections transformed. Unable to embrace the nymph he had chased, he was left with the immutable laurel tree. Overwhelmed by sorrow and loss, Apollo tenderly caressed the tree's bark and, with a vow, declared that the laurel would forever remain evergreen and would stand as a symbol of victory and eternal remembrance. Crafting a wreath from its leaves, Apollo made the laurel an emblem of his undying love for Daphne and a sign of honor and triumph.

From this poignant tale, the laurel became a symbol not only of victory but also of the sacrifices made for one's honor and principles. The Crown of Immortality, often interlinked with the laurel, encapsulates this duality of eternal love and steadfast honor.

The concept of a crown or wreath symbolizing immortality is not confined to Greek mythology. In Roman traditions, victorious commanders during their triumphal processions wore laurel wreaths, representing their ascent to a god-like status. In Christianity, the crown of thorns worn by Jesus Christ during his crucifixion can be viewed as a symbol of eternal life through sacrifice. Similarly, in many cultures, the idea of a circlet or crown representing divine favor, eternal life, or resurrection is prevalent.

Over the ages, the Crown of Immortality has become a popular motif in art, literature, and culture. From Renaissance paintings to modern fantasy tales, the idea of a crown or artifact that bestows eternal life remains a captivating concept. It symbolizes humanity's timeless hope for a life beyond death, a victory over the ephemeral nature of existence.

While the Crown of Immortality might be a mythological construct, its significance is profound. It serves as a reflection of human aspirations, desires, and the age-old quest for understanding life's mysteries. Whether seen as a symbol of eternal love, as with Apollo and Daphne, or the ultimate triumph over mortality, the Crown stands as a beacon of hope in the face of life's transient nature.

Sources/Further Reading:

"Metamorphoses" by Ovid
"The Greek Myths" by Robert Graves
"Greek Art and Archaeology" by John G. Pedley

Draupnir

In the vast and intricate depths of Norse mythology, among gods, giants, and otherworldly beings, there exists a collection of powerful artifacts that have captivated the imagination of many. Among these, one finds Draupnir, a ring of immeasurable value and enchantment.

Draupnir, translating to "the dripper" in Old Norse, is a gold ring steeped in Norse mythology. It's not just any ring, but a symbol of opulence, providence, and the inexhaustible wealth of the gods, particularly the Allfather, Odin. The magic of Draupnir lies in its ability to multiply. Every ninth night, the ring miraculously 'drips' eight new gold rings of equal weight and beauty, reflecting the notion of inexhaustible wealth and divine abundance.

Draupnir's Genesis: A Wager of Deception

The roots of Draupnir's creation lie in a mischievous scheme plotted by Loki, the ever-troublesome trickster god of the Norse pantheon. Loki, having maliciously sheared off the hair of Sif, Thor's wife, found himself at the receiving end of the thunder god's wrath. In a desperate bid to placate Thor and save his own skin, Loki promised to fetch even finer hair made of pure gold for Sif, along with gifts for the gods that would surpass everything they currently possessed.

To fulfill his rash promise, Loki approached the talented dwarf brothers, Brokkr and Sindri. However, ever the mischief-maker, Loki didn't just commission the items; he made it into a competition. He claimed that the brothers could not surpass the craftsmanship of two other dwarfs, sons of Ivaldi, whom Loki commissioned to make gifts for the gods as well. Brokkr and Sindri took on the challenge, with high stakes: if they lost, Loki could take Brokkr's head.

Amidst the fiery depths of their forge, the brothers began their divine craftsmanship. As Sindri worked the bellows, Brokkr operated the forge, crafting marvels one after another. However, Loki, not wanting to lose, transformed into a fly and bit Brokkr in an attempt to disrupt their work. Despite the distraction, the brothers managed to forge three magical items: a boar with golden bristles called Gullinbursti, a ship named Skidbladnir that could be folded and kept in one's pocket, and the magical ring, Draupnir.

Upon completion, both sets of gifts (those crafted by Brokkr and Sindri, and those by the sons of Ivaldi) were presented to the gods for judgment. Each god received a gift, and each gift had its unique marvel. Odin received the ring Draupnir, which dripped eight other gold rings every ninth night, epitomizing endless wealth and prosperity.

In the end, it was deemed that the brothers' gifts held greater value. Loki tried to wriggle out of the bet but was outwitted and endured punishment from Brokkr and his tools.

Draupnir's Odyssey: An Emblem of Endless Grief and Hope

Balder, often called "Baldr" in Old Norse texts, was one of the Aesir gods in Norse mythology. He was the son of Odin, the chief of the gods, and Frigg, the queen goddess.

Balder's death is a pivotal event in Norse mythology and is surrounded by a series of omens and dreams. He began to have nightmares about his own demise, which greatly alarmed the gods. Concerned, his mother Frigg made every object on earth vow never to harm Balder. Everything complied except for the mistletoe, which she viewed as too young and harmless to swear an oath.

Loki, the trickster god known for his cunning and deceit, learned of this oversight. Seeing an opportunity to sow chaos, he crafted an arrow or dart made of mistletoe. Loki then tricked Hodr, Balder's blind brother, into throwing this dart at Balder during a game where the gods amusingly hurled objects at Balder, marveling at how none could harm him. Guided by Loki, Hodr's throw struck Balder, causing his immediate death.

Balder's death sent ripples of despair throughout the Aesir. As the most beloved among them, his absence cast a shadow over their divine realm. The gods and goddesses convened to honor him in a way befitting his glory. As preparations were made for his funeral pyre, tokens of immense value and sentimental significance were chosen as offerings. At the heart of these tokens was Draupnir, the ring that dripped wealth.

Placing Draupnir on Balder's funeral pyre symbolized more than just an offering; it was a heart-wrenching testament of Odin's grief. The ring, which was a manifestation of boundless abundance and prosperity, now bore witness to the ultimate price: the loss of a beloved son. As the flames consumed Balder's mortal form and

Draupnir gleamed amidst the flames, it was as if the ring's luminescence mirrored the tears of the gods, reflecting their sorrow and their hope for a brighter dawn.

Upon Balder's death, the halls of Asgard were enshrouded in grief. Yet, within Odin's heart, a glimmer of hope persisted. He dispatched Hermóðr, a brave god known for his resolve, on a mission to Hel, the realm of the dead, to negotiate Balder's return. Armed with his determination and riding Sleipnir, Odin's swift eight-legged steed, Hermóðr ventured into the cold depths of the underworld.

His journey was fraught with challenges and sights that would deter lesser beings. Yet, Hermóðr pressed on, driven by the combined weight of Odin's hope and the Aesir's longing for Balder. When Hermóðr reached Hel's hall, he found Balder sitting in a place of honor. In Hel, Hermóðr met with its ruler, also named Hel, and pleaded for Balder's release. Hel agreed to release Balder under one condition: everything in the world, living and dead, must weep for him to prove his universal love. If even one thing did not, Balder would remain with her.

The Aesir sent out messengers to request everything to weep for Balder. All did, except for a giantess named Thökk (often believed to be Loki in disguise), who refused. Therefore, Balder had to remain in the underworld. The Draupnir, Odin's self-duplicating gold ring thus ended up in Hel with Balder.

The imagery of Draupnir is profound. In a culture where the essence of life and fate was often seen as interwoven threads, the continuous production of gold from Draupnir symbolized not just physical wealth, but the richness of life, legacy, and memory. The ring, in its endless generation, can also be seen as a representation of the cyclical nature of life, death, and rebirth in Norse cosmology.

Sources/Further Reading:

"The Prose Edda" by Snorri Sturluson
"Norse Mythology" by Neil Gaiman
"The Norse Myths" by Kevin Crossley-Holland

Dyrnwyn

Dyrnwyn, known by its evocative name "White-Hilt", stands as a beacon among the myriad of enchanted objects in Welsh mythology. This isn't just a blade forged for battle; it is a testament to the intricate weave of magic and moral fiber that underscores the ancient Welsh worldview. Beyond its formidable edge, Dyrnwyn boasts mystical qualities that discern the very essence of its bearer, responding fervently to the righteous and recoiling from the unworthy. profound relationship between power and virtue in the lore of the Celts.

Dyrnwyn's legacy is intrinsically bound to its illustrious bearer, Rhydderch Hael. As a beacon of benevolence and grandeur, Rhydderch is immortalized in Welsh history as one of the "Three Generous Men of Britain," a title bestowed upon those of extraordinary magnanimity, as celebrated in the revered Welsh Triads. Yet, the grandeur of the king is further accentuated by Dyrnwyn, his legendary sword.

But Dyrnwyn isn't simply a weapon; it's a mirror reflecting the soul of its handler. Forged from enchantments as ancient as the hills of Wales itself, this blade possesses a unique dichotomy. When unsheathed by a man of genuine nobility and honor, the blade erupts into a brilliant blaze, its fire symbolizing the purity and righteousness of its wielder. This ethereal flame not only augments the sword's might but also serves as a beacon of justice and virtue on the battlefield.

Conversely, in the grip of deceit or malice, Dyrnwyn reveals its wrathful side. Those unworthy of its power, attempting to draw it with ill intentions or a tainted heart, find themselves ensnared by its vengeful flames. Rather than a tool, the sword becomes an arbiter, ensuring that its immense power is channeled only by those who uphold the ideals it represents. In this way, Dyrnwyn stands as a sentinel, guarding the fine balance between might and righteousness in Welsh lore.

Rhydderch and the Quest for Dyrnwyn

In the verdant valleys of Wales, when magic still pulsed through the very earth and skies, Rhydderch Hael, a young prince then, heard whispers of a sword forged from Starfire and imbued with the essence of dragons. This sword was Dyrnwyn, a blade that could blaze with fierce fire when wielded by the worthy and consume with its flames those of wicked intent.

Rhydderch, ever curious and eager to prove himself, set his heart on retrieving the sword. The stories spoke of its last known resting place: nestled within the heart of the treacherous Labyrinth of

Llyn, guarded by ancient spirits and enchantments. Many had entered, seeking the sword's power, but none had returned.

Accompanied by a band of loyal warriors and guided by the wise old Druid, Myrrdin, Rhydderch embarked on his quest. Through thick forests where trees whispered secrets, across vast plains where shadows held mysteries, the prince and his party finally reached the labyrinth's entrance.

The maze was a confounding and shifting puzzle, with walls that moved and paths that vanished. More than once, Rhydderch and his warriors found themselves back at the start, the elusive heart of the maze remaining out of reach. But Rhydderch's determination never wavered. Guided by Myrrdin's wisdom and his own instincts, he began to sing the ancient songs of his ancestors, imploring the spirits of the land to aid him.

It was on the third night, beneath a patchwork of shimmering stars, that the heart of the maze revealed itself. There, upon a pedestal of pure obsidian, lay Dyrnwyn, its blade gleaming with an otherworldly light.

But the sword wasn’t unguarded. From the very shadows, a spectral guardian emerged, a test for Rhydderch's worth. The two clashed, not just in a physical duel, but in a battle of wills and virtues. The prince's courage, honor, and selflessness shone brightly, eventually earning him the respect of the guardian spirit.

With a nod of acknowledgment, the spirit dissipated, leaving Rhydderch to claim his prize. As he held Dyrnwyn aloft, the blade recognized its new master and blazed with a brilliant fire, signifying the union of a worthy soul with a legendary sword.

The tale of "Culhwch and Olwen," a jewel in the crown of the "Mabinogion," is a grand epic of love, challenge, and magic. As with many such stories, the surrounding world and the objects within it provide layers of depth and meaning, adding to the narrative's richness. Dyrnwyn, though not central to Culhwch's quest, holds a poignant significance in this context.

Culhwch's resolve

In the enchanting story titled "Culhwch and Olwen," from a revered collection known as the "Mabinogion," a young man named Culhwch embarks on a noble quest of love and determination. The tale primarily revolves around the love story between Culhwch, a cousin of King Arthur, and Olwen, a stunningly beautiful maiden. Like many captivating stories, the tale is set in a world filled with magic, honor, and legendary items that carry deep significance.

Early in the narrative, Culhwch seeks an audience with the renowned King Arthur. In this meeting, it's crucial for Culhwch to validate his intentions and establish his noble background. To do so, he references notable figures and artifacts from their shared world, much like someone today might cite influential ancestors or famous family artifacts.

One name he mentions is Rhydderch Hael, a revered figure known to possess a magical sword named Dyrnwyn. This isn't an ordinary weapon; it has the unique ability to burst into flames, but only when wielded by someone truly worthy. To those familiar with their world's legends, this sword is a potent symbol of honor, righteousness, and moral integrity.

Although Culhwch's main story doesn't revolve around Dyrnwyn, his mention of it is deliberate. By invoking the sword and its owner, he's not just name-dropping; he's emphasizing the gravity of his mission and underscoring his own noble character. Thus, while Dyrnwyn might not directly influence the events of Culhwch's journey, its invocation is strategic. It serves as a declaration of Culhwch's seriousness and the high stakes of his mission. In a world where one's lineage and connections spoke volumes, referencing a figure like Rhydderch and the legendary Dyrnwyn was akin to staking a claim of both personal worth and the monumental nature of his quest.

While Culhwch's journey would see him face beasts, giants, and tests of character, Dyrnwyn's evocation in the story's beginning served as a testament. It wasn't just about winning a maiden's hand but was about honor, lineage, and proving one's mettle in a world that revered valor above all. Dyrnwyn's silent presence in this narrative was Culhwch's promise to the world: a pledge of bravery, worth, and a challenge thrown to destiny itself.

With the help of King Arthur and his knights, Culhwch embarks on a quest to fulfill these tasks. The narrative recounts their adventures and the challenges they face. Throughout the tale, Olwen remains a symbol of the unattainable, driving Culhwch forward in his endeavors.

What makes Dyrnwyn especially fascinating is its moral dimension. The sword serves as a discerning judge of a person's character, deciding if they're worthy of its power. It reinforces the age-old wisdom that true power isn't just about physical might but moral integrity.

This sword isn't just a weapon; it's a protector of virtue and a punisher of vice.

Sources/Further Reading:

The Mabinogion – Translated by Sioned Davies
The White Goddess by Robert Graves
Welsh Celtic Myth in Modern Fantasy by C.W. Sullivan III

Excalibur

Excalibur is arguably the most renowned sword in literature and folklore. This magical weapon is deeply intertwined with the legend of King Arthur, emblematic of divine kingship, and representing both the might of a warrior and the ethical integrity of a just ruler.

Excalibur is a legendary sword associated with King Arthur, attributed with magical powers, or sometimes associated with the rightful sovereignty of Great Britain. It has been depicted variously as the weapon pulled from the stone to prove Arthur's kingship or as the sword given to Arthur by the Lady of the Lake. Its aura is imbued with the essence of valiance, righteousness, and nobility.

There are two prevailing tales about Excalibur's origin. The first, and perhaps more widely recognized, is the story of the "Sword in the Stone." In another version, after the sword from the stone breaks, Arthur is granted Excalibur by the mystical Lady of the Lake. She emerges from the water, offering the sword to Arthur, its blade gleaming with an otherworldly light.

The Sword in the Stone

Upon the death of King Uther Pendragon, the realm of Britain was rife with uncertainty. The land's unity began to dissolve, and various lords and knights eyed the throne, each believing himself to be the most suitable successor. Yet, without a clear heir, the kingdom was on the brink of descending into anarchy and war.

Amid this turmoil, Merlin, the wise and enigmatic wizard, foresaw a future where Britain would be governed by a king of unparalleled wisdom and justice. But instead of appointing a king himself or letting the lords of the land squabble over the throne, he devised a test of divine selection.

In a churchyard in London, a great stone appeared, and within it was an anvil. Deeply embedded in the anvil was a gleaming sword with an inscription reading: "Whoso pulleth out this sword of this stone and anvil is rightwise king born of all England."

News of the sword's appearance spread throughout the land. Knights and nobles from every corner of Britain flocked to the churchyard, each eager to try his luck and prove his divine right to rule. However, despite their strength, ambition, and confidence, none could budge the sword from its resting place. Days turned into weeks, and the sword remained immovable, further deepening the mystery and despair.

Enter Arthur, a mere boy, unversed in the complexities of politics and power. In some versions of the tale, Arthur was attending a tournament with his foster brother, Sir Kay, and had been sent to fetch Kay's sword. In his search, he stumbled upon the sword in the stone. Unaware of the sword's significance and the trials many had faced in attempting to extract it, Arthur pulled the sword out effortlessly to bring it to his brother.

Upon presenting the sword, the truth quickly dawned on those present. The young, unassuming boy had done what no knight or noble could. After proving his feat by replacing and extracting the sword multiple times, the murmurs began to grow – could this boy truly be the future king Merlin had prophesied?

Though he had retrieved the sword, Arthur's journey had only just begun. Many refused to accept such a young, unknown figure as their king based merely on the sword's testament. But with Merlin's guidance, the loyalty of those who saw his potential, and the power and symbolism of Excalibur, Arthur embarked on a journey to not only claim his throne but to become one of the most legendary kings in history.

In certain versions of the legend, Excalibur is a different sword altogether, gifted to Arthur by the Lady of the Lake. It is this sword that is often attributed with magical properties and is sometimes accompanied by an equally magical scabbard that prevents the wearer from bleeding. Merlin, being a wise counselor and aware of many mystical entities and locations, introduced Arthur to the Lady of the Lake, from whom Arthur received Excalibur.

However, over centuries and through numerous retellings, the distinction between the two swords has blurred in many adaptations, with Excalibur sometimes being referred to as the sword that Arthur pulled from the stone.

The Lady of the Lake

The breaking of Arthur's first sword was a grave moment. With enemies threatening his kingdom and his rule constantly challenged due to his young age and the unconventional manner of his ascension, a strong symbol was needed to bind the kingdom together and solidify his claim.

Enter Merlin, the ever-watchful magician, and guide. Aware of the great trials and tribulations that lay ahead for the young king, he knew Arthur needed not just any weapon, but one with power and prestige. Merlin took Arthur on a journey, the destination of which was unknown to the young monarch.

As they trekked, they reached a tranquil lake, its waters shimmering under the soft light of dawn. It was here, in this seemingly ordinary expanse of water, that the extraordinary occurred. As Arthur and Merlin watched, the lake's surface stirred, and from its depths emerged an arm, clad in white samite, holding aloft a magnificent sword, its blade gleaming with an ethereal light and inscriptions.

This was the Lady of the Lake, a mystical and enigmatic figure with ties to the old magics of the land. As the guardian of Excalibur, she recognized the young king's destiny and his pure heart.

Arthur, taken aback by the sight, approached the water's edge. The Lady spoke, her voice echoing with the deep timbre of ancient wisdom, "Arthur Pendragon, take Excalibur, the sword of kings.

Wield it with justice, honor, and valor. With it comes great responsibility, for its edge can cut through the darkness that threatens your kingdom."

With a reverent nod, Arthur reached out, taking the sword. As he held Excalibur, he felt a rush of power and clarity, an unspoken understanding of the weapon's significance and the weight of the responsibility now placed upon his shoulders.

The Lady of the Lake, having bestowed this gift, sank back into the depths, leaving Arthur with Merlin at the lake's edge. The magician, with a knowing smile, simply stated, "With great power, comes great duty. May you wield it wisely."

From that day forth, Excalibur was at Arthur's side, a beacon of hope for his people, and a symbol of the enduring legacy of King Arthur. The sword would play a pivotal role in many battles, its legend growing with each tale, intertwined with the legend of the once and future king.

Excalibur's Return: The Closing of an Epoch

The fields of Camlann lay strewn with the casualties of war, the once-glistening armors and banners now dulled with the weight of blood and tragedy. Among the fallen was King Arthur, gravely wounded and on the brink of joining the spectral ranks of his fallen knights. The legendary Excalibur, the sword that had once signified his divine right to rule and had aided him in countless battles, now gleamed somberly by his side, its brilliance juxtaposed with the grim tableau of war.

As the weight of his injuries bore down on him, Arthur, with the clarity that often accompanies life's final moments, recognized the need to ensure Excalibur's return to its mystical origins. He called Sir Bedivere, one of his most loyal and trusted knights, to his side. With a voice weakened by pain but firm with purpose, he entrusted Bedivere with a final task: to return Excalibur to the Lady of the Lake.

Bedivere, overwhelmed by the monumental responsibility and the imminent loss of his king, set out towards the lake. As he walked, the weight of Excalibur in his hand was not just of metal but of memories, triumphs, and the legacy of a once-great kingdom. The sword's ethereal beauty under the moonlight, its blade still pristine and its hilt adorned with precious stones, made Bedivere hesitate. Could he truly part with such a treasure? A symbol of their golden era?

Twice, Bedivere approached the lake, and twice his resolve wavered. He concealed the sword and returned to Arthur, fabricating tales of having completed the task. But Arthur, even in his weakened state, saw through the deception. With a mix of disappointment and understanding, he implored Bedivere to honor his final wish.

On his third approach, a battle raged within Bedivere — loyalty to his dying king against the allure of retaining a relic of unparalleled significance. Ultimately, loyalty won. With a heavy heart, he hurled Excalibur into the shimmering expanse of the lake. As the sword sailed through the moonlit night, a sight of wonder unfolded: an ethereal hand, bathed in an otherworldly glow, emerged from the lake's depths, catching Excalibur mid-flight. It held the sword aloft for a brief moment, as if acknowledging the end of an epoch, before disappearing beneath the water's surface.

Returning to Arthur, Bedivere recounted what he'd witnessed. The king, now assured of Excalibur's safe return, found a measure of peace. His reign had come full circle — from a divine gift at its dawn to a mystical farewell at its twilight.

Throughout the tales of King Arthur, Excalibur plays a crucial role. Whether it's aiding Arthur in his battles against the Saxons, its gleam guiding the Knights of the Round Table, or symbolizing the king's divine right and mandate, the sword is much more than just a weapon—it's an emblem of Arthur's legitimacy, his courage, and his moral integrity.

Excalibur has transcended its origin in medieval romances to become a symbol in broader culture. The sword is now emblematic of heroism, rightful power, and nobility. It's been reimagined in countless retellings, films, and references, solidifying its status as one of the most iconic mythical artifacts in history.

Sources/Further Reading:

Le Morte d'Arthur by Sir Thomas Malory
The Once and Future King by T.H. White – A more modern retelling of the Arthurian legends.
The Arthurian Handbook by Norris J. Lacy and Geoffrey Ashe
The World of King Arthur by Christopher Snyder

Eye of Horus

The Eye of Horus often referred to as the "Wadjet", is an ancient Egyptian symbol of protection, healing, and royal power. It resembles a stylized eye, often with the markings of a falcon's eye, a nod to the falcon-headed sky god, Horus. Its legend is deeply rooted in the myths of the Egyptian pantheon, particularly revolving around the conflict between Horus and Set.

The overall shape of the Eye of Horus resembles a stylized eye and eyebrow. The design is highly distinctive, with the central part of the eye resembling a falcon's, which links it to Horus, often depicted as a falcon-headed god. Below the eye, extending towards the cheek, there's a curvy line resembling a stylized version of a tear or a cosmetic marking. This is believed to represent the traumatic injury that Horus sustained, and the subsequent restoration, symbolizing the pain and healing process. Extending from the outer corner of the eye, there is a spiral-like structure that can be interpreted as the braid or tail of a falcon, or even as the falcon's beak, further strengthening the connection between the eye and Horus.

While in many depictions the Eye of Horus is rendered in simple black or monochrome, in more detailed versions, it might be adorned with a variety of colors. Gold might be used to reflect the divinity and purity of the eye, while greens and blues might evoke connections to the Nile, healing, and rebirth.

Ancient Egypt's pantheon was rife with tales of ambition, betrayal, and cosmic rivalries. At the heart of many of these myths stood two gods: Horus, the soaring falcon representing the skies, and Set, the unpredictable deity of storms and chaos. Their destinies were entwined from the very beginning.

The Wadjet's Origin

Osiris, the benevolent king of Egypt and father to Horus, had brought prosperity and peace to the land. However, his rule and legacy were coveted by his brother Set, whose heart brewed with envy and malevolence. Succumbing to his darkest impulses, Set orchestrated a cunning plot, murdering Osiris and usurping the throne.

Osiris' demise was more than a personal loss for Horus; it represented a breach of the divine order. The young god, still coming into his power, now faced the daunting task of reclaiming his father's kingdom from his treacherous uncle. Thus began a series of confrontations, each more intense than the last, as Horus and Set clashed, shaping the fate of Egypt.

One day, as the two gods locked in fierce combat, Set, fueled by rage and desperation, aimed a ferocious blow at Horus. He managed to gouge out Horus's left eye, shattering it into six distinct pieces. This wasn't just a physical assault; the act bore deeper, symbolic implications. Horus's eye represented the moon, and its loss disrupted the cosmic balance, plunging the realm into darkness and chaos.

The fragmented eye, scattered across Egypt, seemed lost forever. Yet, not all were content to watch Egypt's descent into anarchy. Thoth, the god of wisdom, magic, and the moon, recognized the gravity of the situation. With a heart committed to restoring order, he embarked on a quest to find the lost fragments of the eye.

Each fragment he discovered was a puzzle piece, carrying with it a piece of Egypt's soul and prosperity. After a relentless search, Thoth succeeded in retrieving all the pieces. Using his profound knowledge of magic and alchemy, he meticulously reconstructed the eye.

But Thoth went a step further. He didn't just restore the eye to its former state; he imbued it with potent magic, ensuring it held powers of healing, protection, and rejuvenation. The restored Eye of Horus, also known as the "Wadjet" or "Udjat," became a symbol of resilience, rebirth, and divine justice.

With his eye restored, Horus was once again at the zenith of his power. The subsequent battles saw Set defeated and pushed to the outskirts of the realm, restoring Horus's rightful place on the throne of Egypt. The Eye of Horus would thereafter be seen as a beacon of hope, a testament to the indomitable spirit of the gods and their devotion to justice and order. Its symbol became one of the most enduring in all of ancient Egyptian culture, offering protection and blessings to all who invoked its power.

The Eye of Horus became a powerful amulet, used widely by the Egyptians. The Eye was a common symbol in amulets and talismans, believed to protect against the evil eye and to bring safety in the afterlife. Its intricate design carries deeper meanings:

Each part of the Eye symbolizes a fraction, which together adds up to 63/64 – purposefully not making a whole, representing the idea that nothing is perfect. The individual parts of the eye were believed to represent the senses, including touch, thought, hearing, taste, and sight.

Just as it was restored by Thoth, the Eye was seen as a symbol of health and was used in funerary rites to ensure the well-being of the deceased in the afterlife. Pharaohs often had the Eye of Horus inscribed in their tombs or on their person, indicating their divine right to rule and the protection of the gods during their reign.

The Eye of Horus has transcended its ancient origins to become an icon in modern culture. It's found in jewelry, tattoos, and art as a symbol of protection, insight, and health. Moreover, the Rx symbol, used globally for prescriptions, is believed by some to have been derived from the Eye of Horus, underscoring its connotations of health and healing.

Sources/Further Reading:

"The Complete Gods and Goddesses of Ancient Egypt" by Richard H. Wilkinson
"The Oxford Encyclopedia of Ancient Egypt"
"Reading Egyptian Art: A Hieroglyphic Guide to Ancient Egyptian Painting and Sculpture" by Richard H. Wilkinson.

Fairy Flag of Dunvegan

The Fairy Flag of Dunvegan is a treasured artifact with deep roots in Scottish folklore, specifically associated with the Clan MacLeod of Dunvegan Castle on the Isle of Skye

Steeped in legends and tales of old, the Fairy Flag is more than a relic; it's a testament to the deep bond between the supernatural and the mortal, the magic that once intertwined the two realms, and the protective aura that still hovers around the MacLeod clan. The tattered silk flag has seen centuries come and go, but its power and significance remain undiminished.

The origins of the Fairy Flag are clouded in mystery, with multiple legends attempting to explain its creation and power

Gift from the Fairies: A Love Beyond Realms

In the rugged terrains of the Isle of Skye, where the boundaries between the earthly and the ethereal were often blurred, the tale of a mortal chief and an immortal fairy unfolded. Their love story is as timeless as the waves that crash against the cliffs of Dunvegan.

On a fateful misty evening, the young chief of the MacLeod clan, while wandering the moors, was enchanted by the mellifluous voice of a fairy singing. Following the voice, he came upon a glen bathed in moonlight, where the fairy danced with a grace that seemed to make the very stars lean closer to the earth. Their eyes met, and in that fleeting moment, two worlds collided.

Knowing the consequences of consorting with mortals, the fairy initially resisted the chief's advances. But love, with its persistent tug, drew them together. Their meetings in secret glades and hidden coves became their treasured moments, where time stood still. Yet, the fairy often reminded him that their love was ephemeral, bound by the limitations of her ethereal existence.

After a series of stolen moments and whispered promises, the inevitable dawned. The fairy was summoned back to her realm, bound by ancient pacts and age-old duties. The pain of their impending separation was palpable. On their last night together, under a canopy of twinkling stars, she presented him with a gift - a silken flag, delicate yet brimming with magic.

"This flag," she whispered, her voice quivering like a soft breeze, "is imbued with the essence of my realm and the strength of our love. In your direst need, unfurl it, and the magic we've shared shall shield your clan."

The chief, heartbroken but resilient, returned to his duties, often gazing at the flag and reminiscing about their moonlit trysts. The flag, known as the Fairy Flag, became an emblem of protection for the MacLeod clan. Its magic, a testament to a love that transcended realms, and a reminder that even in the face of insurmountable odds, love finds a way to leave its indelible mark.

The flag's magic is believed to have the power to save and protect the clan during its darkest hours, but it can only be used thrice. According to legends, it has already been used twice, and only one usage remains.

First Use: Battle of Glendale - The Flag's Triumph

The Isle of Skye in the 15th century was rife with clan rivalries, age-old feuds, and territorial disputes. In this tumultuous era, the Battle of Glendale stands out, not just for its strategic importance but also for the ethereal intervention that decided its outcome.

The MacLeod clan, one of the dominant clans of Skye, faced mounting pressure from adversaries who sought to diminish their power. Word spread of an impending attack and the MacLeods prepared for battle. However, as the days turned to night and back to day, the sheer number of their enemies became clear. The MacLeods, though fierce and proud, were outnumbered.

In the heart of the battle, with the MacLeods being pushed back, the scene was grim. The air was thick with the clang of weapons, the cries of the wounded, and the chaos of warfare. It was then that the clan chieftain remembered the legend of the Fairy Flag. Passed down through generations, it was said to possess the power to protect the clan in its direst hour.

With a mix of desperation and hope, he called for the flag to be brought forth. And as the Fairy Flag was unfurled, a hush fell upon the battlefield, only for a moment, before an otherworldly energy surged through the MacLeod warriors.

From the flag emanated a brilliant light, so radiant that it seemed as if the fairies themselves had descended onto the battlefield. MacLeod warriors, who were moments ago on the brink of exhaustion, felt a renewed vigor. Legends speak of spectral warriors joining the ranks, summoned by the flag's magic.

The tide of the battle shifted dramatically. The enemies, overwhelmed by the sudden ferocity of the MacLeods and possibly the ethereal warriors among them, began to retreat. The Battle of Glendale, which seemed a certain defeat for the MacLeods, transformed into a resounding victory.

To this day, the Battle of Glendale serves as a testament to the intertwined fates of the MacLeods and the mystical Fairy Flag, a reminder that even in the darkest moments, ancient magic and clan spirit can turn the tide.

Second Use: The Cattle Epidemic

One fateful year, a mysterious ailment began to grip the cattle. One by one, the strong and robust animals grew weak, their usual vitality replaced by a haunting lethargy. Their eyes, once lively, now reflected pain and confusion. As days turned into weeks, the disease spread like wildfire, and the clan watched in growing horror as their lifeline dwindled.

Desperation set in. The clan's healers and wise folk tried various remedies, chants, and rituals, but nothing seemed to halt the progression of the disease. The very foundation of the clan's livelihood was under threat.

In their darkest hour, an elder of the clan recalled the tales of the Fairy Flag's protective powers. The same flag that had turned the tide of battles and showcased its might in times of peril was now their last hope. With a blend of trepidation and faith, the clan decided to invoke the magic of the flag once again.

On a moonlit night, a ceremony was held. At the heart of the gathering, the Fairy Flag was unfurled, its fabric seeming to shimmer with an ethereal glow under the silvery moonbeams. The entire clan, young and old, gathered around, chanting ancient verses, calling upon the spirits of the flag to heal their cattle.

As dawn approached, a soft mist descended upon the land, wrapping everything in a gentle embrace. As the first rays of the sun pierced the mist, something miraculous happened. The cattle, which had been lying listlessly the night before, began to stir. A newfound energy seemed to pulse through them. Over the next few days, the disease that had seemed insurmountable started to wane. The cattle regained their health, their eyes once again sparkling with life. The MacLeod clan celebrated this miraculous recovery with feasts and songs, attributing their fortune to the benevolent magic of the Fairy Flag.

The power of the third and final usage of the flag remains intact, awaiting a dire situation worthy of its deployment.

The Fairy Flag can still be seen today. It resides in Dunvegan Castle, the ancestral home of the Clan MacLeod, carefully preserved as a reminder of the clan's storied past and their mystical protector.

The Fairy Flag of Dunvegan is not just an artifact; it's a symbol of Scottish folklore's enchantment, echoing the times when mortals and mystical beings interacted and when magic was just a heartbeat away. Whether draped in a castle or invoked in battle, its essence reminds us of the wonders of yesteryears and the hope for future miracles.

Sources/Further Reading:

"The Fairy Flag of Dunvegan" by Roderick Charles MacLeod
"The MacLeods: The History of a Clan, 1200-2000" by Alexander MacLeod
"Scottish Myths and Legends" by Judy Hamilton

Fountain of Youth

The Fountain of Youth, a legendary spring that reputedly restores the youth of anyone who drinks its waters, has captured the human imagination for centuries. This timeless myth, a symbol of rejuvenation and eternal vitality, echoes across various civilizations, revealing humanity's enduring obsession with immortality and the fear of aging.

For millennia, tales of such a fountain have bewitched explorers, kings, and common folk alike. This legendary wellspring, a symbol of eternal youth and unparalleled vitality, stands as a testament to humanity's age-old fascination with thwarting the inexorable march of time. Across vast empires and secluded villages, from the whispering sands of the Middle East to the dense jungles of the Americas, stories reverberate of this fountain's allure. It speaks of a collective human dream: the quest for an elixir that promises a life untouched by the weariness of age and the shadow of mortality.

Sequestered in a place where time seems to stand still, the Fountain of Youth is often envisioned as a shimmering pool of crystalline water, ensconced within a lush and untamed grove. The air around it pulsates with an almost ethereal luminescence, hinting at the magic within its depths. Graceful willows might arch over the fountain, their drooping branches skimming the water's surface, which ripples with an iridescent sheen. Every droplet that emerges from this source seems to capture and refract light in a dance of colors, reminiscent of the first rays of dawn or the soft glow of twilight. The sound of the flowing water resonates like a gentle lullaby, promising peace, restoration, and a return to days of unblemished youth. At its heart, the fountain is not just a source of water but a reservoir of hopes, dreams, and the eternal human yearning for a life untouched by the ravages of time.

The origins of the Fountain of Youth myth are scattered across time and geography. Ancient civilizations, from the Greeks to the Chinese, have their own versions of a life-renewing spring. Herodotus, the Greek historian, wrote of a fountain in Ethiopia that gave the Ethiopians an exceptional lifespan. Similarly, the Chinese have tales of the Isles of the Blest, where the immortality-granting waters are protected by the Eastern Dragon.

Herodotus and the Ethiopian Fountain

In the broad collage of stories woven by Herodotus in his "Histories," the tale of the Ethiopians stands out. These were not just any Ethiopians; they were described as the "longest-lived of men." Beyond the known realms and at the very edges of the world as perceived by the Greeks, they inhabited a land where life moved differently.

The secret to their prolonged life was believed to be a sacred spring. Upon reaching a certain age, individuals would partake in a ceremonial bath. As they stepped into the spring's waters, the years would seemingly melt away, restoring them to a younger state. Their skin regained its elasticity, their eyes sparkled, and their vigor returned as if they'd turned back time.

While Herodotus did rely on hearsay, the persistence of such a tale and its resonance with his audience speaks volumes. It suggests that even in ancient times, the human longing for eternal youth and the fear of aging were potent. This Ethiopian tale, layered with mystique, likely became a seed from which later myths, like that of the Fountain of Youth, grew in the collective psyche of the West.

The Chinese Isles of the Blest

Far from the known realms of ancient China, across treacherous seas and elusive mists, were the Isles of the Blest or Mount Penglai. In these paradisiacal lands, the very air was believed to rejuvenate, and its waters held miraculous properties.

The islands, lush and teeming with life, were home not just to mortals but immortals. They lived in harmony, their lives untouched by disease, decay, or death. At the heart of these tales were the springs that flowed through the Isles. Their waters shimmered, and those who drank from them or bathed in them found ailments cured, their youth restored, and the shadows of age dispelled.

But these waters and the secret of the Isles were fiercely guarded. The Eastern Dragon, an emblem of the profound cosmic forces, stood as a protector. This majestic creature, whose scales glistened and whose eyes held the wisdom of ages, ensured that only the worthy approached these waters.

Emperor Qin Shi Huang's quest for these islands wasn't merely about conquering new lands. It was a search for eternity, a bid to escape the inescapable grasp of mortality. Despite the many expeditions, the Isles remained elusive, further elevating their legendary status.

In the context of the New World, Spanish explorer Juan Ponce de León is often associated with the Fountain of Youth. While the popular narrative claims he sailed to Florida in search of these magical waters, historians suggest that this might be a later embellishment, as there's little concrete evidence from his time that supports this quest. Nevertheless, the story has persisted, making de León synonymous with this enduring legend.

Ponce de León and the New World

Juan Ponce de León was an accomplished explorer and a contemporary of Christopher Columbus. Born in Spain, de León was lured by the allure of the New World, seeking not just territories but the promise of wealth and prestige. By the early 16th century, he had already become the first Governor of Puerto Rico, establishing a prominent presence in the Caribbean.

The association of de León with the Fountain of Youth began as stories whispered in the courts of Europe and among the sailors of the New World. They spoke of lands to the north, where waters held the magical property of restoring youth. For European explorers, who often faced perilous journeys and unknown lands, the idea of a fountain that could heal wounds and reverse aging was undeniably tempting.

In 1513, de León led an expedition to the uncharted territories north of Cuba. He landed on the eastern coast of a vast land, which he named "Florida" because of its lush landscape and in recognition of the Spanish festival "Pascua Florida" (Festival of Flowers). It's this expedition that later got intertwined with the legend of the Fountain of Youth.

Historical records from this period, including de León's own writings and official documents, make no mention of a quest for a magical fountain. The primary goal seemed more territorial and wealth-driven. The association with the Fountain of Youth seems to have been popularized later, notably by chroniclers and writers who either aimed to mock de León's ambitions or were captivated by the romance of such a quest. The embellished tales spoke of an aging explorer, desperate to restore his youth, venturing into unknown territories in pursuit of the fountain.

By the time of Washington Irving's writings in the 19th century, the story of de León's quest for the Fountain of Youth was solidified in popular culture. Irving, known for his other fictional creations, included the tale in his historical works, further cementing the myth.

The concept of the Fountain of Youth has metamorphosed over time, aligning with contemporary understandings of science and longevity. Today, the "fountain" is often metaphorically linked to medical breakthroughs, anti-aging products, and technologies that promise increased lifespans.

While the literal existence of the Fountain of Youth remains a matter of myth and legend, its symbolic resonance is undeniable. It underscores humanity's timeless hope for renewal and the lengths to which we might go in our quest for immortality.

Sources/Further Reading:

"The Fountain of Youth: History and Myth" by Brian Fagan
"Ponce de León: Discoverer of Florida" by Rachel Eagen
"Mythologies" by Roland Barthes

Fragarach

The Fragarach, known also as "The Answerer" or "The Retaliator", is a mythical sword from Irish mythology. Rooted deeply within the tales of the Tuatha Dé Danann, the pre-eminent gods of ancient Ireland, this blade possesses qualities that distinguish it from other legendary weapons. Not only is its cut sharp and fatal, but the sword also has the power to command the truth from those it is pointed at, making deceit impossible.

At first glance, Fragarach might appear as a longsword of impeccable craftsmanship. Its blade, forged by divine hands, gleams with a silvery radiance, reflecting light with an ethereal glow. The blade itself is rumored to be so sharp that it could slice through any shield, armor, or barrier, rendering all forms of protection useless against its edge.

Beyond its physical appearance, the Fragarach emits a palpable aura. Those in its presence might feel a mixture of awe and reverence, a sensation of being in the company of something ancient and profoundly powerful. This aura isn't just about its combat capabilities but also its mystical properties. There's an undercurrent of truth to it—a promise that secrets can't remain hidden when faced with "The Answerer."

The Truth of the Fragarach

The annals of Celtic mythology recount that the gods, in their celestial realms, created the Fragarach. These divine beings, with unparalleled knowledge and power, sought to craft a weapon unlike any other—a sword that embodied both unparalleled martial prowess and profound mystical abilities.

Manannán mac Lir, the god of the sea, storms, and the otherworld, was the chosen guardian of this celestial weapon. It is said that the blade echoed with the sounds of the raging seas and the whisper of otherworldly realms, binding Manannán's essence to its very core. With Fragarach at his side, he ruled the waves and controlled the passages to the otherworld, ensuring harmony between realms.

The stories then speak of a time when Manannán, recognizing the potential and destiny of Lugh, decided to pass on the sword to him. Lugh, a multi-talented deity known for his proficiency in various skills and arts, was deemed the perfect heir for such a weapon. The Fragarach complemented Lugh's vast array of talents, making him nearly invincible in combat and challenges. Lugh's adversaries often found themselves not just outmatched in battle, but also cornered by the sword's ability to extract truth, giving Lugh an edge in both warfare and diplomacy.

The most distinct and revered quality of the Fragarach was its ability to make any adversary speak the truth. In many tales, Lugh, leveraging this power, could unveil treacheries, decipher riddles, and understand the mysteries of the world. Many enemies tried to lie or deceive, but once the blade was at their throat, falsehoods melted away, leaving only the raw truth behind.

Throughout Irish myths, there are accounts of Lugh wielding Fragarach in numerous battles, both against mortal enemies and other deities. The blade's sharpness and the terror it instilled made Lugh an indomitable force on the battlefield. Beyond combat, it also became a symbol of justice, order, and the relentless pursuit of truth in the narratives of ancient Ireland.

Lugh's Ascension and the Second Battle of Mag Tuired

Lugh's most famous engagement in myth is the Second Battle of Mag Tuired, wherein the Tuatha Dé Danann, the divine tribe to which Lugh belonged, fought against the oppressive Fomorians. Although Lugh had many skills and multiple weapons at his disposal, Fragarach was among the most potent.

When Lugh arrived at the court of the Tuatha Dé Danann, he initially faced resistance in gaining entrance. He claimed expertise in many crafts, but for each, he was told that the Tuatha Dé already had a member with that skill. When he claimed to have mastery over all crafts, they allowed him entrance. Once inside, his array of talents, and not least among them his possession of the powerful Fragarach, quickly made him a central figure.

The Fomorians, a chaotic and malevolent race, were attempting to reclaim their lost territories, threatening the dominion of the Tuatha Dé Danann. As the Fomorian forces gathered, their leader, Balor of the Evil Eye, summoned a thick mist, blanketing the battlefield, concealing his warriors and leaving the Tuatha Dé Danann virtually blind.

Amidst the confusion, the shouts of warriors, and the clanging of metal, Lugh, resplendent in his armor, unsheathed the Fragarach. The blade shimmered, seemingly unaffected by the obscuring fog. Every swing of the sword cleared swathes of the mist, revealing

Fomorian soldiers, who were promptly dispatched by the Tuatha Dé Danann.

However, Balor's power was not to be underestimated. His evil eye, once opened, could obliterate all in its path. Lugh knew that the key to victory was not just defeating the army but incapacitating Balor. Using the speed granted to him by his otherworldly lineage and the precision of Fragarach, Lugh carved his way through the Fomorian lines, aiming straight for Balor.

Confronting the giant, Lugh found himself momentarily overpowered. But with a swift motion, he placed Fragarach against Balor's throat. Bound by the sword's magic, Balor was frozen. Seizing the opportunity, Lugh questioned him: "How can your eye be sealed forever?" Forced by the blade's compulsion, Balor whispered the secret.

With the knowledge, Lugh, combining his skills was able to defeat Balor, aiming a sling-stone that drove Balor's destructive eye out the back of his head, where it continued its path of destruction among the Fomorian ranks.

In combat, Fragarach isn't just a tool of war but an extension of its wielder's will. Its swings are swift and precise, and its strikes, are devastating. The sword seems to hum with energy, and each time it's unsheathed, it's as if the very air grows tense, anticipating the power it's about to unleash.

In essence, the Fragarach is a masterpiece, a blend of divine craftsmanship and the embodiment of Celtic myths, a weapon that stands as a testament to the tales of gods, heroes, and the eternal quest for truth.

Sources/Further Reading:

"Early Irish Myths and Sagas" translated by Jeffrey Gantz
"The Book of Invasions" by Lebor Gabála Érenn
"Irish Folk and Fairy Tales" by W.B. Yeats

Gáe Bulg

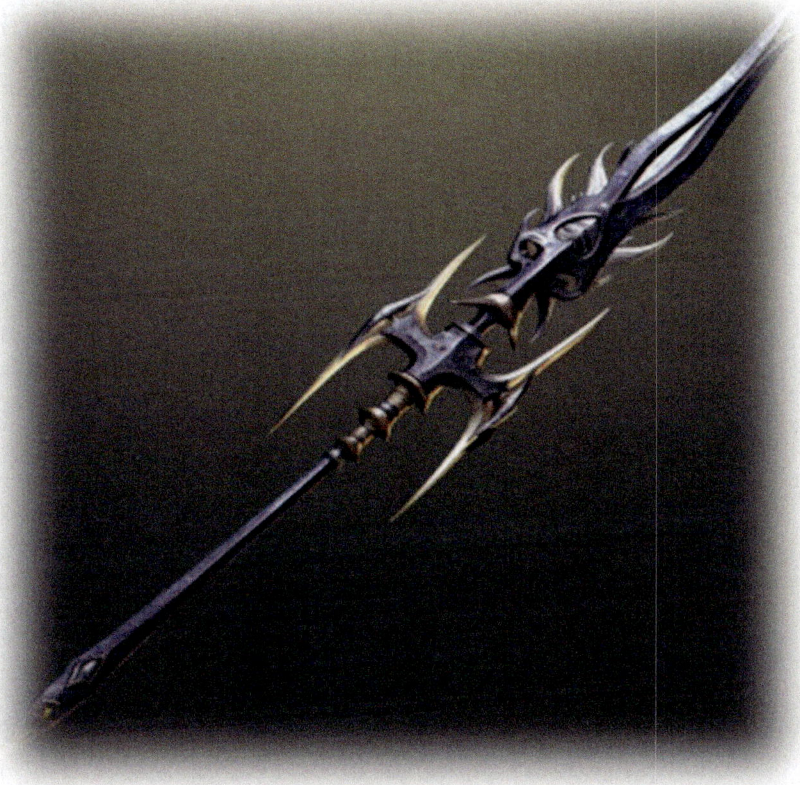

The Gáe Bulg (also spelled "Gáe Bolg" or "Gáe Bolga"), whose name translates to "spear of mortal pain/death spear" or "belly spear", is a legendary weapon from Irish mythology. Most famously, it is associated with the hero Cúchulainn, one of the greatest figures in the Ulster Cycle, a collection of ancient Irish sagas and tales.

The Gáe Bulg is more than just a spear; it holds a unique place in the arsenal of Cúchulainn due to its deadly nature and the lore surrounding its use. A weapon of singular destruction, it was reputedly made from the bone of a sea monster, the Coinchenn, that died while battling another creature.

The Gáe Bulg was no ordinary spear. Once it entered an opponent's body, it was said to unleash barbs, causing grievous, often fatal wounds. Extracting the Gáe Bulg added further injury, making it a weapon of dire consequences. It's described in some accounts as having seven ridges along its length, and when used in battle, it would open inside its victim, releasing multiple barbs, making its removal nearly impossible without causing further harm.

Scáthach's School of Warriors

Perched upon the rugged cliffs of the Isle of Skye, Scáthach's fortress was a place of legends. It was whispered among the bards and warriors of Ireland that those who survived her training would emerge as the finest fighters in all the Celtic lands. Her fortress wasn't just a place for physical training; it was a crucible where character and destiny were forged.

Scáthach, whose name translates to "The Shadowy One", was not just a master of combat but also of the esoteric arts. When Cúchulainn arrived at her doorstep, she recognized the fire in his eyes and the destiny that lay before him.

During Cúchulainn's rigorous training, Scáthach introduced him to a variety of weapons, each with its unique power and technique. However, among them, the Gáe Bulg stood apart. Made from the bone of a sea monster, it was not merely a weapon but a testament to nature's fury and the mysteries of the deep.

Scáthach, aware of the spear's power, entrusted it to Cúchulainn only when she believed he was ready. It was not just about physical prowess but also about maturity and understanding. The Gáe Bulg demanded respect.

The training was grueling. The Gáe Bulg was unlike any other weapon, not just in its make but in its use. To employ it effectively in battle, Cúchulainn had to abandon much of what he knew and open himself up to a completely new style of combat. With Scáthach's guidance, he learned the technique of deploying the spear using his feet, harnessing the strength of his legs to thrust it upwards with deadly precision.

Scáthach, ever the meticulous teacher, also instilled in him the philosophy behind the spear's use. The Gáe Bulg was a weapon of last resort, a final, irrevocable decision. To use it was to commit wholly to the act, understanding the consequences fully.

As the days turned into weeks and weeks into months, a deep bond formed between Scáthach and Cúchulainn. Through sweat, blood, and relentless practice, he not only mastered the Gáe Bulg but also understood its essence. And Scáthach, for her part, saw in Cúchulainn not just a student, but the embodiment of the future of Celtic heroism.

By the time Cúchulainn left the Isle of Skye, he was transformed. Not only did he possess the Gáe Bulg, but he also carried with him the wisdom, techniques, and blessings of Scáthach. He was no longer just a warrior; he was a legend in the making.

Brothers in Arms, Foes in Fate

The plains of Ireland echoed with the clashes of swords and shields as the armies of Connacht sought to take the prized brown bull of Cooley from Ulster. At the heart of this great war was a personal tragedy that pitted brother against brother, friend against friend.

Cúchulainn, the great champion of Ulster, had faced countless foes in defense of his homeland, but none so formidable or heart-wrenching as his dear friend, Ferdia. They had trained together under Scáthach and shared meals, stories, and dreams. Their bond was forged in the fires of camaraderie and mutual respect. But the tides of war, guided by the cunning hand of Queen Medb of Connacht, thrust them into opposing roles.

For three intense days, the two warriors locked horns, neither willing to relent. Their battles were not only a display of unmatched skill but also the emotional turmoil of facing a beloved friend on the battlefield. Each morning, they would greet each other warmly, share tales of old, and then, as duty demanded, cross weapons in fierce combat.

By the fourth day, the duel had taken its toll. Both were weary, not just from physical exertion but from the emotional weight of their predicament. The surrounding landscape bore witness to their struggles, scarred and transformed by the force of their blows.

As the fourth day wore on, it became evident that neither warrior would yield, and their equal prowess meant the battle might continue indefinitely. Cúchulainn, recognizing the desperate situation and the looming threat of the Connacht armies, made the heart-wrenching decision to use the Gáe Bulg, the very weapon he had acquired under the tutelage of Scáthach, and one he knew Ferdia was familiar with.

With a heavy heart and tears in his eyes, Cúchulainn summoned the power of the Gáe Bulg. Using the technique taught by Scáthach, he deployed it with devastating effect, piercing Ferdia's defenses and striking his friend down. The immediate aftermath was silent, save for the mournful cries of Cúchulainn. In the midst of a great war, two friends had shared a deeply personal tragedy. Cúchulainn had won the duel, but the victory came at the immeasurable cost of a friend's life.

Beyond its immediate, terrifying effects in battle, the Gáe Bulg stands as a symbol of the tragic cost of conflict, especially when friends or brothers are set against each other. Its use against Ferdia is one of the most poignant moments in Irish myth, illustrating the sorrowful depths to which warfare can plunge even the greatest of heroes.

Sources/Further Reading:

"The Táin" translated by Thomas Kinsella
"Early Irish Myths and Sagas" translated by Jeffrey Gantz
"Celtic Myths and Legends" by T. W. Rolleston

Girdle of Aphrodite

The Girdle of Aphrodite, a bewitching artifact from ancient Greek mythology, is intrinsically tied to the goddess of love and beauty herself. This belt, often described as being crafted of finely wrought gold, was said to possess the power to kindle irresistible passion and attraction in the hearts of all who beheld its wearer.

As with many artifacts of the gods, the origins of the Girdle of Aphrodite are shrouded in divine mystery. Some legends state it was gifted to her by her husband, Hephaestus, the god of the forge, crafted to accentuate her already breathtaking beauty. Others claim it was one of her original possessions, a part of her divine essence from the very moment of her birth from the sea foam.

But beyond its role as a symbol of Aphrodite's irresistible allure, the girdle also represented her dominion over both love and desire. In several tales, Aphrodite lends her girdle to other goddesses, temporarily granting them the power to inflame love.

The Judgement of Paris: A Contest of Divine Beauty

In the glittering halls of Olympus, where the gods and goddesses resided, peace was often a transient thing. One day, a seemingly minor event sparked a chain reaction that would culminate in one of the most epic wars in mythological history: the Trojan War.

It began with a grand feast celebrating the union of Peleus and Thetis. Almost every deity was invited, except for Eris, the goddess of discord. In her characteristic fashion, Eris sought to create strife. She threw into the midst of the revelers a beautiful golden apple, upon which was inscribed, "To the fairest."

Three goddesses, each peerless in her own right, believed the title of "fairest" belonged to her. Hera, queen of the gods; Athena, goddess of wisdom and warfare; and Aphrodite, goddess of love and beauty, all laid claim to the apple. The ensuing dispute threatened to disrupt the very fabric of divine politics.

To resolve the matter without sparking further chaos on Olympus, Zeus, the king of gods, devised a plan. He chose Paris, a mortal prince of Troy known for his fair judgment, to decide the rightful recipient of the golden apple. Each goddess, in her bid to secure the title, sought to persuade Paris with a tempting offer.

Hera promised him vast kingdoms and unparalleled power. Athena offered wisdom and unparalleled skills in warfare. But Aphrodite, understanding the deep-seated human longing for love and desire, promised Paris the affection of Helen, the most beautiful mortal woman. To further her cause, Aphrodite wore her Girdle, enhancing her divine allure to irresistible levels.

Paris, mesmerized by Aphrodite's beauty and the prospect of love with Helen, awarded the apple to the goddess of love. However, this decision was not without consequences. Helen, at the time, was already married to Menelaus, the king of Sparta. When Paris and Helen eloped, it set the stage for the epic Trojan War, a battle that would see heroes made, cities fall, and the gods themselves taking sides.

Beyond its narrative roles, the Girdle of Aphrodite serves as a potent symbol in mythological analysis. It represents the often-uncontrollable nature of love and attraction, suggesting that these feelings can be as powerful and influential as any physical weapon. It also underscores the idea that beauty and allure can provide a unique form of power, with the potential to sway even the mightiest kings or alter the course of history.

The Girdle of Aphrodite, with its golden gleam and intoxicating influence, stands as a testament to the ancient Greek understanding of love's complexities, its challenges, and its unparalleled significance in the human experience.

Sources/Further Reading:

Hesiod's "Theogony"
Homer's "Iliad"
"The Greek Myths" by Robert Graves
"Mythology: Timeless Tales of Gods and Heroes" by Edith Hamilton

Golden Fleece

The Golden Fleece is one of the most iconic symbols from ancient Greek mythology. It represents royal authority, a divine sanction, and the promise of prosperity and fertility.

The Golden Fleece, a luminous emblem of divine favor and royal intrigue, stands as one of the most sought-after artifacts in ancient Greek mythology. This gleaming pelt, which once adorned a miraculous ram, has come to symbolize quests, valor, and the age-old pursuit of glory and immortality. Beyond its physical splendor, the Golden Fleece represents the pinnacle of challenges for heroes, demanding not just strength but wit, tenacity, and moral resolve.

Emerging from a backdrop rife with godly machinations and human follies, the legend of the Fleece encapsulates a narrative familiar to many cultures: the seemingly insurmountable journey for a treasured artifact, promising power and prestige. Yet, within Greek lore, the Fleece takes on nuanced layers of meaning. It's not just a symbol of kingship or divine endorsement, but also a reminder of familial ties, the fickleness of fate, and the intertwined destinies of gods and mortals.

Intrigue of the Gods and the Birth of the Ram

The tale begins not with the golden ram, but with clouds, gods, and betrayal. Nephele, the cloud nymph, was created by Zeus from a cloud in the likeness of Hera, his wife, to deceive the lusty Ixion. Later, Nephele married Athamas, the king of Boeotia, and bore him two children, Phrixus and Helle. But the whims of the heart are unpredictable. Over time, Athamas lost interest in Nephele and took another wife, Ino.

Ino, driven by jealousy and a desire to secure the throne for her own children, devised a treacherous plan. She induced a famine in Boeotia and then bribed the oracles to proclaim that the famine would only end if Phrixus was sacrificed to the gods. The distraught Athamas, driven by the desperation of his people, agreed.

As preparations for the sacrifice were underway, Nephele, hearing of her children's impending doom, intervened. She sent a miraculous golden ram, created by Hermes, the messenger of the gods. This was no ordinary ram—it was imbued with the ability to speak and fly. The siblings, Phrixus and Helle, mounted the ram just in time, soaring into the skies, away from the clutches of their wicked stepmother and the misguided intentions of their father.

However, the journey was perilous. As they flew over the narrow strait between Europe and Asia, Helle, perhaps overcome by dizziness or fear, lost her grip. She plummeted into the waters below, which thereafter became known as the Hellespont (or "Sea of Helle").

Phrixus, however, held on and eventually landed in the distant kingdom of Colchis, on the eastern edge of the Black Sea. Grateful for the divine intervention and his newfound safety, Phrixus sacrificed the golden ram to Zeus, honoring the god who had indirectly been the source of his salvation. He then presented the ram's gleaming fleece to King Aeëtes of Colchis as a token of gratitude. Recognizing its divine nature and the power it held, Aeëtes placed the fleece in a sacred grove, where it was zealously guarded by a sleepless dragon, ensuring that this divine artifact remained protected from mortal desires and ambitions.

The Quest for the Golden Fleece

In the marbled halls of ancient Iolcus, whispered tales spoke of a golden treasure that lay in the distant kingdom of Colchis – the illustrious Golden Fleece. But to young Jason, the rightful heir of Iolcus, this was not just a treasure; it was a symbol of his stolen birthright, a testament to his claim to the throne usurped by his treacherous uncle, King Pelias.

Aware of a prophecy that foretold his downfall at the hands of a descendant of Aeolus (from which Jason hailed), Pelias devised a scheme. When confronted by Jason about his rightful place as king, Pelias saw an opportunity. He would send Jason on a perilous quest to retrieve the Golden Fleece, believing the journey would be the end of his young challenger.

Undeterred, Jason commissioned the construction of a grand ship, the Argo. And with the promise of glory and adventure, he rallied the mightiest heroes of Greece to his cause. Among them were the demigod Heracles with his unmatched strength, the soul-stirring musician Orpheus, and the celestial twins Castor and Pollux. Together, they formed the Argonauts, setting sail towards destiny.

Their voyage was fraught with perils. They confronted the Symplegades, massive clashing rocks that threatened to crush their ship. With Orpheus' divine music, they evaded the enchanting allure of the Sirens, who lured sailors to their watery graves. Each trial they faced, each monster they battled, only solidified their resolve.

Upon reaching the shimmering coasts of Colchis, the true challenge began. King Aeëtes, sensing Jason's determination and perhaps wary of his band of heroes, set forth three daunting tasks. These included yoking fire-breathing oxen, sowing dragon's teeth into the field, and battling the fearsome warriors that sprouted from the sown teeth.

Yet, in the shadows of the Colchian palace, another story was unfolding. Medea, the king's daughter and a sorceress of unparalleled skill, found herself drawn to the charismatic Jason. Their fates intertwined, and with her help, Jason triumphed over the challenges. But Aeëtes' treachery knew no bounds. Refusing to part with the fleece, he forced the lovers to take drastic measures.

Using her arcane arts, Medea lulled the fierce dragon guarding the fleece into a deep slumber, enabling Jason to retrieve the coveted prize. As dawn broke, the Argo, with its golden cargo and two star-crossed lovers, set sail back to Iolcus.

The journey home was equally harrowing, but with Medea's magic and the might of the Argonauts, they weathered every storm, both literal and metaphorical. Their return to Iolcus marked not just the retrieval of a legendary artifact but also the weaving of a tale of ambition, love, betrayal, and redemption—a story that would echo through the annals of time, immortalizing the quest for the Golden Fleece.

The Golden Fleece was more than just a quest item; it represented a king's legitimacy. By bringing the fleece back to Iolcus, Jason would have demonstrated not only his worthiness as a hero but also his divine right to rule.

Its story, passed down through the annals of time, underscores the lengths to which individuals might go for honor, redemption, and love. It offers a mirror to the societal values and aspirations of the ancient Greeks, casting light on their perceptions of heroism, sacrifice, and the eternal tension between human ambition and divine will. The journey of the Argonauts reflects the challenges of leadership, the nature of heroism, and the complexities of divine and human relationships.

Sources/Further Reading:

"Argonautica" by Apollonius of Rhodes
"The Complete World of Greek Mythology" by Richard Buxton
"The Greek Myths" by Robert Graves

Gungnir

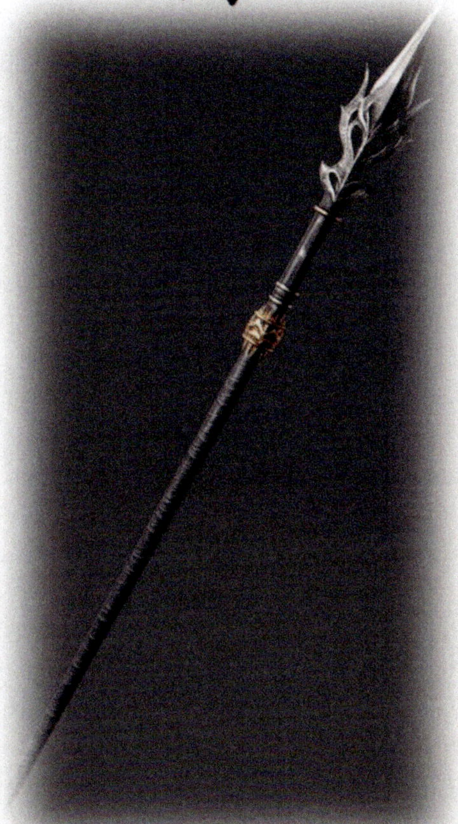

Gungnir, **whose name is believed to mean** "The Swaying One," is more than just a weapon in Norse mythology; it's a symbol of divine authority, precision, and the relentless quest for knowledge. A manifestation of the Norse worldview where tools and talismans held deep symbolic significance, the spear stands as a testament to the might and majesty of the Aesir gods and their dominion over the Nine Realms.

A masterwork of dwarven craftsmanship, Gungnir boasts an exquisite design, with ancient runes etched into its blade, each one narrating tales of valor, wisdom, and the intricate mosaic of fate that binds all beings. But it's the spear's unparalleled accuracy and balance that truly sets it apart. Once thrown, it never misses its target, a testament to both its flawless design and the unwavering intent of its wielder.

Moreover, in the heat of battle, the mere presence of Gungnir, held aloft by Odin as he rode his eight-legged steed Sleipnir, was enough to rally the Aesir and strike fear into the hearts of their adversaries. The spear's reputation was such that it was believed to have a life force of its own, resonating with the pulse of the universe and the heartbeat of its divine master.

Odin's spear, Gungnir, stands alongside other iconic items like Thor's hammer, Mjölnir, Frey's ship, Skidbladnir, and Odin's ring Draupnir, as one of the masterpieces crafted by the talented Dwarven brothers, Sindri and Brokkr. Their skills were challenged in a famous wager with Loki, the trickster god. Loki, after maliciously cutting off the hair of Sif, Thor's wife, was forced to provide even greater treasures to the gods to avoid their wrath. In response, he commissioned other dwarves to create magical items. Meanwhile, Sindri and Brokkr, accepting Loki's bet that they couldn't create items superior to the other dwarves, crafted treasures including Gungnir for the gods. Despite Loki's attempts to sabotage their work, they succeeded in creating artifacts of unmatched power and beauty. As a result, Gungnir became a possession of Odin.

Odin's Quest for Knowledge

Odin, unlike many gods from different pantheons, is ceaselessly driven by a thirst for wisdom and understanding. While he is already known as the chief god and the Allfather of the Aesir in Norse mythology, he continually seeks to deepen his wisdom, often going to great lengths and making personal sacrifices.

In the "Hávamál," Odin describes a profound and self-inflicted ordeal. He hangs himself from Yggdrasil, the immense ash tree that connects all of existence, and pierces himself with his own spear, Gungnir. He hangs in this agonizing state without any sustenance for nine nights, a symbolic number in Norse mythology, representing completion and the cyclical nature of things.

"I know that I hung on a windy tree
Nine long nights,
Wounded with a spear, dedicated to Odin,
Myself to myself."

Amidst the pain and near the brink of death, at the culmination of his sacrifice, Odin experiences a transformative vision. He perceives the runes, ancient symbols imbued with magic and wisdom, which were previously hidden. He then seizes them in an act of ecstatic revelation and, with them, gains new powers and profound knowledge.

"Then I was fertilized and became wise;
I truly grew and thrived.
From a word to a word I was led to a word,
From a work to a work I was led to a work."

Rejuvenated by this newfound wisdom, Odin returns to Asgard, the home of the gods, forever changed. The runes he discovered are more than mere symbols; they are powerful magical tools that play a significant role in many Norse myths and sagas. Skalds (poets) and shamans could invoke their power for divination, healing, protection, and other magical practices.

Gods and Games

In the darkened halls of Valhalla, whispers spoke of a challenge, a contest of skill among the gods. Thor, ever boastful of Mjölnir's might, claimed none could match his hammer's power. Intrigued, Odin proposed a test of accuracy rather than strength, pitting Mjölnir against Gungnir.

At the edge of Asgard, overlooking the vast expanse of Midgard, a target was set: a single golden ring, floating amidst the stars. The challenge was simple: to strike the ring without disturbing its celestial dance.

Thor went first, hurling Mjölnir with a thunderous roar. The heavens trembled as the hammer spun, narrowly missing the ring but causing it to waver slightly in its path. Odin stood next, Gungnir gleaming in the twilight. With a deep breath, he cast the spear. It soared, silent and unwavering, through the cosmos. As the gods watched, Gungnir pierced the center of the golden ring, leaving its dance undisturbed.

The court of Valhalla erupted in awe. While Mjölnir's might was unmatched, Gungnir's precision was unparalleled. It wasn't just the spear's design, but the intent and focus of Odin, the Allfather, that ensured it never missed.

From that day, whenever bards sang of the weapons of the gods, tales of Mjölnir's might were always accompanied by the unerring accuracy of Gungnir, the spear that never missed its mark.

The First Clash of Divinities – Gungnir's Decree

The cosmos of Norse mythology is not only an expanse filled with heroic deeds and treacherous monsters but also the theater of cosmic conflicts. One of the most profound of these was the first war, a celestial clash that pitted the Aesir against the Vanir. These two families of gods, although dwelling in the same realm, held different dominions and values. The Aesir, led by Odin, were gods of war and poetry, while the Vanir were deities of fertility, prosperity, and nature.

As tensions brewed, posturing gave way to open hostilities. The open plains near the cosmic tree, Yggdrasil, became the battleground where divine forces met in a confrontation that would shape the course of mythology. But how does one signify the commencement of a battle between gods? With mortals, a horn might be blown or a flag raised. For the Aesir, it was the might and symbolism of Gungnir, Odin's trusted spear, that would herald the onslaught.

Odin, atop his high vantage point, saw the gathering Vanir in the distance. The air was thick with anticipation, and a charged silence gripped the plains. Then, with a deliberate motion, the Allfather drew Gungnir. The spear, crafted by the cosmos's most skilled hands, gleamed with an ethereal light, its intricate runes shimmering. With the precision that only a god of his stature could muster, Odin hurled Gungnir into the midst of the Vanir.

But this wasn't merely a military maneuver. The act was rich in symbolism. In launching Gungnir, Odin wasn't just making the first move in the skirmish; he was sending a message, imbued with ritualistic significance. The spear's flight, unwavering and true, was a manifestation of the Aesir's resolve, their commitment to the upcoming struggle, and a challenge to the Vanir. It declared, in no uncertain terms, the commencement of the divine conflict.

However, beyond the immediate implications of the battle, the throwing of Gungnir set a precedent. It became emblematic of the beginning of significant confrontations, underscoring the weight of the events about to unfold. The war's aftermath, marked by treaties and exchanges, would reshape the dynamics of the Norse pantheon, but the image of Gungnir, soaring through the air as a harbinger of conflict, remained an enduring symbol of decisive moments in the grand expanse of Norse lore.

More than just a weapon, Gungnir was a symbol of Odin's authority over the cosmos and his role as a war god. It was believed that the mere act of Odin hurling Gungnir over an army would ensure its victory.

Gungnir remains a powerful symbol in Norse mythology, representing not just martial prowess but also the wisdom and authority of Odin. The spear's mythological significance extends beyond battle, symbolizing the lengths one might go to in the pursuit of knowledge and understanding, as exemplified by Odin's own sacrifices.

Sources/Further Reading:

"The Poetic Edda"
"The Prose Edda" by Snorri Sturluson
"Norse Mythology" by Neil Gaiman

Hagoromo

In the rich fabric of Japanese folklore, the Hagoromo, often translated as the "celestial robe," stands out as a symbol of ethereal beauty and otherworldly encounters. Deeply rooted in traditional Japanese literature, drama, and dance, the story of the Hagoromo bridges the world of humans with the divine realm of the heavens.

The Hagoromo is not a mere garment but a magical feathered robe worn by Tennin (akin to celestial nymphs or angels in other cultures). These heavenly beings would often descend from their celestial abode to the earthly realm, especially near bodies of water, leaving behind their Hagoromo on the shores. These celestial maidens are sometimes shown dancing or playing music, embodying both aesthetic and spiritual beauty. They symbolize purity, divinity, and the transient nature of life, often acting as messengers or intermediaries between the human world and the divine realm.

Visually, the Hagoromo is depicted as an ethereal, beautifully shimmering robe that flows gracefully, often adorned with feathers or motifs symbolizing its celestial origin. Its delicate and otherworldly appearance reflects the divine and pure nature of the Tennin who wear it.

Beyond its beauty, the Hagoromo possesses magical properties. The most notable of these is its ability to grant its wearer the power of flight. When donned, the Hagoromo allows the Tennin to ascend to the heavens and traverse between the celestial and earthly realms. Without it, a Tennin would be unable to return to her heavenly abode, making the robe an integral part of her existence.

The most famous tale associated with the Hagoromo takes place in the scenic Miho no Matsubara, near the city of Shizuoka in Japan.

The Tale of Hagoromo

In the picturesque coastal stretch of Miho no Matsubara, the air was often filled with the briny scent of the sea, mingled with the fragrant whispers of pine trees. It was here that an age-old tale unfolded—a tale of love, deception, and longing.

One twilight evening, as the setting sun painted the sky in hues of pink and gold, a group of heavenly maidens, Tennyo, descended from the celestial realm. They were drawn to the beauty of the Earth, and in their joy, they began to dance upon the shimmering sands, their laughter echoing like a melody. As they danced, they shed their Hagoromo, the celestial robes that granted them their divine abilities, and draped them over the nearby pine trees.

Unbeknownst to them, a young fisherman named Hakuryo, known for his mischievous nature, had been wandering the beach and had chanced upon the ethereal scene. Enchanted by their beauty and grace, a wicked thought crossed his mind. Quietly, he approached the pine where the robes lay and hid one, belonging to the most beautiful Tennyo.

As night began to fall, the Tennyo prepared to ascend to the heavens. However, to their dismay, one among them could not find her Hagoromo. Without it, she was bound to the Earth. Desperate, she searched everywhere, while her sisters, unable to delay their ascent, bid her a tearful goodbye, promising to return for her.

Seizing the opportunity, Hakuryo approached the distraught Tennyo and consoled her, feigning ignorance about the missing robe. Over time, as she adjusted to her mortal surroundings, the two grew close. Hakuryo, with his charm and the hidden leverage of the Hagoromo, managed to woo the Tennyo, and soon they were married.

Years passed, and they were blessed with children. Their life together was peaceful, and Hakuryo's initial deception seemed a distant memory. However, the Tennyo often gazed skyward, her heart aching for her celestial home and sisters. One fateful evening, burdened by guilt and moved by the love he genuinely felt for his wife, Hakuryo confessed his deception, revealing the hidden Hagoromo. The Tennyo, a tumult of emotions—anger, sadness, and relief—retrieved her celestial robe. As she donned it, her divine form was restored.

Facing Hakuryo, she spoke of her love for him and their children, but also of her longing for the heavens. With tears in her eyes, she took one last look at her earthly family, and then, with grace, ascended to the skies.

Hakuryo, filled with remorse and love, watched her disappear into the heavens, leaving him with their children and memories of a love that spanned realms. Miho no Matsubara, with its pine trees and golden sands, became a testament to their love, a place where the earthly and the divine had once intertwined.

The ancient tale of the Hagoromo, deeply rooted in Japanese folklore, encapsulates themes of transient beauty, deception, sacrifice, and the profound, sometimes tenuous, connections bridging different realms. Over the centuries, this story has permeated various artistic expressions within Japanese culture, from the dramatic performances of Noh and Kabuki theatre to the intricate designs of ukiyo-e woodblock prints.

In the vibrant world of Kabuki theatre, the celestial dance of the Tennin emerges as a moment of profound emotion and ethereal beauty. Accompanied by traditional music and clothed in the mesmerizing twirls of the feathered Hagoromo, the actress endeavors to convey the heavenly nymph's emotions and the celestial allure. The robe, central to the tale, is rendered in lavish detail, its shimmer and flow meticulously crafted to echo its divine origins. While preserving the essence of the story, Kabuki introduces layers of depth, often adding characters or subplots, enhancing the narrative's drama.

Parallelly, the world of ukiyo-e, or "pictures of the floating world," brings the tale's fleeting moments into sharp focus. These woodblock prints capture the transient nature of the Hagoromo tale with unmatched finesse, be it the Tennin's graceful dance or the poignant moment she discovers her missing robe. Each stroke, each expression immortalizes the story's ephemeral essence.

This enduring tale also finds its celebration in the modern day. Every year, on the second weekend of October, the Hagoromo Festival is held in the city of Shizuoka. Near the ancient pine tree's revered site, the story is remembered and celebrated, bridging the past and the present.

The Hagoromo's legacy, beyond its captivating narrative, lies in its symbolism. It serves as a poignant reminder of the fleeting nature of beauty, the sacrifices made for love, and the mystical threads that bind the celestial to the terrestrial.

Sources/Further Reading:

"Manyoshu":
"The Feather Mantle and Other Stories of Japan" by Miyoko Matsutani

Harp of Dagda

The Harp of Dagda, often simply referred to as Dagda's Harp, is a powerful and magical instrument steeped in Irish mythology. The harp is linked with Dagda, one of the chief deities in the pantheon of Celtic gods, known as the Tuatha Dé Danann.

The Harp of Dagda, known in some legends as "Uaithne," isn't just an instrument. It is a testament to the divine artistry and the deep connection between the gods and the elements of nature in Celtic mythology.

Legends whisper of the origins of the harp, a time when the skies resonated with the ethereal melodies of the universe, and the earth pulsed with the rhythm of life. Drawing inspiration from these cosmic harmonies, the gods desired an instrument that could capture the essence of the world's song.

The harp was carved from the heartwood of an ancient tree, a tree that had witnessed countless sunrises and stood sentinel during innumerable storms. This tree had absorbed the world's tales, and its wood resonated with memories. The frame of the harp was thus not just wood but a chronicle of time itself. The strings, crafted from the golden hair of a maiden, held their own magic. This maiden, often believed to be a demigoddess or a spirit of nature, willingly gave strands of her hair, infusing the strings with her essence. Every strand echoed with her laughter, whispered her secrets, and hummed with her dreams. When plucked, the strings wouldn't merely produce music but evoke emotions, memories, and sensations.

The Harp of Dagda wasn't just a musical instrument; it was a divine artifact, and its appearance reflected its significance. It was adorned with precious gems that gleamed like stars, each representing a celestial body. Intricate patterns and runes, which were said to be words of power and protection, were etched into its frame. These symbols narrated stories of the gods, tales of creation, and sagas of heroes.

The chief deity, Dagda, recognized the harp's value, not just for its beauty but for its capability to resonate with the universe's melodies. In his hands, Uaithne wasn't just an instrument but a bridge between realms, a translator of the universe's language, and a key to the hearts of all who listened.

The harp held significant power. With it, Dagda could command the seasons and influence the order of nature. But most notably, the harp had the power to play three distinct melodies:

The Lament of Sleep: Which could send anyone listening into a deep slumber.

The Laugh of Merriment: Which would make listeners burst into joyous laughter.

The Sob of Sorrow: Which would reduce anyone to tears.

Harmony Disrupted: The Fomorian Scheme

The Fomorians, a race known for their chaotic inclinations, saw the harp not merely as an instrument but as a tool to assert dominion over the natural order. By controlling the harp, they believed they could hold the seasons hostage, turning harvests to famine and day to endless night, thereby bending the Tuatha Dé Danann to their will.

One dark evening, a band of cunning Fomorians infiltrated the halls where the harp was kept. Using dark sorceries and distractions, they managed to snatch away the celestial instrument. As they fled, the world felt the absence of the harp's melodies. Seasons faltered, stars dimmed, and a cold silence enveloped the lands.

Dagda, sensing the disarray and the theft of his beloved harp, assembled a group of deities. Using their collective might, they sought clues, read the stars, and invoked ancient spells to trace the Fomorians' path. The pursuit was fierce, not just a chase in the physical realm but a battle of wits, magic, and intentions.

Upon finally cornering the Fomorians in a desolate cavern, Dagda stepped forward, his eyes fixed on his treasured harp, which was suspended in an arcane barrier. But the bond between Dagda and his harp was unbreakable. With a commanding voice that echoed the primordial sounds of creation, Dagda called out to the harp. Responding to its master's call, the harp broke free, flying towards Dagda, its strings strumming a battle hymn. On its path, it struck down nine Fomorians who dared to obstruct.

With the harp safely in his grasp, Dagda didn't resort to violence. Instead, he played. The first melody lulled the Fomorians, ensnaring their senses in a deep slumber. The second was a lament, so poignant that even these ancient adversaries were moved to tears, their defenses dropping. The final melody was one of joy, a song of the cosmos, which induced uncontrollable laughter among the Fomorians.

With their foes incapacitated, Dagda and his companions retreated, restoring the harp to its rightful place and, with it, the harmonious balance of the cosmos. The tale serves as a reminder that true power lies not in suppression or chaos but in harmony, unity, and the melodies that bind the universe.

Dagda's Harp is not just an instrument but a symbol of order, harmony, and the cyclical nature of existence. The god's ability to command it, even when stolen, showcases the enduring connection between a deity and their source of power. In broader terms, the harp, with its power over emotions, emphasizes the ancient Celtic reverence for music and its transformative abilities.

Sources/Further Reading:

"The Mythological Cycle": Various texts, including the Lebor Gabála Érenn (Book of Invasions), contain the narratives of the Tuatha Dé Danann and their exploits.
"Celtic Myths and Legends" by Peter Berresford Ellis
"Early Irish Myths and Sagas" by Jeffrey Gantz

Headband of Sun Wukong

The headband, often referred to as the golden fillet or tight hoop, is an iconic accessory worn by Sun Wukong, the Monkey King, in the classic Chinese novel "Journey to the West" written by Wu Cheng'en. This golden fillet, while seemingly a mere accessory, encapsulates the tumultuous and transformative journey of Sun Wukong, the celebrated Monkey King. As an emblem of constraint, discipline, and eventual enlightenment, the headband stands as a testament to the trials faced by Wukong and serves as a reminder of the enduring human struggle between impulsive rebellion and the path to self-betterment.

The headband, often depicted as a thin, shimmering golden circlet, is more than just a decorative piece. Its intricate designs might vary depending on the rendition, but its primary function remains consistent. When donned, it fits snugly around Wukong's head, becoming an inseparable part of him. To any observer, it appears delicate and elegant. However, its true power lies in its magical properties.

Made of a unique metal, the headband can neither be removed nor broken, making it an eternal fixture on Sun Wukong's brow once placed. With the utterance of a specific mantra by Tang Sanzang, the headband can constrict, exerting excruciating pressure on Wukong's head. This tightening serves both as a punitive measure and as a tool to rein in Wukong's impulsive tendencies. Let's dive deeper into the story of this unique artifact.

The Monkey King's Ascension and Hubris

Sun Wukong was no ordinary monkey. Born from a stone nourished by the energies of heaven and earth, he rapidly grew in strength, wisdom, and ambition. After acquiring powerful combat skills and mastering the 72 transformations, his audacity knew no bounds. He declared himself the 'Great Sage, Equal of Heaven,' challenging the very celestial hierarchy.

His antics weren't just limited to declarations. Wukong infiltrated the Dragon King's palace to acquire his magical staff, the Ruyi Jingu Bang, and even managed to get his name removed from the Book of Life and Death, effectively granting him immortality. These deeds and his relentless defiance against the celestial order led to multiple confrontations with Heaven's army, and he emerged victorious each time.

The heavens were in turmoil, and the Jade Emperor sought the counsel of the Buddha. Recognizing Wukong's indomitable spirit and power, the Buddha challenged him to a simple task - to leap out of his palm. Confident, Wukong took the leap, reaching what he believed was the world's end. However, upon his return, he found, to his astonishment, that he had never left the Buddha's hand at all. This was a humbling realization. The Buddha then trapped Wukong under a mountain, where he remained imprisoned, pondering his actions for half a millennium.

When the time came for the monk Tang Sanzang to undertake the perilous journey to retrieve the sacred scriptures, he would need protectors to guard against demons and challenges. The compassionate Bodhisattva Guanyin proposed Sun Wukong as an ideal guardian. Yet, given Wukong's previous rebelliousness, measures were needed to ensure his obedience.

Hence, the introduction of the magical golden headband. This wasn't just a tool for control, but also a symbol of Wukong's redemption path. Every time it tightened around his brow, it was a reminder of his vow to serve, protect, and, above all, evolve.

Throughout their journey, Wukong's relationship with Tang Sanzang transformed from that of a mere protector to a devoted disciple. The headband, though a tool of constraint, played a role in Sun Wukong's growth, making him realize the significance of discipline, self-control, and the path of righteousness.

The headband, while a physical restraint, is also symbolic. Sun Wukong's entire journey in "Journey to the West" is a path of redemption and enlightenment. The headband represents discipline, control, and the restraint needed on the path to enlightenment. It ensures that the wild nature of Wukong, which often acts on impulses, is kept in check.

Throughout their journey, the relationship between Tang Sanzang and Sun Wukong evolves. While initially a tool of control, the headband eventually becomes more of a reminder to Wukong of his duty and the promises he made. It's a testament to the transformative power of discipline and commitment on the path to spiritual growth.

In essence, the headband's story is not just about subduing a rebellious spirit but illuminating the path of growth, realization, and eventual enlightenment. It serves as a poignant reminder that sometimes, the most formidable challenges we face are the ones that lead us to our highest selves.

The headband of Sun Wukong has become emblematic of the character. It has been depicted in numerous adaptations of the story, including films, television series, and comics. Its design and the concept of a controlling artifact have even influenced characters in other cultures and stories.

Sources/Further Reading:

"Journey to the West" by Wu Cheng'en
"The Monkey and the Monk: An Abridgment of The Journey to the West" translated by Anthony C. Yu

Heimdalr's Horn

Heimdallr's Horn, often known as the Gjallarhorn, is a significant artifact in Norse mythology. In the intricate web of Norse mythology, where gods, giants, and otherworldly beings entangle in a dance of fate and free will, the Gjallarhorn, or Heimdallr's Horn, stands as a symbol of warning, vigilance, and the impending cataclysm.

Heimdallr, sometimes simply Heimdall, is a god associated with light, foreknowledge, and guardianship in Norse mythology. He stands as the watchman of the gods and is stationed at the Bifrost, the rainbow bridge that connects the realm of the gods, Asgard, to the world of humans, Midgard. Gjallarhorn, when directly translated, means "Yelling Horn" or "Loud-Sounding Horn." This horn is closely tied to Heimdallr's role as the guardian of the gods. Its primary function is to serve as a warning system. When danger approaches Asgard, especially during the events leading up to Ragnarök (the prophesied end of the world), Heimdallr will blow the Gjallarhorn to alert the gods.

Ragnarök's Clarion Call: The Sound of the Gjallarhorn

Ragnarök, often translated as the "Doom of the Gods," is a sequence of events foretold in Norse mythology that signifies the end and rebirth of the world. This apocalyptic prophecy, detailed in the "Völuspá" of the Poetic Edda, encompasses battles, natural disasters, and the eventual submersion of the world in water.

Central to the heralding of this cosmic endgame is Heimdallr's Gjallarhorn, a horn imbued with the gravity of the impending fate of the universe. In the tranquil realm of the gods, where time weaves its own pace and the fabric of reality is thick with intertwined destinies, Heimdallr, with his unmatched vision and acute hearing, perceives the stirrings of chaos long before any actual threat becomes apparent. Yet, he remains a stoic sentinel, awaiting the moment when his horn's call will pierce the stillness.

As the forces of disorder muster strength and the giants, monsters, and malevolent beings begin their march on Asgard (the realm of the gods), Heimdallr takes the Gjallarhorn and readies himself. With a deep breath, he blows into the horn. Its clarion sound, haunting and majestic, reverberates throughout the Nine Worlds, reaching the deepest caverns of Niflheim to the lofty heights of Alfheim. Every being, mortal and divine, recognizes its call, for it signifies not just a battle, but the battle - the culmination of eons of intertwined destinies.

The sound of the Gjallarhorn is not merely an alarm; it's a call to arms, a melancholic song of endings, and a harbinger of rebirth. It encapsulates the Norse worldview - that every ending is a new beginning, that destruction paves the way for creation.

As the Aesir gods prepare for the final confrontation, they do so with the knowledge of their likely doom. The Gjallarhorn's call, though somber, also carries an undertone of hope - hope that, in the cycle of death and rebirth, the new world that emerges post-Ragnarök will be one of peace, prosperity, and harmony. Thus, Heimdallr's horn transcends its role as a mere instrument, becoming a poignant emblem of the cyclical nature of existence and the eternal dance of chaos and order.

In certain versions of Norse myths, during the events leading up to Ragnarök, the Gjallarhorn is said to be hidden away by Heimdallr, and its location is lost to him.

Heimdallr's Quest: The Rediscovery of the Gjallarhorn

As the tapestry of fate wove ever tighter around the gods of the Norse pantheon, foretelling the inevitable doom of Ragnarök, Heimdallr, the vigilant guardian of the Bifröst, faced a profound dilemma. The Gjallarhorn, the very instrument he needed to signal the onset of the end times, was missing.

Ancient myths whisper that Heimdallr, foreseeing the dire events that lay ahead, had once hidden the Gjallarhorn to prevent it from falling into the wrong hands. As the sentry of the gods, he was all too aware of the lurking shadows and the entities that sought to hasten Ragnarök prematurely. Yet, over time, the precise location of the horn slipped from his memory, a secret buried deep within the cosmos.

As omens of the impending cataclysm began to manifest - the sun dimming, winters extending, and a general unrest rippling through the realms - Heimdallr recognized the urgent need to recover the Gjallarhorn. The annals of lore hint that the horn lay hidden near Mímir's Well, a repository of wisdom and knowledge guarded by the decapitated head of the deity, Mímir.

Approaching the well, shrouded in mists and the whispers of ages past, Heimdallr confronted a heart-wrenching choice. Mímir, ever thirsty for knowledge, demanded a price for revealing the horn's location. The watchman had to sacrifice one of his heightened senses. This was no small cost for Heimdallr, whose keen senses were his very essence, allowing him to hear grass growing and see hundreds of leagues away.

Yet, recognizing the magnitude of his duty, Heimdallr agreed. Plunging his hand into the ancient waters, he forfeited his ear, forever altering his existence. In return, Mímir's voice, deep and timeless, revealed the Gjallarhorn's resting place.

With the instrument once again in his grasp, Heimdallr stood ready to fulfill his destiny. The tale of the Gjallarhorn's loss and recovery underscores the recurring Norse theme of sacrifice for the greater good and the inexorable march towards destiny, even in the face of oblivion.

The Gjallarhorn, in its essence, serves as a symbol of warning, readiness, and the inexorable nature of fate in Norse mythology. Just as the gods can't prevent Ragnarök, they can only prepare for it. Similarly, the horn doesn't prevent disaster but serves as an alarm, underscoring the idea of facing one's destiny head-on, no matter how dire.

Sources/Further Reading:

"The Prose Edda" by Snorri Sturluson
"The Poetic Edda"
Academic Analysis: "The Norse Myths" by Kevin Crossley-Holland

Helskor boots

The Helskor, also known as the "Hel-shoes" or "shoes of Hel", are lesser-known items within Norse mythology. These are special shoes given to the dead so they can make their way to Hel, the land of the dead ruled by the entity of the same name, Hel.

The Helskor are a mystifying artifact in Norse mythology, carrying with them the weight of finality and the passage of souls. These are not shoes meant for the living or for grand heroic adventures. Instead, they serve a solemn purpose: to guide the spirits of the departed through the treacherous paths leading to Hel, ensuring their safe arrival to the cold and distant realm of the dead.

Mystical in nature, the Helskor are not your typical footwear. Described in ancient texts as being fashioned from dark, ethereal materials, they embody the essence of the afterlife. Their mere presence emanates a cold, otherworldly aura. Once worn by a spirit, the Helskor light up their path, becoming beacons in the obscurity of the underworld. Their soles, though seemingly insubstantial, are sturdy enough to endure the rocky and treacherous terrains of the nether regions.

While the Helskor might not boast the combative powers of Thor's Mjölnir or the protective abilities of Odin's spear, Gungnir, they hold an indispensable role in Norse cosmology. Every soul, whether of a mighty warrior or a common villager, relies on the Helskor to navigate their afterlife journey.

One of the most tragic tales in Norse mythology is the death of Balder, the beloved god of light and purity. After his untimely death due to Loki's mischief, the gods mourned him deeply. As is customary, Balder was provided with the Helskor to aid his journey to Hel's domain, reflecting thc universal nature of death and the afterlife – even gods aren't exempt. In the sagas, countless unnamed or less significant individuals meet their end in battles, voyages, or simple everyday occurrences. For these souls, the journey to Hel could be daunting. The Helskor served as a comforting assurance, a gift that even in death, the gods provided a means of guidance and safe passage.

The "Visio Godeschalci" (Vision of Godeschalk) is a medieval text that details the vision of a journey to the afterlife experienced by a peasant named Godeschalk from Holstein. This vision is particularly interesting as it comes from a period when Christianity was starting to spread in the region, and the text shows a blending of old Germanic beliefs and new Christian teachings.

One account from Visio Godeschalci details a vision of the underworld and the trials souls face there. This vision emphasizes the theme of judgment, with souls receiving rewards or punishments based on their deeds in life. In this account, the Helskor shoes were believed to aid the souls in their travels through the challenging terrains of the underworld.

The Journey of Astrid

Astrid, a brave warrior from a remote village, had lived a life of honor, defending her people from invaders and ensuring justice prevailed. As she grew old, she was visited by a mysterious seer who spoke of the Helskor boots, an artifact said to help souls navigate the treacherous terrains of the underworld.

Upon her death, Astrid found herself at the beginning of a vast, thorny heath. Remembering the seer's words, she looked around and spotted the radiant Helskor boots hanging from a sacred Linden tree. As she wore them, the thorns retracted, making her path more straightforward.

Guided by the luminescence of the Helskor, Astrid reached the River of Irons. The river, with its sharp, cutting currents, looked insurmountable. But with the Helskor on her feet, Astrid discovered that she could step onto narrow boards that floated atop the waters, allowing her to cross safely.

On the second day, she reached the crossroads. The paths to heaven, hell, and the in-between stretched out before her. The boots, sensing her virtuous life, glowed even brighter, illuminating the way to heaven. But Astrid paused. She remembered souls she had seen struggling on her journey, souls who didn't have the guidance of the Helskor.

She decided to use the Helskor to guide lost souls, ensuring they found their rightful place in the afterlife. And so, Astrid became a beacon for lost souls, her Helskor's light symbolizing hope, guidance, and the eternal bond between the world of the living and the realm of the dead.

Astrid's decision to aid lost souls with the Helskor's guidance epitomizes the narrative's core message: in the vast divide between life and death, it's the acts of compassion and hope that shine the brightest.

The Helskor's tale isn't just about a pair of radiant shoes. It's a story of hope, guidance, and the eternal bonds that link the living with the departed. Through the glow of the Helskor, Norse mythology conveys a comforting message: even in death, one is never truly alone.

Sources/Further Reading:

The Poetic Edda" translated by Carolyne Larrington
"The Prose Edda" by Snorri Sturluson
"The Road to Hel: A Study of the Conception of the Dead in Old Norse Literature" by Hilda Roderick Ellis Davidson

Hliðskjálf

Hliðskjálf is a significant artifact in Norse mythology. It is the high seat of the Allfather, Odin, from which he is able to gaze out across all the nine realms of the cosmos and see everything that occurs. Situated in the god's grand hall, Valaskjálf, this throne symbolizes Odin's omnipresence and omniscience.

Hliðskjálf, often described as the "all-seeing throne," stands in Valhalla, Odin's majestic hall. While the exact appearance of the seat is not elaborated on in great detail in ancient texts, its significance is unquestionable. As the throne of the Allfather, it embodies the god's divine authority and vast knowledge.

The power of the Hliðskjálf is often alluded to when referencing Odin's extensive knowledge. It is through this seat that he keeps an eye on the heroes he has chosen, the valkyries in their tasks, and the ever-looming threats from the giants. Odin's role as a god of war and wisdom is deeply intertwined with his ability to see all, strategize, and act accordingly. Odin, draped in his blue cloak and often accompanied by his two ravens, Huginn (thought) and Muninn (memory), would frequently ascend the throne. Sitting atop Hliðskjálf, he wasn't just the ruler of Asgard; he became the watchful eye of the cosmos. With a single gaze, he could traverse the vastness of the nine realms, from the icy reaches of Niflheim to the fiery pits of Muspelheim, from the human world of Midgard to the stronghold of the giants in Jotunheim.

This power was not just a tool of surveillance but an instrument of governance. Odin's primary responsibility was to maintain the balance of the cosmos and to prepare for the prophesied cataclysm of Ragnarök. Through Hliðskjálf, he monitored the heroes destined to join him in Valhalla, observing their valor, trials, and tribulations. He watched the valkyries, his chosen warrior maidens, as they selected the bravest of the slain to join his ranks in the eternal hall.

But it wasn't just heroes and valkyries that drew Odin's attention. The giants, ancient beings of chaos and wild nature, often plotted against the gods of Asgard. From his throne, Odin could preemptively identify threats, strategize responses, and often dispatch Thor or other Aesir to counteract the giants' moves.

However, the power of Hliðskjálf wasn't just about observation; it was about wisdom and introspection. Odin's ability to see all also meant confronting uncomfortable truths, recognizing the limitations of godly power, and accepting the inevitability of destiny. The throne wasn't just a source of external knowledge but a mirror reflecting Odin's internal battles, challenges, and philosophies.

The Hliðskjálf, while not an active tool like Thor's hammer Mjölnir, plays a vital, passive role in the Norse cosmos. It serves as a constant reminder of the gods' watchful eyes and the interconnectedness of the realms. To sit upon the Hliðskjálf is to bear the weight of responsibility for all the cosmos and to understand the intricate web of fate and free will that weaves through every tale and adventure in Norse mythology.

Freya's Gaze and the Price of Omniscience

In the vast shimmering halls of Valaskjálf, the throne of Hliðskjálf stood tall, radiating an aura of both power and mystery. While the throne was specifically reserved for Odin's use, there were rare instances when its allure proved irresistible even to other gods.

Freya, the radiant goddess of love, beauty, and fertility, was a central figure in the Norse pantheon. Known for her passionate nature and deep emotions, she shared a tumultuous relationship with her husband, Óðr. Óðr was a mysterious figure, often away on long travels, leaving Freya longing and heartbroken in his absence.

On one fateful day, in Odin's absence from his hall, a distressed and lonely Freya was drawn to Hliðskjálf. Whether it was out of curiosity or a hope to catch a glimpse of Óðr's whereabouts, she decided to ascend the throne. As she sat upon it, the vast expanse of the nine realms spread out before her, each secret, every whisper, and every movement laid bare.

It was then that her gaze was captured by a heart-wrenching scene. She witnessed Óðr in a tender moment with another, an act of betrayal that cut Freya to her core. The raw pain of this revelation was compounded by the sacred nature of the throne — it showed truth, unvarnished and undeniable.

This traumatic experience had profound consequences. The heartache drove Freya to weep tears of gold, and she embarked on an extensive search throughout the realms, looking for her husband and seeking answers. Her travels brought her into various adventures and encounters, further enriching Norse tales of her endeavors.

The story of Freya's Gaze offers a deep lesson on the perils of omniscience. It underscores the idea that there are certain truths that might be too painful to bear, especially when they concern matters of the heart. Hliðskjálf, in this context, is not just a throne of power but also a seat of immense responsibility. The ability to see everything comes with its own set of challenges, as knowledge can be both a gift and a curse.

In essence, Hliðskjálf symbolized the dual nature of leadership: the necessity of vigilance and the weight of responsibility. Through Odin's watch, we glimpse the challenges faced by a deity who, despite his vast power, grapples with the complexities of fate, the unpredictability of free will, and the looming shadow of an uncertain future. It serves as a poignant reminder that true leadership isn't just about seeing but understanding, not just about power but the wisdom to wield it judiciously.

Sources/Further Reading:

"The Prose Edda" by Snorri Sturluson
"Norse Mythology" by Neil Gaiman
"Gods and Myths of Northern Europe" by H.R. Ellis Davidson

Horn of Plenty

The Horn of Plenty, also commonly known as the Cornucopia, is one of the most enduring symbols from ancient mythology. It represents abundance and nourishment and is typically depicted as a large, curved horn overflowing with produce, flowers, nuts, and other goods.

The Cornucopia, deriving its name from the Latin words "cornu" (horn) and "copia" (plenty), is deeply rooted in ancient Greco-Roman culture. This horn, brimming with fruits, vegetables, and other bounties of the harvest, has long been a representation of abundance, prosperity, and gratitude. Often associated with particular deities and festivals, its iconography has transcended its origins and has been adopted in various cultures as a universal symbol of Thanksgiving.

Zeus and Amalthea: The Birth of the Cornucopia

The tale begins with a prophecy that struck fear into the heart of Cronus, the Titan king of the universe. It was foretold that one of his children would rise up against him and overthrow his reign. Fearful and paranoid, Cronus took the desperate measure of swallowing each of his offspring as soon as they were born. This gruesome act, while violent, ensured that the prophecy could not come to fruition, or so he thought.

Rhea, Cronus' wife and the mother of the gods, was heartbroken at the loss of her children. When her youngest child, Zeus, was born, she couldn't bear to let him meet the same fate as his siblings. In a bid to save him, she concealed his birth and handed Cronus a stone wrapped in swaddling clothes, which he swallowed, believing it to be his son. Meanwhile, the real Zeus was whisked away to the Diktean Cave on the island of Crete, far from the prying eyes of his dangerous father.

On this secluded island, the young god was entrusted to the care of Amalthea, a gentle goat nymph. She nourished and protected him, providing him with her milk, ensuring Zeus grew strong and healthy. The cave's resonating sounds from the clanging of the shields of the Kouretes, minor local deities, masked the infant's cries, keeping his presence a secret from Cronus.

As Zeus grew, his playful nature emerged. One day, while frolicking in the cave, he accidentally broke off one of Amalthea's horns. Rather than being a moment of distress, this event became a serendipitous twist of fate. The broken horn, touched by the divine nature of Zeus and the selfless love of Amalthea, transformed. It became the Cornucopia, or the Horn of Plenty. This magical artifact had the unique ability to provide endless sustenance to its possessor, representing the nourishment and care that Amalthea provided to Zeus in his most vulnerable moments.

Heracles and Achelous: The Battle for Deianeira

Among the pantheon of Greek heroes, few shone as brightly as Heracles. Known for his incredible strength, bravery, and his twelve labors, Heracles' tales of valor spread far and wide across ancient Greece. However, it wasn't just monstrous creatures and challenging tasks that the hero faced; at times, he grappled with the gods themselves.

The story begins in Calydon, where the beautiful maiden Deianeira had many suitors vying for her hand in marriage. Among these was the river god Achelous, a powerful deity who held dominion over the largest river in Greece. He was deeply smitten with Deianeira's beauty and grace. But so was Heracles. Both desired to wed her, and a fierce rivalry ignited between the two.

Achelous was not a typical god. He had the unique ability to change forms. While he was primarily associated with water and appeared as a serpentine being, he could also transform into a raging bull, embodying the force and might of his river. He would use this form to intimidate his opponents and often to showcase his strength.

One fateful day, the tension between Heracles and Achelous reached its climax. To decide who would win Deianeira's hand, the two engaged in a fierce duel. As the battle raged on, Achelous, sensing an opportunity, transformed into his mighty bull form, thinking that this would give him the upper hand against the mortal Heracles.

But Heracles, with his unparalleled strength and combat experience from his labors, was not easily defeated. Using his might, he grappled with the bull, and in a display of sheer power, managed to wrench off one of its horns.

The torn horn, infused with the divine essence of Achelous and the heroic spirit of Heracles, underwent a magical transformation. From it sprouted fruits, flowers, and grains, and it turned into a Cornucopia, symbolizing abundance and plenty. This Horn of Plenty was different from Amalthea's horn but carried a similar essence of prosperity and blessings.

Defeated and humiliated, Achelous conceded, transforming back into his river form and retreating to his watery domain. Heracles, having bested a god, won Deianeira's hand. However, their story didn't have a happy ending, but that is a tale for another time. As for the Cornucopia, it stood as a testament to Heracles' triumph over the divine, a symbol of man's ability to harness nature's abundance, and a reminder of the thin line between victory and defeat in the battles of gods and heroes.

The Cornucopia, originally rooted in Greek mythology, resonated strongly with the values and beliefs of the Roman civilization. Rome, an empire renowned for its vast territories, diverse cultures, and the ability to assimilate various aspects from these cultures, seamlessly adopted the Cornucopia into its own mythological and cultural landscape.

One of the primary deities with whom the Cornucopia became associated in Rome was Fortuna, the goddess of fortune and the personification of luck. Fortuna was often depicted holding or being accompanied by the Cornucopia, which was a direct representation of the abundance and prosperity she could bring. To the Romans, the overflowing horn embodied not just material wealth but also the unpredictable nature of fortune – an empire could be as overflowing with riches as the Cornucopia or face scarcity if Fortune turned her gaze away. Temples dedicated to Fortuna were widespread in Rome, and during certain festivals, her statues would be adorned with the Cornucopia.

Another deity connected with the Cornucopia was Abundantia, whose very name means "abundance" or "plenty" in Latin. Abundantia was a minor goddess, but her role was clear: she personified the bounty and prosperity of the Roman Empire. Like Fortuna, she was often depicted carrying the Cornucopia, from which flowed an endless supply of grains, fruits, and other harvest goods.

While the Cornucopia originated from Greek myths, its adoption and adaptation by the Romans added layers of significance to it, making it a potent symbol of the vastness, wealth, and cultural amalgamation of the Roman Empire. Through the ages, it evolved to signify not just plenty but also the ebb and flow of fortune and the expansive reach of one of history's most formidable empires.

Over time, the Cornucopia became a symbol not just of food and harvest but of abundance in all its forms - be it wealth, happiness, or success. During the Renaissance, its image was revived, and it appeared in various forms of art, symbolizing the abundance of the land and the prosperity of the times.

In modern culture, especially in the United States, the Cornucopia is closely associated with the Thanksgiving holiday, signifying gratitude for the year's harvest and blessings.

The enduring legacy of the Cornucopia lies in its simplicity. Its curved horn, overflowing with nature's bounties, is a universal testament to the earth's generosity and the cycles of growth and harvest. The Cornucopia reminds us of the importance of gratitude, the interconnectedness of nature and culture, and the perennial human hope for abundance and prosperity. Whether through tales of deities and heroes or the centerpiece of a Thanksgiving table, the Horn of Plenty continues to resonate as a symbol of gratitude and abundance in cultures worldwide.

Sources/Further Reading:

"Metamorphoses" by Ovid
"The Classical Tradition" by Anthony Grafton, Glenn W. Most, and Salvatore Settis
The Theoi Project (theoi.com)

Jade Books in Heaven

The concept of the "Jade Books in Heaven" is deeply embedded in Chinese mythology and Taoist cosmology. These aren't physical books but serve as cosmic ledgers, chronicling the deeds of mortals. They symbolize the meticulous moral order of the universe, wherein every action, intention, and thought is recorded, emphasizing the weight of one's actions and fostering accountability. While they are often depicted or imagined as jade, symbolizing their permanence and sanctity, it's the essence or idea of the books – as cosmic ledgers or records – that's more significant than their physical manifestation.

The Cosmic Significance of the Jade Books

In ancient Chinese tales, celestial scribes, often pictured as stern figures with brushes, record every deed. These records, inscribed with special brushes and inks on jade pages, embody the enduring nature of one's actions. Jade, known for its purity and durability in Chinese culture, denotes the indelible nature of these records. Upon death, these chronicles from the Jade Books help celestial judges determine the fate of souls, be it ascension to a heavenly realm, reincarnation, or descent into punitive realms.

To appease these celestial scribes, rituals, practices, and offerings evolved, all in the hope of achieving a balanced record. This wasn't merely about evading punitive consequences but resonated deeply with the intrinsic concept of cosmic justice. The universe, in all its grandeur, guaranteed that individuals would inevitably confront the outcomes of their actions.

The Jade Books within 'Tian' and 'Dao'

In Chinese cosmology, 'Tian' symbolizes an impersonal cosmic order, unlike the Heaven of Western traditions. This force, while impersonal, gravitates towards righteousness and penalizes wrongs. The concept of "Mandate of Heaven" arises from this, where rulers aligned with 'Tian' are deemed legitimate.

On the other hand, 'Dao' or the Universal Way, central to Daoism, signifies the essence of the universe. Living in tune with the 'Dao' means achieving harmony and balance. In this vast cosmic canvas, the Jade Books are instruments of cosmic justice, ensuring actions and their consequences are aligned, encapsulating the Daoist ideology of causality.

The Celestial Bureaucracy and the Jade Books

Chinese mythology often parallels the earthly with the celestial. Just as the earthly realm had intricate administrative systems, the heavens mirrored these structures. This Celestial Bureaucracy, with the Jade Emperor at its helm, managed a complex hierarchy of deities and spirits.

Central to this bureaucracy were the Jade Books. They were not mere records but were pivotal in maintaining order. Celestial judges, like the Ten Kings of Hell, would use these chronicles during their judgments. Various deities held specific administrative roles, like the God of Wealth overseeing affluence, while the Kitchen God reported on domestic affairs.

This concept deeply influenced ancestral worship and many traditional Chinese festivals. For instance, during the Lunar New Year, the Kitchen God is believed to ascend to the heavens and present his records. Families conduct offerings, hoping for favorable reports.

Sun Wukong and the Jade books

Born from a stone nourished by the winds and the essence of Earth and Heaven, Sun Wukong emerged as a stone monkey, quickly becoming the leader of his fellow primates due to his intelligence and bravery. Over time, he feared the inevitability of death and decided to seek a way to gain immortality.

His journey led him to various sages and teachers, where he learned the ways of Taoism, gained incredible strength, the power to transform, and finally, the secret to eternal life.

His newfound immortality and vast array of powers made Sun Wukong arrogant. After discovering that the celestial Jade Emperor had given him a lowly title, "Protector of the Horses," essentially the keeper of heaven's stables, he rebelled. Feeling disrespected and considering himself equal to the gods, he declared himself the "Great Sage Equal to Heaven."

In his acts of defiance, Sun Wukong decided to further challenge the heavenly order. He stormed into the Hall of Life and Death, where the records of the lifespans of all beings are meticulously maintained in the Jade books. There, he found the Book of Life and Death. Without hesitation, he erased his name and the names of other monkeys from the book. This act granted him and his subjects immunity from death, making them invincible.

This blatant defiance and other mischiefs in Heaven did not go unnoticed. Heaven's forces, including the most powerful deities and warriors, were dispatched to subdue Sun Wukong which led to a series of further adventures.

The Jade Books in Heaven are more than mythological artifacts. They symbolize the intricate relationship between action and consequence, interwoven with cosmic justice. They serve as a reminder of the eternal nature of our deeds and the cosmic balance that governs all. Through the lens of the Jade Books, Chinese mythology offers profound insights into life, death, and the intricate dance between the two, reminding every individual of the indelible footprints they leave in the sands of time.

Sources/Further Reading:

"Tao Te Ching" by Laozi - This foundational text of Taoism offers profound insights into the concept of the 'Dao' and the natural order of the universe.
"Chinese Mythology: An Introduction" by Anne Birrell
"Ancestral Worship in Early China" by John L. Bishop

Járngreipr

Járngreipr, which translates to "Iron Grippers" in Old Norse, are the iron gloves worn by the Norse god Thor. They are a crucial piece of Thor's equipment, as they allow him to handle his primary weapon, the mighty hammer Mjölnir.

In Norse mythology, Thor is the thunder god and the defender of both gods and humans against the forces of chaos. He is most famously known for his mighty hammer, Mjölnir, which was forged by the skilled dwarf brothers, Sindri(also known as Eitri) and Brokkr.

However, Mjölnir was no ordinary hammer. Due to a mishap during its forging, the hammer's handle was much shorter than anticipated, making it difficult to wield. Also, given its immense power, a regular grip wouldn't suffice. Thus, Thor needed the Járngreipr, his iron gloves, to handle and wield Mjölnir effectively.

In the surviving Norse myths and sagas, the detailed origin or creation story of the Járngreipr is not explicitly mentioned. Instead, they are typically listed among Thor's possessions, along with Mjölnir and his belt of strength, Megingjörð.

Given the essential nature of the Járngreipr, allowing Thor to handle the immense power of Mjölnir, we can infer a few things. Just like many other powerful artifacts of the Norse gods, the Járngreipr might have been crafted by the skilled dwarves, the master blacksmiths and artisans of the Nine Worlds. The gloves, being made of iron, are symbolic of both protection and power. Iron was a precious commodity in the Norse world, representing strength and resilience.

By wearing the Járngreipr, Thor could harness the full power of Mjölnir without being overwhelmed by its might. Since the gloves are so intrinsically tied to the wielding of Mjölnir, they might have been crafted around the same time as the hammer. Recognizing the challenge the short handle presented, the dwarves might have crafted the Járngreipr to aid Thor in effectively wielding the hammer despite its flaw.

While many tales revolve around Thor's feats with Mjölnir, direct mentions of the Járngreipr are relatively scarce in the sagas and the Eddas. However, given the constant need for Thor to use Mjölnir, whether in battles against the Jötnar (giants) or in defending the realms, it's understood that Járngreipr was an ever-present aid to Thor.

The theft of Mjolnir and the might of the Járngreipr

In the quiet realm of the gods, Asgard, a shocking discovery was made: Mjölnir, the mighty hammer of Thor, was missing. Without this powerful weapon, Asgard was vulnerable to the threats of giants and other foes. Panic ensued, and the gods convened to discuss the mysterious disappearance. It was soon revealed by Loki, the trickster god, that the hammer had been stolen by Þrymr, the lord of the giants.

But Þrymr didn't just want to weaken the gods; he had a specific ransom in mind. He desired the beautiful goddess Freyja to be his bride. If the gods wished to see Mjölnir returned, they had to send Freyja to Jotunheim, the land of giants.

Horrified at the thought of marrying the fearsome giant, Freyja vehemently refused. The gods, desperate for a solution, convened to discuss alternatives. It was then that Heimdall, the ever-watchful guardian of Asgard, proposed a daring plan: Thor should disguise himself as Freyja, go to Jotunheim, and retrieve Mjölnir.

Thor was initially resistant to the idea, fearing mockery. However, understanding the gravity of the situation, he eventually agreed. With the help of the other gods, Thor was transformed. He donned a bridal gown, a veil, and Freyja's famed necklace, Brísingamen. Loki, seeing an opportunity for mischief and fun, offered to accompany Thor, disguised as a handmaiden.

The two gods then set out for Jotunheim. When they arrived, Þrymr was overjoyed, thinking he was about to wed Freyja. However, during the feast, "Freyja" displayed rather un-ladylike behaviors, consuming vast amounts of food and drink, raising a few eyebrows among the giants. Loki, quick on his feet, explained that Freyja's unusual appetite was due to her excitement and anxiety about the wedding, and the giants were convinced.

The moment of truth arrived during the wedding ceremony. As per custom, Þrymr ordered Mjölnir to be brought forth to sanctify the union. The hammer was placed on "Freyja's" lap as a symbol of blessing. Seizing the opportunity, Thor slipped on his Járngreipr, the iron gloves that enabled him to wield Mjölnir. With the gloves on and his mighty hammer in hand, Thor's disguise fell away. He stood tall and fierce, the god of thunder in all his might.

What followed was a battle of epic proportions. With the power of Mjölnir combined with the might of Járngreipr, Thor unleashed his wrath upon Þrymr and his court, laying waste to the giants who dared threaten the realms of the gods. The hammer was retrieved, and Asgard was once again safe. The tale concluded with Thor and Loki returning to their realm, with one more adventurous tale added to their repertoire, and a lesson about underestimating the cunning and might of the gods.

Járngreipr is a testament to the intertwining of power and responsibility. Just as Mjölnir represents Thor's raw power, Járngreipr signifies the control over that power. It is a reminder that possessing great power also requires the means and wisdom to wield it effectively. While not as famous as Mjölnir, the Járngreipr plays a crucial role in Thor's pantheon of tools. It serves as a vital counterpart to the mighty hammer, ensuring that the thunder god can use his weapon to its fullest potential and maintain the balance of power against the forces of chaos.

Sources/Further Reading:

The Poetic Edda

The Prose Edda: Written by Snorri Sturluson

"The Norse Myths" by Kevin Crossley-Holland

Kusanagi no Tsurugi

Also known simply as the Kusanagi, the Kusanagi no Tsurugi is one of the three Imperial Regalia of Japan, alongside the Yata no Kagami (mirror) and the Yasakani no Magatama (jewel). These sacred treasures represent the three primary virtues: valor (the sword), wisdom (the mirror), and benevolence (the jewel). The Kusanagi no Tsurugi holds a significant place in Japanese mythology and history, symbolizing the divine right and legitimacy of the Japanese Imperial family.

The sword's blade is traditionally straight and double-edged, reminiscent of the ancient Japanese swords before the development of the curved katana. The blade is often depicted as gleaming or shimmering, emphasizing its divine and mystical nature.

The name "Kusanagi no Tsurugi" can be translated to "Grass-Cutting Sword." This name is associated with its legendary ability to control the wind. The Kusanagi's origins are deeply intertwined with the legends of the storm god Susanoo and his battle with the eight-headed serpent Yamata no Orochi.

The Storm God and the Eight-Headed Dragon

Susanoo, the impetuous god of sea and storms, found himself banished from the heavenly realm due to his unruly behavior, which disturbed the peace of the other deities and even threatened the world's order. Although expelled from the heavens, Susanoo's spirit remained unbroken.

Upon his descent to Earth, he arrived in the province of Izumo. It was here, by the banks of the Hi River, that Susanoo encountered an elderly couple weeping inconsolably alongside a young maiden. The atmosphere was thick with sorrow and dread.

Moved by the sight, Susanoo approached them and inquired about their grief. The couple, who were earthly deities, revealed a heart-wrenching tale: Each year, the monstrous eight-headed serpent, Yamata no Orochi, emerged from the waters and demanded one of their daughters as a sacrifice. The serpent had devoured seven of their daughters over seven years, and now, only their youngest, the beautiful Kushinada-hime, remained.

Susanoo, sensing an opportunity for redemption and eager to put his divine prowess to use, offered to slay the dragon. However, he had one condition: upon saving Kushinada-hime, he wished to marry her. The desperate parents readily agreed.

To ensure the maiden's safety, Susanoo transformed Kushinada-hime into a comb, tucking her securely into his hair. He then prepared for the serpent's arrival. Knowing of the beast's penchant for sake, Susanoo set up eight large vats, filling each with the potent brew. His plan relied on the serpent's voracious appetite and the intoxicating power of the sake.

Like clockwork, Yamata no Orochi emerged, its eight heads swaying menacingly. Drawn to the sake, each head drank voraciously from a vat. The serpent, overwhelmed by the intoxication, became drowsy and vulnerable.

Seizing the opportunity, Susanoo unsheathed his sword. With precision and force, he descended upon the beast, striking at its heads and monstrous body. The battle was fierce and echoed with the roars of the beast and the god's war cries. Finally, as the dust settled, the fearsome Yamata no Orochi lay defeated.

But the story did not end there. As Susanoo was dissecting the beast's tail, his blade struck against something hard and resonant. Upon investigating, he found a sword of unparalleled beauty and craftsmanship. This was no ordinary weapon; it radiated with a divine aura and seemed to hum with power. Susanoo named it "Ama-no-Murakumo-no-Tsurugi" (Sword of the Gathering Clouds of Heaven).

In an act of reconciliation and gratitude, Susanoo presented the sword to his sister, Amaterasu, the sun goddess. This divine blade, later known as the Kusanagi no Tsurugi, would go on to become one of Japan's revered Imperial Regalia, symbolizing the divine right and legacy of the Japanese emperors.

In another legend, Prince Yamato Takeru, a legendary Japanese hero, was given the sword for protection.

The Naming of Kusanagi

After the sword was discovered by Susanoo in the tail of the Yamata no Orochi and presented to Amaterasu, it was kept at the Ise Grand Shrine, one of the most significant Shinto shrines in Japan dedicated to the sun goddess Amaterasu. Yamato Takeru received the sword from Yamato-hime, the high priestess at the Ise Grand Shrine, during his visit to the shrine. Recognizing the young prince's valor and the perilous journey ahead, the sword was entrusted to him for protection.

As Yamato journeyed across the provinces, he caught the ire of a cunning warlord who viewed the prince's influence and growing power as a threat. Eager to rid himself of this potential rival, the warlord invited Yamato to a seemingly innocent feast in a vast, open grassy field. However, this invitation hid a nefarious intention.

As Yamato enjoyed the festivities, the warlord's men set the dry grass ablaze, surrounding the prince in a rapidly closing ring of fire. The thick smoke rose, and the fierce flames threatened to engulf Yamato, leaving him with seemingly no escape.

It was at this dire moment that Yamato, driven by instinct and desperation, drew the Ama-no-Murakumo-no-Tsurugi. As the blade was unsheathed, it revealed its hidden power. A gust of wind, fierce and directional, emerged from the swing of the sword. With each calculated swing, Yamato manipulated the wind, pushing back the encroaching flames and carving a path of safety

The grass, which was fuel for the flames that sought to end Yamato's life, was now being cut down, granting him an escape route. The prince emerged unscathed, with the once-threatening inferno now at his back, a testament to the sword's power.

In awe of the blade's ability to "cut" through the grassy field's flames and the wind's manipulation, Yamato Takeru renamed the sword "Kusanagi no Tsurugi", honoring its life-saving power. The name, translating to "Grass-Cutting Sword," became emblematic of its role in that pivotal moment, forever tying the legendary prince's tale to the blade's legacy.

The renamed sword, with its deep-rooted history and newfound significance, continued to be revered, symbolizing not just divine might but also the indomitable spirit of heroes like Yamato Takeru.

While the Kusanagi no Tsurugi is a central symbol of the Japanese Imperial family's divinity and power, its whereabouts are shrouded in mystery. It's traditionally believed to be housed at the Atsuta Shrine in Nagoya. However, like the other Imperial Regalia, it's not on public display, and its existence in its current form remains a topic of debate among historians and scholars.

The Kusanagi no Tsurugi, beyond its intriguing legends, symbolizes the virtues of bravery and valor in Japanese culture. As part of the Imperial Regalia, it signifies the ancient lineage and divine roots of the Japanese monarchy.

Sources/Further Reading:

Kojiki: The earliest chronicle in Japan.
The Sun Goddess and the Storm God in Ancient Yamato by Matsumae Takeshi.
Japanese Mythology by Juliet Piggot.

Kaumodaki

The Kaumodaki is the divine mace (gada) of the Hindu god Vishnu. As with many weapons and accessories of the Hindu deities, Kaumodaki is not just an instrument of battle but a symbol of divine power and Vishnu's ability to preserve order in the cosmos.

Kaumodaki is often depicted as a large, heavy mace with a cylindrical head. In many images and idols, Vishnu is shown holding the mace in one of his four hands, representing his power and his role as the preserver and upholder of dharma (righteousness or moral order).

The mace, as a weapon, is a symbol of authority, power, and sovereignty. In the hands of Vishnu, it signifies the god's power to destroy materialistic or evil tendencies (represented by demons in various tales) and to protect his devotees.

The name "Kaumodaki" itself has a significance. Derived from the Sanskrit term 'Kaumudi', which means moonlight, the mace's name can be seen as an embodiment of the soothing yet potent power of the divine, much like the serene light of the moon that dispels darkness.

While Kaumodaki is often portrayed simply as a mace, there are instances where it takes on a more anthropomorphic form, represented as a female figure known as Gadadevi or Gadanari in Vishnu's sculptures. In these artistic renderings, Vishnu's hand is typically placed atop her head. Furthermore, she might be holding the mace, emerging from it, or have the design of the mace intricately etched onto her headgear or crown.

While the Sudarshana Chakra (Vishnu's discus) often gets a more prominent role in tales of Vishnu's combats, Kaumodaki too has its moments. One of the most notable mentions is during Vishnu's incarnation as Krishna.

The gift from the Varuna

In the Hindu epic, the Mahabharata, there lies a tale of how Krishna came to possess the Kaumodaki. The honorable Pandava princes were bestowed the vast Khandava Forest, envisioning it as the foundation for their grand kingdom. However, the forest was not just a mere expanse of flora and fauna. For the fire god Agni, plagued by crippling indigestion, the forest was his salvation, a remedy he yearned to consume with his engulfing flames. Yet, a challenge lay ahead. Indra, the mighty king of gods and protector of Khandava, would undeniably oppose Agni's plans.

Desperate for a solution, Agni approached Arjuna, the skilled Pandava prince, and his divine ally, Lord Krishna. He pleaded for their assistance against any interference from Indra. Recognizing the weight of the task ahead, Krishna and Arjuna sought divine armaments to ensure their success. It was then that the sea god Varuna intervened, presenting Krishna with the Sudarshana Chakra and the formidable Kaumodaki mace. Arjuna, on the other hand, was bestowed the legendary bow, Gandiva, accompanied by a quiver of ethereal arrows.

As the duo prepared for what lay ahead, the heavens rumbled in anticipation. When confrontation arose, the celestial weapons shone with might and fervor. Against the combined prowess of Krishna and Arjuna, even the mighty Indra found himself overwhelmed. With the king of gods subdued, Agni set forth, consuming the forest with his insatiable flames.

From the ashes of Khandava, a new era arose. The land, once dense with woods, now stood ready to embrace its destined glory — the grand capital of the Pandavas, Indraprastha.

Krishna and Dantavakra

In the Mahabharata, Dantavakra was a king of the Adhirajas and a cousin of Lord Krishna. Their enmity wasn't just a random occurrence; it had deep-rooted karmic reasons. According to legends, in their previous births, Dantavakra and Shishupala were doorkeepers, Vijaya and Jaya, in the divine realm of Lord Vishnu. Due to a curse by the sage Sanaka, they were reborn multiple times as demons opposing the incarnations of Vishnu on Earth. In their last birth in the Dvapara Yuga, Dantavakra became the adversary of Krishna.

Dantavakra's animosity towards Krishna was amplified when he learned about the death of his close friend, Shishupala, at the hands of Krishna. Consumed by rage and seeking revenge, Dantavakra marched towards Krishna's capital city, Dwarka. Without waiting for any formalities or challenges, he stormed directly into the city, his intentions clear - to kill Krishna. Krishna, aware of Dantavakra's intentions and their shared destiny, stepped out of his palace to confront him. The streets of Dwarka became the battleground for this epic clash.

In many battles, Krishna utilized his Sudarshana Chakra, a weapon known for its swiftness and precision. However, against Dantavakra, Krishna chose his mace, Kaumodaki. The two clashed, with their maces creating sounds akin to thunderbolts. The fight was intense and evenly matched for a while, but it was evident that Krishna had the upper hand.

Dantavakra managed to strike Krishna on the head with his mace. But this attack, despite its force, did not harm Krishna. Seizing the moment, Krishna swung Kaumodaki with such force that it crushed Dantavakra's chest, ending the life of the tyrannical king and fulfilling the curse that had started ages ago.

The battle between Krishna and Dantavakra is emblematic of the constant cosmic play between good and evil. While Dantavakra was a powerful king and warrior, his animosity and pride were his downfall. Krishna, embodying dharma, stood firm against oppression, showcasing not only his physical prowess but also the significance of righteousness.

Furthermore, Lord Krishna's choice of weapon in this battle underlines the importance of the Kaumodaki mace. It's not just a tool of war but a symbol of the strength and power that upholds justice and cosmic order.

Vishnu's depictions, whether in ancient sculptures, temple carvings, or paintings, often include Kaumodaki. It serves as an immediate identifier for the deity, alongside his other attributes like the Sudarshana Chakra (discus), Padma (lotus), and Shankha (conch).

Kaumodaki is not just a weapon but a symbol of the timeless and cosmic power of Lord Vishnu. It emphasizes his role as the protector of the universe, upholding the principles of righteousness and order.

Sources/Further Reading:

"Mahabharata" by C. Rajagopalachari
"Jaya: An Illustrated Retelling of the Mahabharata" by Devdutt Pattanaik

Lance of Longinus

The Spear of Destiny, also known as the Holy Lance or the Lance of Longinus, is a legendary artifact associated with Christian history and folklore. This spear is believed to be the one that pierced the side of Jesus Christ during his crucifixion.

As its name suggests, the Spear of Destiny is often said to grant its wielder the power to shape or determine the course of history or their own destiny. Beyond simple invincibility, it's believed that whoever possesses the spear is guaranteed victory in their endeavors, particularly in conquests or battles. On the flip side, there's a legend that says if the spear is lost or taken away from its possessor, downfall or even death will soon follow.

The Origin of the Spear of Destiny

In the heart of Christian lore, there lies a tale not just of divine sacrifice but also of a Roman soldier and the weapon he wielded—a spear that would go down in history as the Spear of Destiny or the Lance of Longinus.

The crucifixion of Jesus Christ is a cornerstone event in Christian belief, and it's recorded in the New Testament of the Bible. The Gospel of John provides a detailed account of Jesus' last moments on the cross. According to tradition, to expedite the death of those crucified, Roman soldiers would often break the legs of the crucified person. This prevented the person from lifting themselves up to breathe, leading to a quicker death due to asphyxiation

However, in the case of Jesus, the Gospel recounts a divergence from this brutal norm. As the soldiers approached Jesus, they observed that he seemed to be already dead, negating the perceived need to break his legs. To verify his death, one of the soldiers thrust his spear into Jesus' side, and immediately, blood and water poured out, a phenomenon that has been the subject of much theological discussion and interpretation.

The name of this Roman soldier isn't provided within the canonical scriptures. However, as is the nature of such significant events, tales, and traditions outside the canonical texts, often called "apocryphal" or "extra-biblical," began to emerge. Among these is the story of Longinus.

Longinus, according to later Christian tradition, was said to be this Roman centurion. His act of piercing Christ's side was not just a testament to his duty but would define his future. In some traditions, Longinus was believed to have been afflicted with poor vision or perhaps was even blind. It's said that upon piercing Jesus' side, some of the blood or water from the wound touched his eyes, miraculously restoring his sight. Recognizing the divine nature of the man he'd pierced, Longinus is said to have converted to Christianity and, in some tales, met the fate of many early Christian converts—martyrdom.

The spear he used, due to its direct contact with the divine blood of Christ, was believed to have inherited special powers and was thus venerated as a relic of great significance. This relic, now associated with the name of the soldier, became widely known as the Lance of Longinus or the Spear of Destiny.

As with many ancient artifacts and stories, the lines between myth and history blur. The Lance of Longinus became a beacon for both the faithful and those seeking power, merging the spiritual with the temporal in its long journey through the annals of time.

Over the centuries, numerous legends and tales have surrounded the Spear of Destiny, attributing to it mystical and divine powers.

One of the most enduring legends is that whoever possesses the spear has the power to control the world, but losing it would mean imminent death or downfall. This belief led many leaders and conquerors, including Adolf Hitler and Napoleon Bonaparte, to seek it.

Ownership and Pursuit

For much of the Middle Ages, the Holy Roman Empire was a central political entity in Europe, claiming to be the continuation of the ancient Roman Empire but with a Christian orientation. The title of Holy Roman Emperor was highly prestigious, and the rulers often sought legitimacy and divine endorsement of their rule. Possessing religious relics was one way to assert this divine authority.

The Holy Lance, believed to have pierced Christ's side, was one of the most sought-after of these relics. It symbolized not only a connection to Christ but also the divine right of the ruler to lead the Christian world. The relic was thus more than a mere artifact; it was a representation of the unity of temporal power with spiritual authority. The Holy Lance, along with other relics and royal items, became part of the Imperial Regalia of the Holy Roman Empire. These items were used in the coronation ceremonies of the emperors, further enhancing the divine validation of their rule.

By the 15th century, the Imperial Regalia, including the Holy Lance, were kept in Nuremberg, one of the empire's most important cities. They were stored in the Church of the Holy Spirit, and their presence made Nuremberg a significant city in the Holy Roman Empire.

However, the tumultuous times of the late Middle Ages and the Reformation led to concerns about the safety of the Imperial Regalia. In the early 19th century, as Napoleon's influence spread across Europe and the Holy Roman Empire was dissolved, the relics were moved to Vienna for protection. They have remained there since, with the Hofburg Palace in Vienna housing the treasury that contains the lance among other imperial artifacts.

Over the centuries, many scholars and enthusiasts have debated the authenticity of the lance in Vienna. Is it truly the Spear of Destiny from biblical times, or is it a later medieval creation? Despite the uncertainty, the Holy Lance's status as a symbol of divine authority and its association with the legacy of the Holy Roman Emperors is undoubted.

Adolf Hitler and many of his inner circle, including Heinrich Himmler, were known to have a fascination with the occult, ancient relics, and esoteric traditions. Himmler, in particular, was deeply engrossed in mysticism and sought to integrate these beliefs into the ideological fabric of the Nazi party. The SS, under Himmler's guidance, even conducted numerous expeditions to search for artifacts and ancient texts that might bring power or validation to the Nazi cause.

According to some accounts, Hitler first encountered the spear as a young man in the Hofburg Museum in Vienna. He was allegedly captivated by it, seeing it as a symbol of power and destiny.

During World War II, when Germany annexed Austria in the Anschluss of 1938, it's said that Hitler took possession of the spear, which was then in Vienna. The relic, along with other treasures, was allegedly moved to Nuremberg, Germany, for safekeeping.

However, as the tide of war turned against the Nazis, the relics' safety became uncertain. In 1945, American troops are said to have discovered the spear in Nuremberg. According to legend, Hitler's death by suicide coincided with the exact moment the U.S. forces took possession of the spear, further fueling the myths surrounding its power.

While the tale of Hitler's obsession with the Holy Lance is captivating, it's essential to approach it with skepticism. Ravenscroft's book and similar accounts have faced criticism for their lack of concrete evidence and reliance on esoteric and unverifiable sources. Additionally, while the Nazis' interest in the occult is well-documented, direct evidence linking Hitler to a pursuit of the Holy Lance remains elusive.

Armenia and the Spear of Destiny

Armenia, a nation with a rich history and one of the earliest Christian civilizations, has its own claim to the Spear of Destiny. The lance, referred to as the "Geghard" in Armenian, is intrinsically linked to Armenian religious traditions and history.

According to Armenian tradition, the spear was brought to Armenia by the Apostle Thaddeus, one of the twelve apostles of Jesus. The spread of Christianity in Armenia is traditionally attributed to Thaddeus and another apostle, Bartholomew, and thus, Armenia prides itself on being the first nation to adopt Christianity as its state religion in AD 301.

The spear's name "Geghard" is shared with a famous monastery in Armenia called the Geghard Monastery or "Monastery of the Spear." The monastery, a UNESCO World Heritage site, gets its name from this relic. It's believed that for a significant period, the spear was kept at this monastery, which is carved out of the cliffs and surrounded by towering cliffs on all sides.

Today, the spearhead, believed by many in Armenia to be the true Holy Lance that pierced Jesus' side, is housed in the treasury of the Echmiadzin Cathedral, the spiritual center of Armenia and the seat of the Armenian Apostolic Church. It's a revered relic, not just for its biblical connection but also for its significance in the early Christian history of Armenia.

Over the years, the lance in Echmiadzin has been the subject of various investigations and studies. Some suggest that the design and make of the artifact align with Roman lances from the 1st century, giving credence to its authenticity, while others approach it with skepticism.

There are several spears today that claim to be the authentic Spear of Destiny. As with many religious relics, the authenticity of any of these spears remains a matter of faith and belief rather than empirical evidence.

The Spear of Destiny's allure isn't just in its biblical origin or its alleged mystical properties, but also in its journey through time — a journey steeped in faith, power, and the ever-burning human desire to be part of a larger, divine narrative.

Sources/Further Reading:

The Spear of Destiny: The Occult Power Behind the Spear which pierced the side of Christ" by Trevor Ravenscroft

The New Testament, The Gospel of John

"Hitler's Holy Relics: A True Story of Nazi Plunder and the Race to Recover the Crown Jewels of the Holy Roman Empire" by Sidney Kirkpatrick

Mandrake

The Mandrake, while often considered a magical plant in folklore and mythology, is actually a real plant known scientifically as Mandragora. This plant, particularly its root, has been steeped in myth and legend for centuries.

Mandrakes are herbaceous perennials that produce large, brown roots that can often resemble the human form. The plant's leaves are rosette-shaped, and it produces small, bell-shaped flowers which vary from white to purple.

The mandrake root can sometimes look eerily human, with bifurcations that resemble arms and legs. This resemblance is most pronounced in the species Mandragora officinarum. Because of this, the plant was often associated with superstitious beliefs and practices. In some tales, it was believed that the mandrake would grow under the feet of a hanged man, drawing life from the fallen body.

Due to its human-like appearance, there were beliefs in some cultures that the mandrake was imbued with a form of life or consciousness. Some stories spoke of the mandrake having the power to illuminate hidden treasures if it was uprooted under specific lunar phases. Legend had it that if a human tried to uproot a mandrake, the plant would release a piercing scream. This scream was said to be so powerful that it could cause madness, deafness, or instant death. Because of this, specific rituals evolved around the harvesting of the mandrake to ensure safety.

To avoid the lethal effects of the mandrake's scream, an intricate ritual was devised. A person would dig around the root until its tip was exposed. They would then tie the exposed root to a dog, often using meat to lure the animal. When the dog moved forward to get the meat, it would pull the mandrake from the ground. As the plant was uprooted, it would emit its deadly scream, killing or harming the dog but leaving the human harvester unharmed. The human could then safely collect the mandrake root.

Fertility and Love

This story from Genesis provides an indirect link between the mandrake and fertility.

Leah and Rachel were sisters, both married to Jacob. While Leah bore many children for Jacob, Rachel remained barren for a long time, causing distress and jealousy. One day, Leah's son Reuben found mandrake roots in the field and brought them to his mother. Knowing of their reputed fertility-enhancing properties, Rachel, desperate to bear a child, asked Leah for the mandrakes. Leah agreed, but in exchange asked for a night with their shared husband, Jacob.

Rachel's willingness to try the mandrake reflects the deep human yearning and the lengths to which people might go when faced with desperate situations. Whether or not the mandrake was effective, Rachel's actions demonstrate the hope and faith people place in remedies, especially in times of distress.

Besides the biblical account of Leah and Rachel, various ancient texts mention the mandrake. The ancient Greeks, for instance, referenced the plant in their literature, associating it with love and seduction. Theophrastus, an ancient Greek philosopher, and botanist, wrote about the use of mandrakes in love philtres.

The Love of Hermes and Crocus

Hermes, the wing-footed messenger of the gods, was known for his various adventures and escapades. However, amid all his tales, one stands out not for its mischief but for its heartbreak: his love for Crocus.

Crocus was not a god or a hero but a stunningly beautiful youth. With his radiant allure, he captured the heart of Hermes, known for his swift movements and swift passions. The two shared tender moments, their bond strengthening with every passing day. The world seemed brighter and more beautiful when they were together.

One fateful day, as Hermes and Crocus were playing a game, a tragic accident occurred. Hermes, with his godly strength, threw a discus. Crocus, either misjudging its trajectory or too engrossed in the game, was struck by the discus. The blow was fatal.

Hermes rushed to his beloved's side, but it was too late. Crocus lay motionless, his life having ebbed away in mere moments. Despair gripped Hermes' heart. How could such a fleeting moment steal away something so precious?

As Hermes held Crocus' lifeless body, tears flowed from his eyes, and the blood of Crocus seeped into the earth. From this union of godly sorrow and mortal blood, two plants emerged. Where Crocus' blood touched the ground, the first saffron crocus sprouted, its radiant crimson stigma symbolizing the vibrant life force of the youth. This saffron crocus would become the source of the prized saffron spice, known for its intense color and aroma.

A few steps away, where Hermes' tears merged with the earth, the first mandrake took root. Its human-like form was a reminder of the beautiful youth and the god's overwhelming grief. The plant, with its dual nature of being beneficial and poisonous, became a symbol of the passionate love and heart-wrenching tragedy that birthed it.

The mandrake root, or fragments of it, was carried as an amulet or charm to promote conception. Such amulets were particularly favored by women who hoped to become pregnant. The practice of placing a mandrake root beneath the bed of a childless couple was not just about physical proximity to the plant. It was symbolic, representing the couple's hopes and prayers for a child. This act was a blend of the mystical and the intimate, seeking both divine favor and the potent energy of the mandrake.

Beyond just fertility, the mandrake was believed to offer protection against negative energies or evil spirits that might interfere with conception. It was not just about inducing pregnancy, but also about shielding the couple from any adverse influences.

The mandrake's association with fertility rites and practices provides a fascinating insight into how ancient cultures interpreted the natural world around them, attributing sacred and potent meanings to plants based on their appearance and the effects they believed them to have.

Sources/Further Reading:

"Mandrakes and Mistletoe: A Historical Look at Plants in Folk Magic" by Corinne Boyer
"The Natural History" by Pliny the Elder

Mauis Fishhook

Maui's Fishhook, also known as Manaiakalani, is a famed artifact in Polynesian mythology. Maui is a demigod, central to many legends in Polynesian, Maori, and Hawaiian traditions. The fishhook symbolizes his strength and cunning and plays a significant role in his adventures.

Maui's fishhook was said to be crafted from his ancestor's jawbone. It wasn't just any tool but a magical artifact that allowed Maui to perform incredible feats. One of the most famous stories related to Maui's fishhook is about the creation of the islands.

The Creation of the Islands: Te Ika-a-Māui

Maui, the youngest of five brothers, was known for his mischievous yet heroic endeavors. Though often underestimated due to his status as the youngest, his cunning and bravery outmatched any disrespect he faced.

One day, after growing tired of catching tiny fish, Maui proposed to his brothers that they embark on a deep-sea fishing expedition. Intrigued, they set sail in a waka (canoe) into the uncharted ocean, far beyond their regular fishing grounds.

As night approached, Maui concocted a plan. He cast a spell, making his brothers fall into a deep sleep, allowing him to row the waka even farther out to sea. By dawn, they were in the deep waters of the Pacific Ocean. When his brothers awoke, they were surprised to find themselves so far from land.

With the boat now steady in the profound depths, Maui took out his fishhook. For bait, he struck his own nose and let his blood drip onto the hook. This was no ordinary fishing expedition, and the bait had to be just as extraordinary.

Casting his line deep into the waters, Maui began a chant, calling to the gods and ancestors to aid him in his quest. After some time, he felt a mighty tug on his line. Realizing that he had caught something enormous, he urged his brothers to row as he began pulling up his catch. The task was arduous, with the strength of the catch challenging the combined might of Maui and his brothers.

After much struggle, what emerged from the ocean wasn't a fish but an enormous landmass. According to the Maori tradition, this land was the North Island of present-day New Zealand. The shape of the North Island was said to resemble a fish, and thus it was named Te Ika-a-Māui, which translates to "The Fish of Maui."

Astounded by their catch, Maui cautioned his brothers to wait before setting foot on the land, as he wished to offer thanks to the gods for their bountiful catch. However, the brothers, overwhelmed by greed, didn't heed Maui's advice. They began to carve out pieces of the island, marking territories for themselves.

This act of defiance against the gods and Maui's wishes resulted in the creation of the various mountains, valleys, and uneven terrains of the North Island.

Over time, Maui's adventures became the stuff of legend, passed down through generations. And central to each of these tales was his fishhook.

Maui and the Whispering Winds

In the heart of the Pacific, on the islands that Maui himself had fished from the ocean's depths, the people reveled in the land's abundance and the sea's bounty. The ocean and winds were their highways, connecting the islands and their inhabitants, allowing them to travel, trade, and share tales.

However, a strange phenomenon began to envelop the islands. A stifling stillness settled, and the once predictable and dependable winds vanished. Without these winds, the sails of the islanders' canoes hung limp, grounding their voyages and disrupting their way of life. The fishermen couldn't venture out into the deep sea, traders couldn't move between islands, and the storytellers couldn't share tales from one shore to another.

Despair crept in as days turned into weeks. The once joyful songs of the islanders were replaced by prayers, asking the gods to breathe life back into the still skies.

Maui, ever the hero of the people, felt the weight of their desperation. Recognizing the gravity of the situation, he decided to intervene. Rumor had it that the winds were not just absent but trapped by an ancient spirit, jealous of the islanders' harmony with nature. These winds were now mere whispers, ensnared within the mountain caverns.

Determined to free them, Maui took to the highest peak of the islands. With the mighty fishhook, which had once pulled land masses from the ocean's belly, he began to carve pathways and channels into the mountainsides. Every swing and every incision were made with purpose and precision. As he carved, faint murmurs of the trapped winds began to stir.

Finally, after what felt like an eternity, a gust broke free, rushing down the mountains and filling the air with its cool embrace. One by one, as Maui continued his task, the winds of every direction were liberated. They danced through the channels Maui had created, caressing the land, filling the sails of waiting canoes, and once again connecting the people of the islands.

The islanders rejoiced as their world was set into motion again. Grateful chants and songs echoed across the archipelago, celebrating Maui and the return of the winds.

After taming the winds to benefit his people, Maui turned his attention to another celestial challenge: the blazing sun, which he believed raced too quickly across the sky, shortening the days for his people.

Maui Slows the Sun: A Battle for Longer Days

Maui, ever the hero of the people, noticed a recurring problem. The days seemed too short. The sun rushed across the sky, leaving the people with very little daylight to complete their tasks. Fishermen had insufficient time to fish; farmers struggled to tend their crops, and artisans couldn't finish their crafts. Nightfall came too quickly, and the people lamented the fleeting daylight.

Determined to solve this problem, Maui sought counsel from his elders and learned about the path of the sun. With this knowledge, he decided to capture the sun and make it move more slowly across the sky. For this daring task, Maui needed a sturdy rope. His sisters came to his aid, cutting their long, black hair and braiding it into a robust rope. With the braided rope and the fishhook, Maui journeyed to the peak of Haleakalā, the "House of the Sun."

Reaching the peak, Maui waited for dawn. As dawn approached, Maui fastened the fishhook to the rope, holding the other end tightly. As the sun began its ascent, sending its first rays across the horizon, Maui cast his fishhook, ensnaring the sun.

Drawing on his strength and determination, Maui engaged the sun in a fierce battle. He demanded the sun move more slowly across the sky, giving the earth longer days. The sun, recognizing Maui's determination and fearing his strength, attempted to negotiate. The sun argued that during certain seasons, the land needed shorter days for rest, while at other times, longer days were beneficial. A compromise was struck. The sun agreed to move more slowly for half the year, granting longer days, and move faster during the other half, ensuring shorter days.

Triumphant, Maui returned to his people, who rejoiced in the longer daylight hours. Thanks to Maui's bravery, they had more time for their daily tasks, festivals, and celebrations.

The stories of Maui and his fishhook are more than just entertaining tales; they contain moral lessons, and explanations about natural phenomena, and offer cultural identity and unity to the Polynesians. These myths are passed down from generation to generation and have recently been introduced to a global audience through Hollywood movies.

Sources/Further reading:

"Maori Myths and Legendary Tales" by A. W. Reed: A detailed account of Maori mythology, including the tales of Maui.
"Hawaiian Mythology" by Martha Beckwith.
"Polynesian Mythology and Ancient Traditional History of the New Zealanders" by George Grey:

Megingjörð

Megingjörð is a name from Norse mythology that translates roughly to "Power Belt." It is one of the three key artifacts belonging to Thor, the thunder god, the other two being Mjölnir (his iconic hammer) and Járngreipr (his iron gloves). The Megingjörð is essential in magnifying Thor's already prodigious strength, ensuring he can wield Mjölnir to its full potential.

While many Norse myths emphasize the raw, elemental power of Thor, especially his strength and bravery, the Megingjörð underscores that even this powerful god has aids that enhance his abilities. This belt, when buckled on, was believed to double Thor's enormous godly strength, making him nearly invincible in battle.

While the specific origin of the Megingjörð is not as extensively covered in the myths as Mjölnir's, its mention is scattered throughout various sagas, underscoring its importance in several of Thor's adventures.

Gríðr's Gift

In a tale that weaves intrigue with myth, it is whispered that the mighty Thor didn't just find or create his belt of strength; instead, it was a gift, shrouded in mystery, bestowed upon him by a giantess named Gríðr.

In the land of gods and giants, Loki's penchant for mischief often led to unforeseen circumstances. On one particular occasion, his tricks left Thor, the god of thunder, venturing without his iconic hammer, Mjöllnir, and the Járngreipr. As Thor journeyed, a looming threat became clear: an unavoidable confrontation with the fearsome giant, Geirröðr.

Aware of his predicament and the peril he faced, fortune favored Thor as he encountered the wise giantess, Gríðr. Recognizing the danger that lay ahead for the thunder god, Gríðr, mother to Víðarr, one of the Aesir, offered him objects of great power: a magical belt, a pair of iron gauntlets, and her enchanting staff, Gríðarvölr.

With the belt strapped, Thor's already godly strength was further magnified, echoing the might of Megingjörð. The gauntlets, perfectly crafted, readied him to grip and swing his mighty hammer, Mjöllnir, once it came within his grasp.

As Thor entered the hall of Geirröðr, the air was thick with tension, for both parties knew that their meeting wasn't a cordial one.

Without wasting time, Geirröðr decided to test Thor's mettle. With a swift motion, the giant grabbed a molten lump of iron with a pair of tongs. The glowing, red-hot iron illuminated the hall momentarily as he hurled it with all his might towards the thunder god.

For any ordinary being, even the sight of such a weapon would be enough to instill fear. But Thor was no ordinary god. Thanks to the foresight of the giantess Gríðr, Thor was equipped with iron gloves. As the molten projectile raced toward him, time seemed to slow. With unwavering focus and the aid of Gríðr's gloves, Thor caught the molten lump, his hands unscathed. The hall filled with gasps of disbelief from the watching giants.

Using his godly strength, further amplified by Gríðr's magical belt, Thor retaliated. He hurled the still-glowing iron back at Geirröðr with even greater force. The giant had little time to react. The molten metal struck him, and the impact was lethal. As the smoke cleared, Geirröðr lay defeated.

Some sources indicate that the belt given by Gríðr to Thor during his encounter with Geirröðr is not the original Megingjörð, but it served a similar purpose in enhancing his strength. The sagas and ancient texts sometimes mention multiple items or artifacts with similar attributes, and over time, they might get conflated or become more widely recognized under a single popular name or narrative.

The Poem Thórsdrápa, attributed to the skald Eilifr Godrunarson, narrates one of Thor's many adventures, shedding light on his encounters with giants, his unyielding spirit, and his undeniable might, often augmented by his legendary belt.

Thórsdrápa: The Journey and The Belt of Strength

As the tale unfolds, Thor, accompanied by Loki and his servant Thjalfi, sets out on a perilous journey. Their voyage is no ordinary one: they must cross vast, icy waters, which some interpretations suggest might represent the North Atlantic Ocean, a formidable barrier between the realms of gods and giants.

While Thor possesses immense strength, even he isn't immune to the challenges thrown his way. As the icy waves churn and threaten to overpower them, Thor's belt, known for its ability to enhance the strength of its wearer, plays a pivotal role. Thjalfi, Thor's loyal servant, is described as "he who benefited from the girdle of strength." This isn't just a poetic embellishment; it provides a vivid imagery of Thjalfi clinging desperately to Thor's belt as they navigate the tumultuous waters. The belt not only amplifies Thor's strength but also acts as a beacon of hope and security for Thjalfi amidst the chaos.

The crossing of the ocean is just one of the many trials the trio faces. Thor's encounters with the giants, his battles, and his eventual triumphs are chronicled in vivid detail in the poem. Each challenge thrown their way, whether it's treacherous waters or menacing giants, only reinforces the significance of Thor's belt. It isn't merely a tool for strength; it's a symbol of perseverance, protection, and divine power.

Megingjörð's presence in the Norse sagas and tales is subtler compared to Mjölnir, but it's a constant reminder of Thor's position as one of the most powerful beings in the Norse pantheon. As with many elements from Norse mythology, the Megingjörð has found its way into modern media and pop culture. It's often portrayed in literature, games, and movies that draw inspiration from Norse tales, emphasizing Thor's unmatched might.

Sources/Further reading:

The Poetic Edda specifically the "Skáldskaparmál"
The Prose Edda by Snorri Sturluson.
"Heimskringla" by Snorri Sturluson
"The Norse Myths" by Kevin Crossley-Holland.

Mjolnir

Mjölnir is one of the most iconic and powerful symbols in Norse mythology. It is the thunderous war hammer wielded by Thor, the Norse god of thunder, storms, and protection. With a handle notoriously shorter than intended and a head that embodies devastating power, Mjölnir isn't just a weapon; it's a testament to Thor's role as protector of gods and men.

Mjölnir, which translates to "the grinder" or "the crusher" in Old Norse, was no ordinary hammer. The very name "Mjolnir" resounds with the thunderous force it represents, echoing through the pages of ancient sagas and across generations of storytelling.

Loki's Mischief and the Crafting of Mjölnir

The tale begins in Asgard, the realm of the gods. Loki, ever the trickster, decided to entertain himself at the expense of others. In a mischievous act, he stealthily cut off the golden hair of Sif, Thor's beloved wife. When Thor discovered the deed, his rage was uncontrollable. He seized Loki, threatening to break every bone in his body.

Desperate for a solution, Loki promised to provide Sif with even more beautiful hair, made of pure gold, that would grow just like real hair. Not wanting to face Thor's wrath, Loki quickly made his way to Svartálfar, the realm of the Dwarves, known for their exceptional blacksmithing skills.

There, he approached the brothers Brokkr and Sindri (also known as Eitri). In an attempt to ensure the best treasures for the gods (and perhaps further his own mischief), Loki made a bet. He wagered his own head, boasting that the brothers couldn't craft items greater than those of the sons of Ivaldi, another pair of skilled dwarf craftsmen.

Eager to prove their unmatched skills, Brokkr and Sindri accepted the challenge. While they toiled, Loki sought ways to ensure that the sons of Ivaldi would produce better items. But he also couldn't help but interfere with Brokkr and Sindri, aiming to disrupt their creations and win his bet.

As Sindri put raw materials in the forge, Brokkr worked the bellows, ensuring a constant air supply for the furnace. Loki, recognizing an opportunity, transformed into a biting fly. As Brokkr worked, Loki bit him, trying to disrupt the dwarf's rhythm. Despite bleeding from the bites, Brokkr continued, unwavering.

However, during the crafting of Mjölnir, Loki bit Brokkr on the eyelid, causing a drop of blood to fall into Brokkr's eye. This momentary distraction caused Brokkr to stop pumping the bellows just long enough for the metal in the forge to be slightly affected.

The result? Mjölnir's handle turned out shorter than intended. Despite this flaw, the hammer possessed immense power, symbolizing Thor's role as protector and warrior. While Loki's interference had caused a slight imperfection in the hammer, it did not diminish its inherent might or significance in the Norse pantheon. It had the power to level mountains and crush foes. Its enchanted nature means only those deemed worthy can lift it. This worthiness is often tied to one's character, valor, and intentions.

Another feature of the hammer is its unfailing ability to return to Thor's hand once thrown. This makes Mjölnir a boomerang-like weapon, allowing Thor to strike enemies from a distance and then immediately ready himself for the next blow.

The Challenge from the Stone Giant

In the vast realms of Norse mythology, few giants dared to brazenly challenge the might of the Aesir gods, let alone in their own domain. But Hrungnir was no ordinary giant. With skin of stone, a heart crafted from hard granite, and unparalleled strength, he was the very embodiment of brute force among the Jotunn, the giants of Jotunheim.

One day, through a twist of fate and the deceptive nature of Loki, Hrungnir found himself in Asgard. The gods, initially hospitable, began to grow wary of their unexpected guest, especially after Hrungnir started boasting about his strength and his desire to destroy Asgard, claiming the goddesses Freyja and Sif as his own.

The gods' tolerance ran thin, and it was Thor, ever the defender of Asgard and its honor, who took the most offense. He challenged the stone giant to a duel, setting the grounds for an epic confrontation that would shake the realms.

The battleground chosen was Grjotunagardar, a place far from both Asgard and Jotunheim. As the two titans faced off, Hrungnir had with him a massive heart-shaped shield of stone and his weapon of choice: a huge whetstone.

Thor, on the other hand, had his trusted hammer, Mjölnir – a weapon that had never failed him.

As the battle commenced, Hrungnir hurled his massive whetstone with all his might towards Thor. Simultaneously, Thor released Mjölnir, setting it on its deadly trajectory. The collision was cataclysmic – Mjölnir shattered the whetstone, with one part of it becoming the flint we find in the earth and the other half embedding itself in Thor's head.

But Mjölnir, undeterred by the collision, continued on its path, striking Hrungnir right between the eyes. The mightiest of all giants fell dead, crushed by the unparalleled power of Mjölnir.

However, the battle left Thor pinned beneath the fallen giant's heavy leg, and it took the strength of his son, Magni, who was only three days old, to free him.

The encounter between Thor and Hrungnir became legendary in the halls of Asgard. Not just a testament to Thor's strength and courage, it was also a story that showcased Mjölnir's unmatched power. The hammer, despite its seemingly flawed creation, proved time and again that it was a force to be reckoned with, capable of defending the Aesir against even the mightiest of foes.

Mjölnir was not just a tool of destruction, it could also be used to hallow, bless, and revive.

Resurrection of Tanngrisnir and Tanngnjóstr

During one of Thor's journeys to Jotunheim, the realm of the giants, he and his trickster companion Loki sought shelter for the night. They came upon a humble farmhouse, occupied by a peasant family. Being guests, Thor decided to provide dinner and brought forth his two magnificent goats, Tanngrisnir and Tanngnjóstr, which pulled his chariot.

With a heavy heart but recognizing the need, Thor slaughtered the goats, preparing them as a feast for all to share. However, he had specific instructions for the bones: they were to be carefully preserved, unbroken, and placed alongside the goat's skins.

The peasant family, particularly the children Þjálfi and Röskva, watched in awe. Under Loki's influence, Þjálfi, either out of curiosity or hunger, cracked one of the goat's leg bones to suck the marrow during the meal.

Come dawn, Thor took his hammer, Mjölnir, and held it high above the goat skins and bones. With a whispered incantation and the might of his intent, he channeled the hammer's power to breathe life into the still remains. To everyone's astonishment, the goats sprang back to life. But there was an issue: one of the goats was limping, its leg now weakened.

Realizing that the bone had been tampered with, Thor's anger blazed. His eyes fixed upon the trembling Þjálfi, who confessed his transgression. To appease the furious Thunder God and to repay for the harm done to the goat, the peasant offered his children, Þjálfi and Röskva, to Thor as his servants.

Beyond these mythological adventures, Mjölnir held cultural significance for the Vikings. As Christianity began making inroads into Scandinavia, the Norse wore Mjölnir amulets, paralleling the Christian cross. This wasn't just an act of defiance; it symbolized Thor's protection, emphasizing the belief in the thunder god's guardianship against malevolent forces.

Mjölnir, with its tales of valor, protection, and resurrection, serves as a poignant reminder of Thor's undying duty towards the realms and its inhabitants. It's a symbol of hope, strength, and the enduring spirit of the Norse gods, a testament to their battles, sacrifices, and undying legacies. In the echoing halls of Valhalla and Midgard's expansive landscapes, Mjölnir's legends continue to resonate, forever immortalized in the annals of Norse mythology.

Sources/Further Reading:

"The Prose Edda" by Snorri Sturluson
"Norse Mythology: A Guide to the Gods, Heroes, Rituals, and Beliefs" by John Lindow

Nanteos Cup

The Nanteos Cup is a wooden chalice that originates from Nanteos Mansion, near Aberystwyth in Wales. This artifact is steeped in local legend and is said by some to possess miraculous healing properties. It's also reputed by some to be the Holy Grail, the cup used by Jesus at the Last Supper.

The cup is a simple wooden bowl made from wych elm, a common European tree. It has been worn down with age, making its original shape and size difficult to discern. Some believe the wear and tear to be a result of it being used by countless individuals seeking its purported healing powers.

The cup is famed for its healing abilities. People would often travel great distances to take a sip of water from the Nanteos Cup in hopes of curing their ailments. The cup was particularly sought after for its rumored power to heal the sick and infirm. In some tales, those who drank from the cup would be cured of their ailments, reinforcing its reputation as a relic of immense power.

The lore surrounding the Nanteos Cup and its association with the Holy Grail is an intricate web woven from religious faith, Arthurian legends, and the tumultuous history of Britain. While this tale has captured the imagination of many, it's important to note that historical accuracy and evidence for such claims are often elusive.

The Holy Grail: Journey from Jerusalem to Nanteos

After the crucifixion of Jesus, Joseph of Arimathea, a disciple and possibly a relative of Jesus, is said to have collected Christ's blood in the Grail. Fleeing persecution in the Holy Land, Joseph sought refuge in the distant isles of Britain, a land with which he had prior connections due to his trade in tin. With him, he brought the Grail.

Joseph is believed to have landed on the shores of ancient Britain at a place now known as Glastonbury. It's said he planted his staff, which miraculously blossomed into the Glastonbury Thorn, a hawthorn tree that blooms twice annually, once in winter and once in spring. Glastonbury, already steeped in pagan traditions, soon became a Christian spiritual center. The Grail was rumored to be buried there, possibly near the Chalice Well, a natural spring with iron-rich waters that flow red, symbolizing the blood of Christ.

For centuries, the Grail was said to be safeguarded by the monks of Glastonbury Abbey, a place that also claimed to be the burial site of King Arthur. The Abbey, like many religious sites, was believed to be a place where the veil between the mortal realm and the divine was thin. The presence of the Grail only added to its mystique.

The 16th century brought tumultuous changes to England. Henry VIII, in his bid to control the church's wealth and power in England, ordered the dissolution of the monasteries. Glastonbury

Abbey was not spared. In 1539, the abbey was sacked, its abbot executed, and its treasures confiscated. Amidst this chaos, the Grail's whereabouts became a mystery. Legend has it that the sacred relic was secretly handed to the stewardship of the Stedman family to protect it from being desecrated or lost. They were entrusted with the safekeeping of the Grail, which was believed to hold divine power and significance. To ensure its safety, the family eventually moved to Nanteos Mansion in Wales, a more remote and secure location. Within the mansion's walls, the Grail found a new sanctuary, now taking the form of the Nanteos Cup.

Over time, the Nanteos Cup became deeply woven into local lore. Pilgrims and those seeking miracles would travel vast distances, hoping for a glimpse or perhaps a sip from this storied chalice. And while skeptics abound, questioning its authenticity as the true Holy Grail, the Nanteos Cup's legend as a beacon of hope and faith remains undiminished. However, historical documentation supporting this legend is scant, and the line between myth and reality remains blurred. The story embodies the enchantment and mystery that myths often carry, touching upon themes of faith, spirituality, and the profound connection between history and belief.

The Vanishing Chalice: The Theft of the Nanteos Cup

In a tale that seems to be straight out of a modern mystery novel, the Nanteos Cup, disappeared in 2014, only to be found under rather dramatic circumstances.

In 2014, news began to circulate that the storied Nanteos Cup had been stolen. The cup, at that time, was not housed in any museum or secured location. Instead, it resided with a woman in Herefordshire. The exact reasons why the cup was with her remain somewhat shrouded in mystery, but it's believed she might have been a caretaker or a descendant of the lineage that had been safeguarding it for generations.

The theft sent shockwaves throughout Britain, especially among those who revered the cup for its spiritual significance. Theories about the theft ran rampant: Was it stolen for its potential monetary value? Did the thief believe in its powers and desired it for personal reasons? Or was there some other more nefarious, unknown motive?

While police and local authorities were vigilant in their hunt for the relic, it was almost a year before a significant clue emerged. In 2015, the cup was discovered, not in a thief's hideout or an underground market, but rather in a most unexpected place: submerged within a body of water in the West Midlands.

It was wrapped securely in a bag, perhaps to protect it from the water or perhaps to conceal its identity. One can only wonder at the motivations of the individual who chose to discard it in such a manner. Was it a realization of the weight of the theft? A sudden pang of guilt or fear of getting caught? Or perhaps the thief found that possessing a relic of such significance was not as rewarding as they'd imagined.

The return of the cup was celebrated, with many seeing its recovery as a testament to its enduring mystique and spiritual power. The incident also reignited discussions about the importance of securing such artifacts, not just for their historical or monetary value, but for the cultural and spiritual heritage they represent. The cup's journey from a woman's home to the depths of a lake and back again adds yet another layer to its rich tapestry of tales, making its story even more intriguing for generations to come.

The story of the Nanteos Cup's journey, from the deserts of Jerusalem to the green valleys of Wales, is more than just a tale of a relic. It's a testament to the enduring human spirit, the lengths we go to protect what we hold dear, and the timeless allure of the divine. The cup's journey through time, surviving the perils of history, mirrors the eternal quest for faith and understanding, a quest that remains as relevant today as it ever was.

Sources/Further Reading:

"The Quest for the Holy Grail" by Norris J. Lacy
"Nanteos: The Dipping Bowl and Cwpan Nanteos" by Robert Mirylees

Necronomicon

The Necronomicon—its name alone evokes an aura of mystery, eldritch power, and forbidden knowledge. Often dubbed the "Book of the Dead," this fictitious tome stands distinct and should not be confused with the ancient Egyptian "Book of the Dead," a collection of spells and incantations meant to assist the deceased in their journey to the afterlife. Born from the mind of H.P. Lovecraft, the Necronomicon represents the pinnacle of forbidden lore, a book said to hold the secrets of the cosmos and the arcane rituals to summon ancient and powerful entities.

Although purely a work of fiction, its legend has grown to such an extent that it's sometimes mistaken for a real, historical grimoire.

Over the decades, its alleged contents and the mere idea of its existence have fueled imaginations, inspired a plethora of derivative works, and tantalized those drawn to the esoteric and the occult. The Necronomicon's shadowy reputation, combined with its elusive nature, has solidified its place as one of the most iconic and enigmatic books in horror literature, with its influence reaching far beyond the written page.

The contents of the Necronomicon are described as being vast and varied. It holds spells, incantations, and rituals—some for summoning these ancient entities, others for protecting oneself from their influence. Beyond this, the book also delves into the history of these cosmic horrors, the nature of the universe, and the dark arts.

In the early 20th century, amidst a backdrop of shifting societal norms and the harrowing reality of World War I, emerged an author who would reshape the landscape of horror fiction: Howard Phillips Lovecraft. A native of Providence, Rhode Island, Lovecraft crafted a universe brimming with ancient, indescribable horrors that lurked just beyond the veil of human perception. Within this universe, he planted the seed of the Necronomicon, a book that would grow to be as enigmatic as its creator.

"The History of the Necronomicon" is a short prose piece that H.P. Lovecraft wrote, not as a story in the traditional sense, but more as a fictional historical account of the book's origins and travels through time. It serves as an exploration of the Necronomicon's fictional history and its evolution through various translations.

The History of the Necronomicon

The Necronomicon was originally titled "Al Azif," a reference to the nocturnal sound of insects believed to be the howling of demons. It was written by Abdul Alhazred, a poet from Sanaá in Yemen. He lived during the time of the Umayyad caliphs and was often referred to as the "Mad Arab" due to his heretical writings and behavior. Alhazred's travels brought him to the ruined cities of Babylon and the subterranean secrets of Memphis, leading to encounters with forbidden knowledge. Lovecraft suggested that Alhazred might have worshiped the Lovecraftian entities Yog-Sothoth and Cthulhu.

The "Mad Arab" met a gruesome end in 738 A.D. in the marketplace of Damascus, where an invisible monster tore him to pieces in broad daylight, leaving onlookers in shock. This was believed to be divine retribution for his heresies.

The text, over the years, was translated and transcribed multiple times. The first known Greek translation was made around 950 A.D., renaming the book "Necronomicon." Later, in the 13th century, Olaus Wormius made a Latin translation, which was, like many other copies of the book, banned by the Church and most of them burned.

Lovecraft weaves a compelling myth around the book's cursed nature. Many individuals involved in the translations or even in possession of the book met mysterious or horrific fates. This added a layer of terror to the mere act of reading or translating the Necronomicon.

By the 20th century, the book had apparently vanished or was kept in secret locations. Few authentic copies were believed to exist in Lovecraft's tales. Institutions like the Miskatonic University in Arkham and the British Museum were said to house some of these rare editions, locked away from the public due to their dangerous content.

Lovecraft's "The History of the Necronomicon" brilliantly cements the tome's authenticity in his fictional universe. It bridges the world of ancient horrors with the modern age and creates a continuous, eerie feeling that these cosmic horrors lurk just outside of human understanding. Through this pseudo-history, Lovecraft made the Necronomicon more than just a prop; he made it a living, breathing entity that has its dark saga.

Lovecraft often referenced the Necronomicon in his works, treating it with an air of reverence and fear. The mere act of reading from its pages or seeking its forbidden knowledge often led to dire consequences for his characters: insanity, doom, or worse. Its presence in multiple stories gave it a sense of continuity and authenticity, leading many readers to wonder if, perhaps, such a tome might truly exist.

"The Dunwich Horror" is one of Lovecraft's most chilling tales, intertwining the rustic eeriness of a rural town with cosmic terror and the looming presence of the Necronomicon.

The Dunwich Horror

The tale unfolds in the isolated, decaying town of Dunwich, a place seemingly forgotten by time but imbued with an oppressive sense of antiquity and malevolence. The landscape itself is rugged and wild, with some areas considered cursed and avoided by the local folk.

Central to the story is the Whateley family. Lavinia Whateley, a deformed, albino woman, gives birth to a son, Wilbur, whose father remains a mystery. As Wilbur grows (at an unnaturally accelerated rate), it becomes apparent that he is far from ordinary. With a grotesque appearance and an insatiable interest in the occult, Wilbur becomes the talk of the town.

His grandfather, Old Whateley, is a known sorcerer and together with Wilbur, they engage in bizarre rituals on their farmhouse, leading the locals to view them with a mix of fear and awe. Their intent is gradually revealed: they seek to call forth ancient, powerful entities from beyond our dimension.

Wilbur's endeavors hinge on the Necronomicon. He possesses a decayed Latin version, but to fully understand and utilize its knowledge, he seeks the complete English translation. This obsession leads him to the Miskatonic University in Arkham. Here, he hopes to access their guarded copy of the tome. His appearance and demeanor alarm the university staff, and his request is denied, setting the stage for subsequent events.

Wilbur's dark intentions become clear when he seeks to open a portal to another dimension, bringing forth an unimaginable horror from beyond. This creature, the Dunwich Horror, is a monstrous, invisible entity that terrorizes the town, leaving destruction in its wake. The horror's origins are deeply entwined with the Whateley family's practices, the Necronomicon, and the dark powers they've harnessed.

As the horror wreaks havoc, it becomes evident that combating this otherworldly threat requires a combined effort. Researchers from Miskatonic University, along with locals, devise a plan to confront the creature using knowledge from the Necronomicon. The story reaches its climax as they engage in a battle against the horror, aiming to banish it back to its dimension.

"The Dunwich Horror" is a masterclass in atmospheric horror. Lovecraft skillfully weaves the eerie rural setting with cosmic dread, with the Necronomicon acting as a conduit between man's understanding and the incomprehensible realms beyond. Through this story, Lovecraft explores the fragility of human understanding in a universe dominated by incomprehensible cosmic entities.

Numerous tales in the Lovecraftian oeuvre either subtly allude to or place the Necronomicon at the forefront. Among the most illustrious of these narratives are:

The Call of Cthulhu - Perhaps one of Lovecraft's most famous stories, it introduces the cosmic entity Cthulhu and the concept of ancient beings beyond human comprehension.

At the Mountains of Madness - This novella details an Antarctic expedition's terrifying discovery of an ancient alien city and the horrifying truths it uncovers about Earth's prehistoric past.

The Thing on the Doorstep - A tale of body-swapping and dark rituals, it delves into themes of identity, forbidden knowledge, and ancient evils.

The Festival - A man visits the town of Kingsport and experiences its bizarre and ancient Yuletide celebration, revealing dark, ancestral connections.

The Whisperer in Darkness - The protagonist becomes embroiled in a correspondence with a reclusive scholar, leading to shocking revelations about extraterrestrial entities in rural Vermont.

The Shadow Over Innsmouth - The story's narrator embarks on a visit to the town of Innsmouth, only to uncover its dark secrets, ancient pacts, and his own terrifying connection to its inhabitants.

The concept of the Necronomicon has proven so compelling that it has been referenced and incorporated into a vast array of other media. From movies, like Sam Raimi's Evil Dead series, to role-playing games and even other books, the Necronomicon's influence is vast.

Several writers, both during Lovecraft's life and after his death, have penned their versions or interpretations of the Necronomicon, attempting to craft an actual book from Lovecraft's scattered references.

Despite its fictional origins, many have come to believe in the real existence of the Necronomicon. Some occult bookstores even claim to have copies for sale. However, any existing versions are undoubtedly products of more recent authors and not the ancient, malevolent tome described by Lovecraft.

The Necronomicon stands as a testament to Lovecraft's ability to blur the lines between fiction and reality. While it remains a product of fiction, its chilling influence continues to inspire fear, curiosity, and reverence in those who encounter the name. As with many elements of Lovecraft's mythos, it serves as a reminder of the vast, unknowable universe and the mysteries it holds.

Sources/Further Reading:

H.P. Lovecraft: The Complete Fiction
"The Necronomicon Files: The Truth Behind Lovecraft's Legend" by Daniel Harms and John Wisdom Gonce III
"Lovecraft's Library: A Catalogue"

Pandora's Box

Pandora's Box is one of the most famous artifacts in Greek mythology, and its story serves as an allegory for the human traits of curiosity and hope.

Pandora's Box is not actually a box, but a jar (often referred to as "Pithos" in Greek). It is an artifact in Greek mythology, connected with the myth of Pandora, the first woman on Earth. The term "Pandora's Box" has become a metaphor used in modern times to mean any source of great and unexpected troubles or, alternatively, a present which seems valuable but which in reality is a curse.

The First Woman and Her Fateful Gift

In the age of gods and mortals, a slight to the divine was met with swift retribution. The tale of Pandora finds its roots in such a transgression. The titan Prometheus, against the will of Zeus, stole fire from the heavens and gave it to mankind. This act, which brought warmth, civilization, and knowledge to humanity, angered Zeus, king of the gods, who vowed to deliver a counter-gift—a gift that would harm humans.

To exact his revenge, Zeus ordered Hephaestus to craft Pandora, the first human woman. According to the annals of Greek mythology, she was sculpted from the earth by the blacksmith god. Zeus then summoned the gods, requesting from each of them a unique quality. With their combined powers, they molded Pandora. Each god bestowed upon her a gift: Aphrodite granted her beauty, Apollo gave her musical talent, Hermes bestowed her with cunning and persuasive charm, Athena, in her wisdom, dressed her and imparted the skills to navigate the world as a formidable woman, while other gods provided traits of curiosity and generosity.

Her name, "Pandora," translates to "all-gifted," symbolizing the various divine gifts she received. Yet, these gifts were not just blessings. They were also tools of seduction, meant to allure mortals and, in the process, bring about their undoing.

With Pandora perfected, Zeus gave her another gift: a jar. This was not an ordinary container, for it was sealed, holding within its confines all the world's suffering—sickness, death, toil, and every evil known and unknown. This jar, through the quirk of translation over time, became widely known as "Pandora's Box."

Zeus's instructions to Pandora were clear and unequivocal: she must never open the jar. However, as with all stories of warnings and prohibitions, this command was more a challenge than a restriction. Along with her many gifts, Pandora had also been endowed with insatiable curiosity.

Pandora's daily life in the world of mortals was tinged with an ever-present temptation: the sealed jar given to her by Zeus. While she was surrounded by the joys of life and the blessings from the gods, the jar represented a mysterious unknown, a challenge to her innate curiosity. Each day, it whispered to her, the weight of its secret pressing upon her, urging her to discover what lay inside.

One fateful day, overcome by a desire that couldn't be quenched, Pandora approached the jar. With trembling hands, she unsealed it, hoping perhaps for more gifts or perhaps some profound wisdom. But as the lid was lifted, a gust of dark wind erupted, and out poured sorrows, sicknesses, and a multitude of miseries. The sky darkened, and the earth seemed to tremble, as these afflictions spread out, finding homes in every corner of the world.

Distraught, Pandora desperately tried to close the jar, to undo her action and contain the unleashed horrors. But it was too late. The evils once trapped inside had tasted freedom and now roamed the world, bringing with them pain, suffering, and hardships.

Yet, the tale does not end in complete despair. After the whirlwind of evils had left the jar, a soft, glowing entity remained at the bottom: Elpis, the spirit of Hope. Some versions of the myth suggest that Pandora released Hope into the world, while others say she resealed it in the jar, either to protect it or to keep it close. Regardless of its fate, Hope's presence offers a crucial counterbalance. While the jar brought forth countless woes, the enduring spirit of Hope suggests that no matter how dire circumstances may seem, there is always the potential for resilience, recovery, and renewal.

Pandora's Box is a multi-layered symbol with a range of interpretations. It illustrates the pitfalls of human curiosity and the consequences of defying the will of the gods. This tale warns against the pursuit of forbidden knowledge and the potential for unforeseen disasters that can result. Metaphorically, Pandora's Box serves as a commentary on the nature of existence. The release of all evils except hope into the world mirrors the coexistence of suffering and optimism in human life. This duality reflects the complexities of the human experience and the inevitability of facing challenges.

The myth of Pandora's Box has endured through millennia, influencing literature, art, philosophy, and psychology. It has been explored in countless adaptations, from ancient Greek theater to modern literature and film. The metaphor of "opening Pandora's Box" is commonly used to describe the unintended consequences of an action that unleashes a series of troubles.

In psychology, the concept of the "Pandora Complex" has been coined to describe the fear of potential negative consequences associated with curiosity and exploration. The myth's themes of temptation, curiosity, and unforeseen consequences continue to resonate with people across cultures and generations.

Pandora's Box stands as a timeless metaphor, cautioning against the pursuit of forbidden knowledge and exploring the complexities of human nature. Its enduring presence in various forms of artistic and intellectual expression showcases its significance as a symbol that transcends time and culture, reminding us of the eternal interplay between curiosity and consequence.

Sources/Further Reading:

Hesiod's "Works and Days" – This ancient Greek text contains one of the earliest versions of the Pandora story.
"The Oxford Companion to World Mythology" by David Leeming
"The Greek Myths" by Robert Graves

Pasha

The Pasha is a symbolic and mythical artifact often depicted as a magical noose or binding knot. This enchanted lasso is believed to have the power to capture and bind anything it's thrown upon, rendering the ensnared entity powerless.

Within the Hindu pantheon, the Pasha is often associated with Lord Ganesha and Lord Varuna. Ganesha, the elephant-headed god of wisdom, beginnings, and obstacles, is sometimes depicted with the Pasha in one of his hands, symbolizing his ability to remove obstacles and ensnare all difficulties. The Pasha in Ganesha's hand represents his power to bind and free obstacles, ensuring the success of his devotees.

The Binding of Basmasura: A Tale of Deception and Divine Intervention

In the cosmic realms, where gods and asuras (demons) continuously vied for supremacy, boons and curses played a pivotal role in determining the fate of battles and allegiances. Basmasura, a mighty and ambitious asura, was no exception in his quest for power.

Desiring invincibility, Basmasura undertook severe penances to please Lord Shiva. Days turned into years, and his unwavering devotion finally moved the great ascetic god. Appearing before Basmasura, Lord Shiva granted him a wish.

With malevolent intent gleaming in his eyes, Basmasura requested a unique boon: anyone upon whose head he placed his hand would instantly be reduced to ashes. Lord Shiva, bound by the cosmic laws of granting boons to sincere devotees, acceded to the asura's request.

No sooner had he received his newfound power than Basmasura's intentions took a dark turn. Wanting to gauge the magnitude of his boon, he turned to Lord Shiva, looking to test the power on the very deity who granted it. Realizing the grave error he had made by granting such a perilous boon and the immediate danger he was in, Lord Shiva began to flee.

The chase was on. Across celestial mountains, through dense forests, and over cosmic rivers, Basmasura pursued Shiva relentlessly, with the singular intention of placing his hand on the deity's head and achieving the ultimate victory over a god.

As the chase continued, the situation grew dire. But just when all seemed lost, Lord Ganesha, the ever-watchful son of Shiva and Parvati, became aware of the unfolding drama. Knowing that his father was in mortal danger, Ganesha decided to intervene.

Manifesting himself at a strategic point, Ganesha, with the divine Pasha in hand, lay in wait for the approaching asura. As Basmasura raced past him, Ganesha skillfully cast the Pasha, ensnaring the unsuspecting demon and halting his relentless pursuit.

With Basmasura temporarily incapacitated, Lord Shiva found the respite he needed. He regrouped, preparing himself for a confrontation. When Basmasura finally managed to free himself from Ganesha's Pasha, he was met not by a fleeing Shiva but by a prepared and formidable deity.

The skies darkened, and ethereal winds howled, sensing the magnitude of the showdown. Celestial beings, rishis, and other gods watched from the distant realms, unsure of the outcome but knowing the very balance of the universe was at stake.

With every step Basmasura took, the ground quaked, and fires sparked, manifesting his fury and the power of his deadly boon. He believed he had the upper hand and attempted multiple times to lay his hand on Lord Shiva, aiming to turn him to ashes.

However, Lord Shiva, being one of the Holy Trinity in Hindu mythology, possessed not only immense power but also unparalleled wisdom. He danced around Basmasura, moving with grace and agility, avoiding the asura's deadly touch. The dance was hypnotic, with Shiva's every move echoing the rhythms of the cosmos, often reminding onlookers of his cosmic Tandava dance, which is said to bring about both creation and destruction.

Seeing that brute force would not allow him to touch Shiva, Basmasura tried to outmaneuver him. But Shiva was always one step ahead, leveraging his deep knowledge of the asura's boon. With every failed attempt, Basmasura's frustration grew.

Seizing the moment, Lord Shiva employed a clever ruse. He challenged Basmasura to a dance-off, stating that if the demon could mimic his every move perfectly, he would willingly allow himself to be touched. Eager to prove his superiority and see Shiva defeated, Basmasura agreed.

As the dance-off commenced, Basmasura copied every one of Shiva's moves. However, Lord Shiva, in his infinite wisdom, made a move where he placed his hand on his own head. Without realizing the implications, Basmasura, in his attempt to mimic the deity, placed his own hand on his head. The very power he sought, the deadly boon he was granted, was turned against him. In an instant, Basmasura was reduced to ashes.

Thus, through the timely intervention of Lord Ganesha and his Pasha, a grave cosmic catastrophe was averted, reaffirming the divine order and showcasing the profound bond between father and son in the pantheon of Hindu deities.

The Ganesha Purana and Mudgala Purana, narrate various stories of Lord Ganesha and often provide deeper insights into the symbolism and use of his weapons. A notable tale recounts the instance when Ganesha captured the moon.

The Humbling of the Moon: Ganesha's Assertive Display

In the ethereal realms, where gods and celestial bodies existed, there unfurled a tale that showcased Ganesha's might and the perils of mockery.

Lord Ganesha, with his insatiable appetite, had just finished partaking in a grand feast. The food, both sumptuous and plentiful, had satiated him but also distended his belly, making it protrude amusingly. Content and satiated, Ganesha decided to take a nighttime ride on his trusted vahana, the tiny mouse.

However, as they journeyed, the mouse was startled by a snake, causing it to stumble. This unexpected jolt threw Ganesha off balance, and he tumbled, his belly bursting open upon the fall, spilling the consumed feast onto the ground. This sight, of a god in a rather uncompromising and comedic position, was witnessed by none other than the moon.

Chandra, the Moon God, known for his luminous beauty, couldn't hold back his amusement. He laughed heartily, his silvery laughter echoing through the cosmos. Each ripple of laughter was a sting to Ganesha's pride. While many gods would have been embarrassed, Ganesha's reaction was one of anger at being ridiculed.

In a swift move, filled with righteous indignation, Ganesha unfurled his Pasha. The noose-like rope, imbued with celestial power, shot up towards the moon. Chandra, who was still laughing, suddenly found himself ensnared, being yanked from his celestial perch. The entire cosmos watched in awe as Ganesha, with the Pasha, demonstrated his authority by pulling the moon closer, making him realize his vulnerable position in the grand scheme of things.

The moon's laughter ceased, replaced by pleas for mercy. He realized the folly of his actions – mocking a god, especially one as revered as Ganesha, was a grave mistake.

Ganesha, having made his point and asserted his authority, released the moon but not without imposing a curse - causing the moon to wax and wane, a constant reminder of his hubris. Chandra, chastised and humbled, faded away, promising never to mock anyone again.

The Paṣha is more than just a tool or weapon; it's deeply symbolic. It represents the idea of binding, controlling, or eliminating negative forces, obstacles, or enemies. Additionally, it can symbolize the concept of fate or karma in some traditions, emphasizing the inescapable nature of one's actions and their consequences.

As with many mythical artifacts, the Pasha is rich in symbolism and varies in its depiction and significance across different cultures. Whether seen as a tool of control, a symbol of divine authority, or a representation of fate's inescapable grasp, the Pasha stands as a powerful emblem in the realm of mythology.

Sources/Further Reading:

"Mythological Objects of India" by M.P. Pandit
"The Book of Hindu Imagery: Gods, Manifestations, and Their Meaning" by Eva Rudy Jansen
"Hindu Myths: A Sourcebook Translated from the Sanskrit" by Wendy Doniger

Philosopher's Stone

The Philosopher's Stone, steeped in the annals of history, has consistently captivated humanity with its dual promise of boundless wealth and the allure of eternal life. This enigmatic substance, variously depicted as a stone, powder, or even a liquid, has shone brightly as a beacon in the world of alchemy. For centuries, its purported capabilities have ignited the imaginations of scholars, fervent dreamers, and those who thirst for power.

Yet, the stone's allure isn't solely grounded in its material benefits. Deeply symbolic, the Philosopher's Stone represents an intense spiritual odyssey. Its crafting, referred to as the Magnum Opus or the Great Work, is more than just an alchemical endeavor; it mirrors the transformative journey of the alchemist's soul toward enlightenment and spiritual transcendence. Every step in its creation, from rigorous processes to the purification of elements, reflects the soul's striving for ultimate perfection.

The practice of alchemy, seen as the forerunner to contemporary chemistry, spanned across continents—from Europe and the Middle East to Asia. At the heart of this ancient practice lay the Magnum Opus, symbolizing not just the crafting of the Philosopher's Stone but a profound spiritual transformation.

Perhaps the most renowned power of the Philosopher's Stone is its potential to transmute common metals—like lead—into invaluable ones, especially gold. Beyond this, legends whisper of its ability to concoct an elixir granting eternal life and immortality. However, to alchemists, the stone's true value was more profound. Its creation epitomized the pinnacle of spiritual growth, symbolizing a state of pristine perfection and a profound connection with the divine.

Throughout history, various texts have mentioned or hinted at the Philosopher's Stone, often enveloped in symbolic and coded language. From the works of medieval European alchemists to Islamic scholars like Jabir ibn Hayyan and Chinese alchemical texts, the stone has been described with a blend of mysticism and proto-scientific exploration.

Hermes Trismegistus and the Emerald Tablet: A Bridge Between Realms

Hermes Trismegistus, a figure shrouded in the mists of time and legend, is often perceived as a synthesis of two deities: the Greek god Hermes and the Egyptian god Thoth. Both these deities were associated with writing, magic, and wisdom. The confluence of Hellenistic and Egyptian cultures under the Ptolemaic dynasty led to the fusion of their pantheons, birthing this unique figure—Hermes Trismegistus, or "Thrice-Great Hermes."

The "Emerald Tablet" is perhaps the most illustrious work attributed to him. This concise, cryptic text, typically inscribed upon a slab of emerald or green stone, holds secrets that have mystified and intrigued alchemists and scholars for centuries. While its content is compact, its implications and breadth of knowledge are vast, serving as a cornerstone for Western alchemical thought and the Hermetic tradition.

The tablet's most iconic axiom, "As above, so below; as below, so above," encapsulates a profound spiritual and philosophical truth. It implies that the microcosm and the macrocosm are intricately connected; what exists in the vast cosmos is reflected in the minuscule, and vice versa. This statement speaks to the idea that the workings of the universe are mirrored within one's own soul and that by understanding oneself, one can begin to understand the universe.

In the context of alchemy, this axiom reinforces the notion that the processes used to transform base metals into gold or to create the Philosopher's Stone are not just physical but deeply spiritual. The outer alchemical work on materials mirrors an inner alchemical process of spiritual purification and enlightenment.

Furthermore, the "Emerald Tablet" doesn't just offer a recipe for the Philosopher's Stone—it hints at the interconnectedness of all things and the inherent divinity of the universe. It suggests that the secrets of transformation, whether of metals, the soul, or the cosmos, are all bound by the same universal principles.

Over the centuries, the teachings of the "Emerald Tablet" and its reputed author, Hermes Trismegistus, have influenced a wide array of disciplines, from alchemy and astrology to Gnosticism and the Renaissance Hermetic revival. Its allure is timeless, and its wisdom, though cryptic, continues to inspire seekers of knowledge and spiritual growth.

Perhaps the most iconic figure entwined with the legend of the Philosopher's Stone is Nicholas Flamel. This 14th-century French scribe and alchemist, whose historical existence is well-documented, has become the stuff of legend. His reputed success in discovering the secrets of the stone and his quest for eternal life passed down through generations, have made his name synonymous with alchemical pursuits and the mysteries of the arcane.

Nicholas Flamel and the Quest for Immortality

In the cobblestone streets of medieval Paris, the name Nicholas Flamel was known primarily for his successful scribal business. However, centuries after his death in 1418, his name would become forever entwined with alchemy, the Philosopher's Stone, and the pursuit of immortality.

The legends began to spread in the 17th century, approximately 200 years after Flamel's death. These tales suggested that Flamel had stumbled upon a mysterious, ancient book: The Book of Abraham the Jew. This tome, allegedly penned by an Egyptian sage, was said to contain the hidden knowledge of the Philosopher's Stone. Since it was written in a language and filled with symbols that Flamel initially couldn't decipher, he became obsessed with unlocking its secrets.

After years of studying, the stories recount how Flamel traveled to Spain, a hub of alchemical and esoteric knowledge due to its confluence of Christian, Jewish, and Muslim traditions. There, he met a wise, learned scholar who assisted him in decoding the book's enigmatic content.

Returning to Paris, armed with this newfound knowledge, Flamel and his wife Pernelle purportedly embarked on the process of creating the Philosopher's Stone. Their efforts, if legends are to be believed, were successful. Not only did they manage to transform base metal into pure gold, but they also produced the Elixir of Life, granting them the gift of immortality.

What added fuel to these tales was the undeniable wealth that Flamel and his wife acquired over their lifetimes. They became notable philanthropists, funding the construction of hospitals, churches, and other charitable establishments. Skeptics argue that their wealth was accrued through Flamel's work as a scribe and his real estate ventures, but believers whisper that such affluence was a testament to the power of the Stone.

Further intrigue surrounds Flamel's death—or supposed death. When grave robbers later exhumed his tomb, hoping to find treasures, they reportedly found it empty, giving rise to speculations that Flamel and his wife never truly died but continue to live on, thanks to the Elixir of Life.

Nicholas Flamel's legacy is cemented in the Marais district of Paris, where one can find a street bearing his name. His former residence, at 51 rue de Montmorency, is said to be the oldest stone house in Paris. But perhaps the most curious relic is his tombstone, discovered in the 19th century, bearing enigmatic symbols. These designs, which bear a resemblance to alchemical symbols, have been scrutinized by many but understood by few, adding another layer of mystery to Flamel's already enigmatic life.

In the end, while historical documents confirm the existence of a scribe named Nicholas Flamel in 14th-century Paris, the veracity of his alchemical adventures remains the stuff of legend, captivating those who yearn for mysteries and the promise of eternal life.

While Flamel's tale grew legendary across Europe, references to the Philosopher's Stone echo in numerous other stories from diverse cultures.

Islamic scholars like Jabir ibn Hayyan and Al-Razi wrote extensively on alchemy. Many of their texts contained references to a stone or elixir capable of miraculous transformations, although interpretations often leaned towards spiritual enlightenment rather than literal gold-making.

In Daoist traditions, the quest for an elixir of immortality was a prominent theme. While not called the "Philosopher's Stone" directly, the goal of many Chinese alchemists was to create a substance or elixir that granted eternal life, drawing parallels to the Stone's mythos in the West.

In some European tales, the Philosopher's Stone is symbolically represented as the "Red Lion" which can cleanse all impurities. This "Red Lion" would be devoured by the "Green Lion," which is another allegory for the dissolution of copper by sulfuric acid, symbolizing the first step in the creation of the stone.

The concept of the Philosopher's Stone is no longer pursued in the literal sense in modern times. However, it remains a powerful metaphor in literature, representing self-improvement, transformation, and the pursuit of the seemingly impossible. One of the most popular references in modern culture is J.K. Rowling's "Harry Potter and the Philosopher's Stone," where the stone offers immortality and endless wealth.

While the physical quest for the Philosopher's Stone may have waned with the rise of modern scientific understanding, its symbolic allure remains undiminished. It stands as a testament to humanity's perennial quest for knowledge, perfection, and the transcendence of our earthly limitations.

Sources/Further Reading:

The Alchemical Body by David Gordon White
The Alchemy Reader: From Hermes Trismegistus to Isaac Newton edited by Stanton J. Linden
"Nicholas Flamel: His Exposition of the Hieroglyphical Figures"

Ring of Gyges

The Ring of Gyges is a mythical artifact that stands at the crossroads of temptation, power, and morality. Hailing from ancient Greek lore, it's not just an object of invisibility but a symbol that probes deep philosophical questions regarding human nature and ethical behavior. The story of this ring emerges from Plato's philosophical work, the "Republic," and serves as a thought experiment discussing justice and the nature of human morality.

The story of the Ring of Gyges is recounted by Glaucon in Book II of Plato's "Republic". Glaucon, Plato's older brother, uses the tale as a way to challenge Socrates on his views about justice, arguing that people are only just because of the consequences of being unjust, not because they believe in justice for its own sake.

The Tale of Gyges

Gyges was a humble shepherd in the service of the king of Lydia. One day, an earthquake revealed a cave in the place where he was feeding his flock. Curious, Gyges decided to explore the mysterious cavern.

Inside the depths of the chasm, the light reflected off an unusual object, catching Gyges' attention. As his eyes adjusted to the subdued lighting, he discerned the shape of a magnificent bronze statue in the form of a horse. The craftsmanship was exquisite, the details of the horse meticulously etched, giving it an almost lifelike appearance.

Gyges approached the statue with a mixture of curiosity and reverence. On closer inspection, he noticed that the statue was not solid, but hollow. What he found inside was as astonishing as the statue itself. There lay a corpse, not decayed by time but preserved in an eerily perfect state.

But what truly caught Gyges' eye was the gleam of gold from the corpse's hand. A beautifully crafted gold ring adorned one of the fingers. Its design was simple yet captivating. Despite the chilling atmosphere and the uncanny nature of his discovery, Gyges was drawn to the ring. Perhaps it was greed, or maybe just sheer curiosity about such a fine artifact, but after a moment's hesitation, he reached out and carefully slid the ring off the finger of the ancient corpse, claiming it for himself.

Slipping the ring onto his finger, Gyges felt an unusual sensation. As he turned the collet inward, the world around him remained the same, but he himself vanished from sight, rendered completely invisible. Experimenting further, he turned the ring's collet outward and found himself once again visible to the world. The realization was immediate and profound: he possessed a ring of invisibility.

With such power literally at his fingertips, Gyges' aspirations grew. The ring's capabilities weren't just a marvel; they were a tool, a means to an end. And so, in the shadowed corridors of the royal palace, he hatched a plot most treacherous. With the ring's power, he seduced the queen, turning her against her own husband. Together, they conspired, and under the cloak of invisibility, Gyges approached the unsuspecting king and committed regicide.

With the king out of the picture and the queen by his side, Gyges swiftly ascended to the throne of Lydia. The shepherd, once a mere pawn in the grand scheme of things, had become the most powerful man in the kingdom, all thanks to a ring discovered by chance in a forgotten cave.

The Ring of Gyges is not just a tale of magical invisibility; it's a profound philosophical thought experiment. Glaucon posits that if two such rings existed, and one was given to a just person and the other to an unjust person, both would end up committing acts of injustice. This is because the power to act without consequences would override any moral compunction.

For Glaucon, this story underscores the idea that people are just only because they fear the repercussions of injustice, not because they see inherent value in being just. The crux of his argument is to challenge the idea of justice being something sought for its own sake.

The legend of the Ring of Gyges and its moral implications have reverberated throughout centuries of philosophical thought. Its echoes can be seen in modern concepts about the corrupting nature of unchecked power and the moral dilemmas posed by anonymity. It poses the eternal question: Would we maintain our moral compass if there were no consequences to our actions?

Sources/Further Reading:

Plato's "Republic": To truly grasp the depth of the story and its philosophical implications, Plato's work is essential.
Modern philosophical critiques and commentaries on the "Republic" will provide a more detailed analysis of the Ring of Gyges and its role in the larger discourse on justice.
"The Lord of the Rings"

Ruyi Jingu Bang

The Ruyi Jingu Bang, often translated as the "As-You-Will Gold-Banded Cudgel" or "Compliant Golden-Hooped Rod," is a mythical weapon wielded by Sun Wukong, the Monkey King, a prominent figure in Chinese mythology and literature. This artifact is best known from the classic 16th-century novel "Journey to the West" by Wu Cheng'en.

At first glance, the Ruyi Jingu Bang appears as an iron rod. However, its seemingly simple exterior conceals its enchanted nature. With innate adaptability, this artifact can change its size at the wielder's will. It can be as minuscule as a sewing needle for easy storage or as vast as a celestial pillar, extending to touch the very heavens. Despite its variable size, its formidable weight remains constant at approximately 13,500 pounds.

The Discovery of the Staff

In the multifaceted montage of Chinese mythology, Sun Wukong, the Monkey King, stands out with his audacious spirit and unparalleled might. Born from a stone, Sun Wukong's powers grew as he learned Taoist magic, combat techniques, and the secret to immortality. His defiance reached its peak when he brazenly declared himself as the "Great Sage, Equal of Heaven," a title that was neither conferred upon him nor accepted by the celestial pantheon. This audacious claim was not just an empty boast, and Sun Wukong knew that to reinforce his self-declared title, he needed a weapon worthy of his extraordinary prowess.

His quest for this ultimate weapon led him to the majestic underwater palace of Ao Guang, the Dragon King of the Eastern Seas. The palace was a trove of heavenly weapons, from shimmering swords to mighty halberds, each with its own unique power and history. But as Sun Wukong inspected each one, he found them wanting. They either felt too insubstantial, almost like toys in his hands, or too cumbersome to be wielded effectively.

Growing increasingly impatient and perhaps a touch amused by the Monkey King's dismissive attitude, Ao Guang casually referred to an ancient black iron pillar situated in the abyss of his palace. This pillar, he mentioned, had a divine purpose: it tethered the waters, maintaining the balance of the seas. It was an object of immense weight and power, and no being, celestial or otherwise, had ever managed to budge it.

Curiosity piqued, Sun Wukong approached the colossal pillar. To the astonishment of all present, not only did he lift it with relative ease, but he also discovered its magical nature. It was the Ruyi Jingu Bang. This wasn't just any staff; it was a staff that seemed to share a connection with Sun Wukong. It responded to his thoughts and whims, expanding to touch the skies or shrinking down to the size of a sewing needle. Despite its ability to alter its size, its weight remained constant. Yet, for the mighty Monkey King, wielding it felt as natural as an extension of his own limbs.

This discovery wasn't just about finding a weapon; it was a declaration. The heavens might not recognize his title, but with the Ruyi Jingu Bang in hand, they could not ignore his power. The staff became an inseparable part of Sun Wukong's identity, a symbol of his journey from a mischievous monkey to a deity that even the heavens learned to respect, if not fear.

In the grand saga of "Journey to the West," Sun Wukong's exploits are nothing short of legendary, and his loyal staff, the Ruyi Jingu Bang, plays a pivotal role in shaping these tales. As the narrative unfolds, it becomes clear that this staff is not merely a weapon; it's an embodiment of Sun Wukong's indomitable spirit and an unwavering ally in his quest.

Embarking on a divine mission to retrieve sacred Buddhist scriptures from the West, Sun Wukong is accompanied by the monk Tang Sanzang and fellow disciples like Zhu Bajie and Sha Wujing. The journey is fraught with trials and tribulations, teeming with an array of formidable adversaries, from cunning demons who wish to devour the monk for immortality to celestial beings testing the resolve of the travelers.

In every challenge, the Ruyi Jingu Bang proves to be an invaluable asset. When facing foes that seem insurmountable, Sun Wukong wields the staff with unparalleled mastery, its size and weight adapting fluidly to his combat style. Its strikes, whether a gentle tap or a thunderous blow, always carry the might of the Monkey King, sending adversaries flying or quelling them into submission.

Beyond the heat of battle, the staff's versatile nature shines in other ways. Its transformative abilities often rescue the travelers from dire situations. When confronted with vast bodies of water or treacherous rivers that threaten to halt their progress, Sun Wukong enlarges the staff, using it as a bridge or a raft, ensuring safe passage for his companions. In terrains where the path ahead is uncertain or where stealth is required, the staff can shrink to a minuscule size, allowing for easy concealment or carrying.

But perhaps, more than its physical attributes, the Ruyi Jingu Bang serves as a testament to Sun Wukong's growth and his commitment to the journey. Every time he wields it, he's reminded of his past defiance, his eventual redemption, and the promise he made to protect Tang Sanzang at all costs. It stands as a symbol of his oath, his duty, and the path of enlightenment he treads alongside his companions.

Throughout the numerous tales and adventures in "Journey to the West," the Ruyi Jingu Bang is not just an instrument but a character in its own right. It resonates with the spirit of the journey, echoing the perseverance, resilience, and undying hope of the travelers as they march towards their divine destiny.

The Ruyi Jingu Bang stands as one of the most iconic weapons in Chinese literature, emblematic of Sun Wukong's adventurous spirit and unparalleled might. Its legacy resonates not just as a tool of battle, but as a testament to the Monkey King's journey from rebellious trickster to devout protector of the Buddhist faith.

Sources/Further Reading:

"Journey to the West" by Wu Cheng'en

Sampo

The Sampo stands as one of the most mysterious and central artifacts in the Finnish national epic, the "Kalevala." It is a magical object often described as a mill, which brings good fortune to its holder. The exact nature and appearance of the Sampo have been topics of much speculation and debate, but its significance in Finnish mythology is unquestioned.

Origin and Creation

The tale of the Sampo begins with the skilled blacksmith, Ilmarinen.

Ilmarinen is not just any blacksmith. In the "Kalevala," he's often referred to as the "eternal craftsman," a master of his art, and one of the chief characters in the epic. His skills are so profound that they're considered divinely inspired, and his forge is believed to have the power to create anything.

Louhi, the powerful witch-queen of the northern realm of Pohjola, is a formidable figure in Finnish mythology. As the "Kalevala" unfolds, she comes to learn of Ilmarinen's unmatched skill as a blacksmith. With a cunning plan in mind, she puts forth a challenge, promising the hand of her beautiful daughter in marriage to whoever can craft the mysterious and much-coveted artifact known as the Sampo.

Though several might have heard of this legendary artifact, none had dared to craft it, for its creation was believed to require not just unmatched skill, but also divine inspiration.

Drawn by the dual allure of crafting the most legendary of artifacts and winning the hand of Louhi's daughter, Ilmarinen decides to take on the task. The scenes at his forge are described with great intensity. Fire blazes, hammers clang, and the entire universe seems to hold its breath as Ilmarinen embarks on his divine act of creation.

Days turn into nights and nights into days, as Ilmarinen labors, pouring all of his skill, passion, and divine inspiration into his work. He uses special ores and materials, some of which are said to be from the celestial realms, making the task even more challenging.

And then, after what seems like an eternity, the Sampo is forged. Unlike any artifact ever crafted, it's described as a magical mill, shimmering and luminous, with the power to produce endless grain, salt, and gold. Its creation is not just a testament to Ilmarinen's unmatched skill but also to the idea that human endeavor when coupled with divine inspiration, can achieve the impossible.

The creation of the Sampo sets forth a series of events that would see it becoming a central motif in the "Kalevala." While Ilmarinen has successfully crafted it, retaining it and ensuring it's used for the benefit of all becomes a challenge, leading to quests, battles, and profound lessons on power, greed, and sacrifice.

The Quest for the Sampo

In the cold, mysterious landscape of Pohjola, the Sampo sat concealed, but its presence was far from secret. As news of its abilities spread, tales of its wondrous nature began to captivate the hearts of many. The power to produce endless grain, salt, and gold made it not just a treasure, but the embodiment of abundance itself.

While many might have heard of the Sampo's wonders, three legendary figures felt its call more intensely than others. Väinämöinen, the wise sage and master of songs; Ilmarinen, the master blacksmith who first forged the Sampo; and Lemminkäinen, the audacious adventurer. Each, in their own way, saw the Sampo as a beacon of hope and the answer to their people's prayers for prosperity. The trio, representing the heart and soul of Finnish folklore, became intrinsically linked with the quest for the Sampo.

At the forefront of this pursuit was Väinämöinen. As a central figure in Finnish lore, his character melds wisdom with ambition. His connection to the Sampo wasn't just the allure of its treasures; it was a deeper, spiritual yearning. For Väinämöinen, retrieving the Sampo was a mission to restore balance, to bring prosperity where there was want, and to fulfill a destiny that seemed written in the stars.

The journey to Pohjola was fraught with challenges. The path was neither straight nor easy, reflecting the complexity of human desires and the trials one must undergo to achieve greatness. Each challenge faced by Väinämöinen and his companions wasn't just a physical barrier but a test of their spirit, resolve, and the purity of their intent.

More than a mere quest for an artifact, Väinämöinen's journey became a pilgrimage. The challenges along the way, from treacherous terrains to confrontations with guardians of the

Sampo, were as much about self-discovery as they were about the external world. Each step taken, each song sung, and each battle fought revealed more about the character of the heroes and the depth of their determination.

Upon reaching the frozen heart of Pohjola, the heroes found themselves standing at the gates of Louhi's stronghold. The land, shrouded in a foreboding aura, echoed with whispers of the power contained within. The stage was set for an epic confrontation.

Louhi, having sensed their approach, had already marshaled her defenses. As the keeper of the Sampo, she was well aware of its allure and the lengths to which intruders would go to claim it. But she was no ordinary foe; Louhi was a powerful sorceress, capable of summoning the elements to her aid and bending the very fabric of reality.

As Väinämöinen, Ilmarinen, and Lemminkäinen stood before her, a palpable tension hung in the air. It was a moment where ambition, honor, greed, and duty stood face to face, each weighing the worth of their journey against the risks of the battle ahead. The ensuing clash was not just of swords and spells, but of ideals and beliefs. Each side represented different facets of human nature, with the Sampo standing as the prize and the symbol of their deepest desires.

The battle, though fierce, eventually saw the heroes gaining the upper hand, managing to seize the Sampo. Their victory, however, was short-lived. As they embarked on their journey back to their homeland, they soon realized that they were not alone. Louhi, in her desperation to reclaim the Sampo, summoned a massive tempest to hinder their path.

Amid the roaring waves and raging winds, the vessel bearing the heroes and their prize was rocked violently. In the ensuing turmoil, the Sampo, unable to withstand the forces around it, was shattered. Its fragments, imbued with the essence of boundless prosperity, scattered into the depths of the sea. The heroes could only watch in despair as the object of their quest, the symbol of abundance, was lost to them.

Yet, even in its fragmented state, the Sampo did not lose its power entirely. The sea into which its pieces fell became rich and fertile, bringing prosperity to the lands nearby. However, the full magnitude of its potential, the promise of endless grain, salt, and gold, was never to be realized again.

The narrative underscores the idea that even in fragments, the influence of a powerful symbol can persist, echoing through generations.

The tale of the Sampo captures the spirit of Finnish mythology and cultural identity. It reflects the eternal human pursuit of abundance and the price one must pay for such boundless desires. The fragmented Sampo serves as a reminder that while the full power of an artifact may diminish, its legacy endures, influencing the course of events and the lives it touches.

Sources/Further Reading:

"The Kalevala" – This is the primary source for any study related to the Sampo.
"The Sampo: Myths and Traditions" by John Abercromby.
"Finnish Folklore" by Leea Virtanen and Thomas DuBois.

Scythe of Cronos

The Scythe (or sickle) of Cronos (or Kronos) is an ancient symbol and artifact from Greek mythology. While exact descriptions vary across sources and artistic interpretations, the scythe of Cronos is typically depicted as a large, crescent-shaped blade, which is curvilinear and sharp-edged. The blade itself is forged from adamant, an indestructible mythical substance, reinforcing its strength and permanence.

The Scythe is primarily associated with the act of castration that Cronos carried out on his father, Uranus.

Cronos and His Scythe

Uranus was the primordial god of the sky, and his union with Gaia, the Earth, produced many offspring. Among them were the first generation of Titans, the Cyclopes, and the monstrous Hecatonchires. The Cyclopes were one-eyed giants, skilled in forging weapons, while the Hecatonchires were fearsome creatures with a hundred hands and fifty heads.

As the children were born, Uranus viewed some with disdain, particularly the Cyclopes and the Hecatonchires, fearing their strength and unique abilities. He believed that these children posed a threat to his dominance over the cosmos. To maintain his unchallenged reign and out of revulsion, he imprisoned these offspring deep within the Earth, in the hidden abyss of Tartarus. This caused immense pain to Gaia as they writhed within her.

The continuous suffering of her children and the unchecked tyranny of Uranus pained Gaia. Seeking an end to her torment and yearning to free her children from their dark prison, Gaia envisioned a plan to overthrow Uranus. She forged a great adamant sickle, sharper and harder than any weapon, capable of carrying out the act she plotted.

Hoping to find an ally among her other children, the Titans, Gaia implored them to rise up against their oppressive father. However, the Titans hesitated, fearing Uranus's wrath. Only the youngest, Cronos, driven by ambition, courage, or perhaps even desperation, chose to stand against his father.

Secretly arming Cronos with the mighty sickle, Gaia set her plan in motion. She advised her son to wait in ambush for the opportune moment.

That fateful night, as the sky (Uranus) descended to meet the Earth (Gaia), Cronos sprang forth from his hiding spot. Using the sickle, in one swift and brutal act, he castrated his father. This heinous act symbolized the transfer of power from Uranus to Cronos, marking the beginning of the reign of the Titans.

The blood from Uranus, spilling onto Gaia, birthed various entities. From the drops that splattered the Earth, the Erinyes (Furies) - deities of vengeance, and the Gigantes - great giants, were born. The severed genitals, when cast into the sea by Cronos, produced a white foam. From this foam emerged Aphrodite, the goddess of love, beauty, and fertility, floating to the shore on a shell, marking a significant moment of beauty and creation from an act of violence.

Thus, the overthrow of Uranus by Cronos set into motion a cyclical pattern of succession struggles, hinting at the inherent volatility and ever-changing dynamics of divine rule in Greek mythology.

The act of castration symbolizes a transfer of power. In many ancient cultures, virility was a direct representation of strength and rulership. By castrating Uranus, Cronos was not merely enacting vengeance but was strategically debilitating the source of Uranus's generative and ruling might, thereby signaling the end of one era and the commencement of another.

The crescent shape of the sickle is evocative of the waxing and waning moon. The moon, in various mythologies, is often linked with cyclical changes, femininity, and transformation. The act carried out with a tool that symbolizes the moon accentuates the cyclical nature of power dynamics—how one reign ends for another to begin, much like the phases of the moon.

In essence, the sickle in the story of Cronos and Uranus is not just a weapon; it's a potent symbol that captures the essence of cyclical power dynamics, the consequences of one's deeds, and the inevitability of change.

Sources/Further Reading:

"Theogony" by Hesiod
"Greek Religion" by Walter Burkert
"The Greek Myths" by Robert Graves

Sudarshan Chakra

The Sudarshan Chakra is a legendary spinning disc-like weapon in Hindu mythology, used by Lord Vishnu, one of the principal deities in the Hindu pantheon. It's known to be one of the most powerful divine weapons ever created. The Sudarshan Chakra is an emblematic, disc-shaped weapon. Made of divine metal that shines with a radiant glow, it is characterized by its sharp, serrated edge adorned with 108 or sometimes 1,000 spikes, though traditional accounts often describe it with 28 prominent spikes.

Though it can be wielded in varying sizes, it is often depicted proportionate to Vishnu's stature when he holds it. More than just a weapon, the Sudarshan Chakra stands as a symbol of time, righteousness, and the divine order that Vishnu upholds in the cosmic cycle.

According to some myths, the Sudarshan Chakra was crafted by the divine architect Vishwakarma. After the Samudra Manthan, or churning of the ocean, Vishnu received the discus from the architect, who had crafted it using the dust of the sun and the scraps left from the creation of Lord Shiva's trishula (trident).

The Sudarshan Chakra is not just a weapon but also a symbol of the infinite power of Lord Vishnu. It's said to possess a will of its own and can chase its target once set into motion. The discus spins rapidly on Vishnu's finger and can be thrown with precision, always returning to its master's hand. It can also produce flames, adding to its destructive power.

The Death of Shishupala

Shishupala was born with three eyes and four arms, a sight that alarmed his parents due to its association with ill omens. Soon after his birth, a prophecy declared that the extra eye and arms would disappear upon being held by the very person destined to kill Shishupala. When Krishna, a cousin to Shishupala, visited and held the baby, the extra limbs and eye vanished, signifying Krishna as the destined slayer. Shishupala's mother, aware of this prophecy, pleaded with Krishna to spare her son's life. Krishna, known for his benevolence, promised that he would pardon Shishupala's transgressions up to a hundred times. However, he also cautioned that he would not tolerate the hundred-and-first offense and would kill Shishupala.

Shishupala grew up to become the king of Chedi. Throughout his life, he harbored animosity towards Krishna for various reasons. This deep-seated hatred became evident at the Rajasuya Yagna (a grand sacrifice) conducted by the Pandava king, Yudhishthira. Here, amidst many kings and noble souls, the honor of the first worship was offered to Krishna, deeming him the most virtuous and deserving among all present. This decision deeply offended

Shishupala, who viewed himself as a better choice. He stood up and hurled a barrage of insults at Krishna, denouncing him and questioning his legitimacy to receive such a venerable honor. As Shishupala continued with his tirade, Krishna remained calm, keeping track of the number of offenses. The assembly watched in a mixture of horror and fascination as Shishupala's audacity knew no bounds.

As Shishupala's offenses reached the count of a hundred, Krishna's patience began to wear thin. Upon the hundred-and-first insult, Krishna deemed that Shishupala's time had come. With a calm demeanor, he invoked the mighty Sudarshan Chakra. The spinning disc, radiant and sharp, flew from Krishna's finger, honing in on its target with unerring precision. Before the assembly could fully comprehend what was happening, the Chakra decapitated Shishupala, thus fulfilling the prophecy of his death.

While Krishna's compassion was vast, allowing Shishupala a hundred chances, justice was eventually served. The Sudarshan Chakra's role in this story cements its position as a divine instrument of judgment and retribution.

In another story, the Sudarshan Chakra played a crucial role in helping Dhruva, a devoted prince, achieve liberation from the mortal realm.

Liberation of Dhruva

Dhruva was the son of King Uttanapada and his wife, Suniti. However, he was not the favored child, as the king favored his other queen, Suruchi, and her son more. One day, when Dhruva tried to climb onto his father's lap, Suruchi scolded him, stating that if he wished to be truly accepted, he'd have to undergo severe penances and seek blessings from Lord Vishnu. Heartbroken and driven, Dhruva left the palace with the aim to meditate and please Lord Vishnu.

In the forests, Dhruva began his meditation. His intense devotion and unwavering concentration moved the heavens. Pleased by the young prince's dedication, Lord Vishnu appeared before him, granting him not only a place of honor in the celestial realms but also making him a guiding star (the Pole Star) that would forever shine brightly in the sky.

Time passed, and Dhruva grew to be a mighty and just king. However, a conflict arose between him and the Yakshas after his brother, Uttama, was killed during a hunt, presumably by a Yaksha. Enraged and seeking revenge, Dhruva waged a war against them. The Yakshas were formidable adversaries, and the battle between them and Dhruva was intense.

Seeing his devoted follower in distress, Lord Vishnu didn't hesitate. He released the Sudarshan Chakra, a weapon of immense power and speed. The chakra whizzed through the battlefield, annihilating the Yakshas who posed a threat to Dhruva.

After the battle, Dhruva was approached by the sage Suka, who made him realize the futility of revenge and the transient nature of life. Realizing his mistakes and with a heart full of repentance, Dhruva sought liberation from the cycle of life and death. Given his deep devotion and the merits he had accumulated, Dhruva achieved Moksha, liberating his soul from the mortal realm.

Throughout this story, the Sudarshan Chakra stands not just as a weapon of destruction but also as a protector of the righteous and devout. It signifies divine intervention and the idea that unwavering devotion attracts divine protection.

The Sudarshan Chakra symbolizes the protection of the good and the destruction of the evil. It embodies the concept of time, which is cyclical in nature and is the ultimate force in the universe that's responsible for the creation and annihilation of all things. The Chakra's constant spinning represents the eternal and timeless nature of the soul and the divine.

Sources/Further Reading:

"Mahabharata"
"Hindu Myths: A Sourcebook" by Wendy Doniger O'Flaherty

Talaria

The Talaria, commonly known as the Sandals of Hermes, are a legendary pair of winged sandals worn by Hermes, the ancient Greek god of messengers, travelers, and thieves. These sandals granted him the incredible ability to fly and move with unmatched swiftness, making Hermes one of the speediest of all the Olympian deities. Their iconic design and mythological significance link them to the idea of swift communication and the traversing of boundaries.

Hermes' swiftness, amplified by the Talaria, often came to the aid of other gods and heroes. For instance, when Zeus sought to free

Io from the watchful eye of the hundred-eyed giant Argus, it was Hermes who was dispatched. Using his cunning and the advantage of his speed, Hermes lulled Argus to sleep and freed Io.

The Talaria were crafted by the god Hephaestus, the divine blacksmith and craftsman of Olympus. Hephaestus was known to create various magnificent items for the gods, and the winged sandals were among his most iconic inventions. They were typically described as being made of imperishable gold and gave Hermes the ability to move freely between the mortal and divine realms, making him a mediator and messenger for the gods.

The First Talaria

Born in a cave on Mount Cyllene to Maia, one of the Pleiades, and Zeus, Hermes was a precocious child, showcasing his cunning and adventurous spirit from the very beginning. On the day of his birth or, by some accounts, when he was merely a few days old, Hermes decided to undertake a daring venture.

Late at night, while Maia rested, Hermes sneaked out of their cave. Using his inherent wit, he crafted shoes from palm and tamarisk leaves to disguise his tracks. In some versions, these are considered an early form of the Talaria. With these, he was able to walk in various deceptive patterns, sometimes backward, ensuring no one could trace his path.

Hermes soon reached Pieria, where Apollo kept his radiant cattle. Quickly, the mischievous infant hid fifty of Apollo's cows, driving them to a distant location. As an extra measure to ensure the cattle wouldn't leave tracks, he made them walk backward. Furthermore, Hermes crafted a lyre from a tortoise shell during his journey, showcasing his inventive nature.

When Apollo discovered the theft, he was incensed. However, tracing the thief was a challenge because of the confusing tracks Hermes left. Thanks to his prophetic abilities, Apollo soon realized it was Hermes who had stolen his cattle. However, proving it was another matter, given Hermes' careful steps to cover his mischief.

Apollo confronted Hermes, but the young god played innocent, emphasizing his youth and claiming he was just born and knew nothing of cattle. Their arguments reached the ears of Zeus, who found the situation amusing but asked Hermes to return the cattle.

Before the tale concludes, Hermes played the lyre he had crafted for Apollo, enchanting the Sun God with its melodies. In exchange for this beautiful instrument, Apollo allowed Hermes to keep several of the cows. This mutual exchange marked the beginning of a lifelong bond between the two gods, with Hermes becoming an ally to Apollo and often serving as his messenger.

Throughout this tale, the early form of the Talaria—those leafy shoes—served as a testament to Hermes' cunning, resourcefulness, and audacious nature, emphasizing his role as a trickster god even from infancy. The sandals, or his innovative foot coverings, were key to his scheme's success, allowing him to baffle even the wise Apollo temporarily.

Hermes' primary role was as the messenger of the gods. With the Talaria on his feet, he could swiftly deliver messages, orders, and divine decrees from Olympus to any destination, be it another divine realm, the world of mortals, or even the Underworld. Apart from his duties as a messenger, Hermes also guided the souls of the deceased to the Underworld. The Talaria facilitated his movement between the realms, ensuring the souls reached their final destination with Hades.

The Rescue of Persephone

The story begins with Persephone, the daughter of Demeter, the goddess of agriculture, and Zeus. One day, while Persephone was gathering flowers in a meadow, the ground beneath her opened up. From this chasm, Hades, the lord of the Underworld, emerged and abducted her, taking her to his dark realm to be his queen. The act was not entirely random; Hades had previously sought Zeus' permission to marry Persephone. However, neither god had involved Demeter or Persephone in this decision.

Devastated by her daughter's sudden disappearance, Demeter searched the earth for her. When she learned of the deception by Zeus and the abduction by Hades, her grief turned to anger. In her despair, Demeter neglected her divine duties. The earth became barren, crops withered, and famine spread. This state of affairs alarmed the other gods, for humanity's prayers and offerings ceased as they struggled to survive.

Zeus, realizing the severity of the situation and hoping to appease Demeter, decided to intervene. He dispatched Hermes, the messenger god, to the Underworld to broker Persephone's release. Adorning the Talaria, those winged sandals granting him swift and safe passage between realms, Hermes descended to the shadowy depths of Hades' domain.

In the Underworld, Hermes delivered Zeus' command to Hades, urging him to release Persephone. Hades, not one to be easily swayed, agreed but not before he tricked Persephone into eating pomegranate seeds. According to ancient lore, consuming food or drink of the Underworld bound the soul to that realm. Because Persephone had eaten a few pomegranate seeds, she was compelled to spend a portion of each year, typically the colder months, with Hades as the queen of the Underworld. For the rest of the year, she was free to return to the world above and her grieving mother.

Hermes, with the speed and assurance provided by the Talaria, escorted Persephone out of the dark confines of the Underworld and reunited her with Demeter. The earth once again flourished as Demeter, in joy, resumed her divine responsibilities. However, the annual cycle of growth and retreat—summer and winter—was established, reflecting Persephone's dual life between the Underworld and the world above.

The Talaria, as a symbol, represents more than just speed. They emphasize the fluidity with which Hermes operates - moving between realms, bridging the gap between gods and mortals, and ensuring that boundaries, no matter how formidable, can be crossed. The sandals also symbolize the omnipresence of divine will and the rapidity with which fate can change in Greek mythology.

Though they might seem like a simple pair of sandals at first glance, the Talaria are imbued with a deep significance in Greek mythology. They not only amplify the attributes of Hermes but also serve as a reminder of the interconnectedness of the world, the realms, and the ever-watchful gaze and reach of the divine.

Sources/Further Reading:

"Theogony" by Hesiod
"Hermes the Thief: The Evolution of a Myth" by Norman O. Brown
"Greek Myths" by Robert Graves

The Boots of Seven Leagues

The Boots of Seven Leagues are a legendary artifact from European folklore, specifically from French fairy tales. As their name suggests, these enchanted boots grant the wearer the ability to take strides that cover seven leagues (roughly 21 miles) in a single step. This allows for swift travel across vast distances, making them an incredibly valuable item for those embarking on epic quests or attempting to evade pursuit.

The Boots of Seven Leagues are mentioned in several European fairy tales, but they are most famously associated with French folklore. The origin of these boots is not tied to a single narrative, but rather, they are recurring items that various heroes come across during their adventures.

Hop-o'-My-Thumb and the Boots of Seven Leagues

In Charles Perrault's classic tale, Hop-o'-My-Thumb is the smallest and cleverest of seven brothers. Born no bigger than his father's thumb, he possesses an acute sense of wit and intelligence that compensates for his diminutive stature. The family, impoverished and struggling for food, makes the heartbreaking decision to abandon their children in the forest, thinking it would be a kinder fate than starvation.

Lost and forlorn, the brothers come upon a grand house in the middle of the woods. Little did they know, it belonged to a terrifying ogre who has a propensity for eating children. Hop-o'-My-Thumb, sensing the danger but also seeing an opportunity, devises a plan to save himself and his brothers. He convinces the ogre's wife to let them stay for the night, and when the ogre returns with the intention of feasting on the brothers, Hop-o'-My-Thumb switches the gold crowns of the sleeping ogre's daughters with the nightcaps of his brothers. The ogre, fooled by this ruse, ends up killing his own daughters instead.

Realizing his grave mistake and filled with rage, the ogre decides to pursue the brothers. Hop-o'-My-Thumb notices a pair of magical boots in the ogre's home – the Boots of Seven Leagues. Recognizing their value and potential for escape, he steals them. These boots, which allow the wearer to cover seven leagues in a single step, give Hop-o'-My-Thumb a significant advantage.

With the Boots of Seven Leagues, Hop-o'-My-Thumb swiftly leads his brothers away from the ogre's clutches. The ogre, despite his size and strength, cannot match the speed granted by the magical boots. In his desperate pursuit, the ogre eventually exhausts himself and falls into a ravine, meeting his end.

Thanks to the Boots of Seven Leagues and Hop-o'-My-Thumb's ingenuity, the brothers safely return home, and with treasures taken from the ogre's home, they lift their family out of poverty. The story concludes with the family living happily ever after, their bond stronger than ever and their home full of joy and prosperity.

"The Red Ettin" by George Douglas, is a Scottish fairy tale that is found in collections of folktales and fairy stories, particularly those gathered by folklorists in the 19th and early 20th centuries. In this tale, the protagonist embarks on a challenging quest, during which he is gifted the Boots of Seven Leagues, a magical artifact that allows him to traverse vast distances with a single step.

The Quest of the Red Ettin

In a land shrouded in sorrow, a nefarious creature known as the Red Ettin kidnapped the beloved princess. The king, desperate to have his daughter returned, proclaimed that anyone who rescued her would have her hand in marriage and inherit the kingdom. Among the many suitors, a young and brave hero, devoid of title or riches, stepped forward, determined to rescue the princess and win her heart.

As the young hero began his quest, he encountered an old woman with piercing eyes and a knowing aura. She listened to his tale and, seeing the determination in his eyes, decided to aid him. "In your journey, you'll face treacherous landscapes and deadly obstacles," she said. With those words, she handed him the Boots of Seven Leagues. These were no ordinary boots; they held the power to allow the wearer to cover vast distances in mere moments.

With the boots aiding him, the hero tackled dense forests, vast mountains, and arid deserts, all within days instead of the months it would've taken him. The Red Ettin's lair was located atop a massive mountain surrounded by an impassable moat, but with the Boots of Seven Leagues, such challenges were trivial.

Reaching the lair, the hero discovered the Red Ettin was not just a kidnapper; he was a sorcerer with the power to summon creatures from the underworld. But the hero, with his quick wit and the agility provided by the boots, dodged every spell and creature the Ettin sent his way.

As the battle raged on, the hero managed to find the source of the Ettin's power - a magical staff. With a swift motion, he used the boots' speed to snatch the staff away, rendering the Ettin powerless. Defeated and at the hero's mercy, the Red Ettin pleaded for his life, promising to never harm another soul.

The hero freed the princess, and together, with the Boots of Seven Leagues, they quickly returned to the kingdom. The land rejoiced at the return of their princess and the defeat of the Red Ettin. True to his word, the king offered the hero his daughter's hand in marriage and the right to the throne. The kingdom celebrated the union and the hero's bravery, and they all lived happily ever after. The Boots of Seven Leagues were safely kept, reminding all of the lengths one would go to for love and honor.

The Boots of Seven Leagues symbolize the ability to overcome obstacles and traverse challenging paths. In many tales, they serve as a tool of empowerment, granting the protagonist the means to face larger threats, surpass insurmountable barriers, or achieve seemingly impossible tasks. Just as other magical items in folklore often have deeper meanings, the boots can be seen as a representation of resourcefulness, determination, and the human spirit's ability to journey through and overcome hardships.

Sources/Further Reading:

"The Complete Fairy Tales of Charles Perrault"
"Scottish Fairy and Folk Tales" by George Douglas
“Folk and Fairy Tales: A Handbook” by D.L. Ashliman

Yasakani no Magatama

The Yasakani no Magatama is a sacred jewel or comma-shaped bead. The magatama's shape, which is somewhat similar to a curved bead with a tail, has ancient origins and has been found in prehistoric sites in Japan, often made of jade. Over time, the magatama came to possess religious and ceremonial significance.

As one of the Three Sacred Treasures, the Yasakani no Magatama is also a symbol of the Japanese Imperial line's legitimacy and divine authority.

While it doesn't offer powers like invisibility, flight, or invulnerability, the Yasakani no Magatama's profound spiritual significance and its role in Japan's foundational myths imbue it with a different kind of "power" – that of deep cultural resonance and divine connection.

Amaterasu and the Yasakani no Magatama

In the expansive panorama of Japanese mythology, the tale of Amaterasu's seclusion stands out as a poignant tale of conflict, despair, and eventual reconciliation.

The story begins with a fallout between Amaterasu, the radiant sun goddess, and her impulsive younger brother, Susanoo, the storm god. Susanoo's disruptive antics, which included throwing a flayed horse into Amaterasu's weaving hall, deeply upset the sun goddess. Distraught and feeling disrespected, Amaterasu retreated into the Amano-Iwato cave, shrouding the world in darkness and leaving the myriad gods and humanity in a state of desolation.

The deities convened to devise a plan to bring back the sun. Among their number was the clever goddess Ame-no-Uzume. Realizing the severity of a world devoid of sunlight, she orchestrated an elaborate plan to coax Amaterasu out.

Near the entrance of the cave, the gods hung the Yasakani no Magatama, along with the Yata no Kagami, a sacred mirror. Ame-no-Uzume, known for her wit and energy, began an entertaining and provocative dance, causing uproarious laughter among the gods. Their joy, combined with the mysterious allure of the glowing jewel and the captivating reflection in the mirror, piqued Amaterasu's curiosity.

Slowly, the sun goddess peeked out to see the source of the merriment. As she did, she caught sight of her own radiant reflection in the Yata no Kagami and was further drawn by the allure of the Yasakani no Magatama. Another god took the opportunity to pull her out completely, and another secured the cave so she couldn't retreat again.

With Amaterasu's emergence, light and warmth returned, breathing life back into the world. The Yasakani no Magatama, along with the other sacred treasures, were not just instruments in this tale, but potent symbols. The jewel, with its deep lustrous glow, represented both the allure and the importance of harmony, underscoring the need for balance and reconciliation among conflicting forces.

The Magatama has been used since ancient times in Japan, predating even the story of Amaterasu. These comma-shaped beads have been found at various archaeological sites in Japan, and they are thought to have been used as religious objects, signifying a connection with the spiritual world, or used as protective amulets. The unique shape of the Magatama has led some to associate it with a representation of the soul or life force.

The jewel's presence in various Shinto rituals underlines its importance as an instrument connecting humanity, deities, and the spiritual realm. It signifies a bridge or a medium in these rituals.

The actual location of the Yasakani no Magatama, like the other Imperial Regalia, remains one of Japan's closely guarded secrets. They are believed to be housed in the Shinto Grand Shrines of Ise in the Mie Prefecture but are not available for public display.

Sources/Further Reading:

"The Kojiki"
"Japanese Mythology" by Juliet Piggott
"Shinto: The Kami Way" by Sokyo Ono

Yata no Kagami

The Yata no Kagami, translating to "Eight Span Mirror," is one of the Three Sacred Treasures of Japan. Along with the Yasakani no Magatama (jewel) and the Kusanagi no Tsurugi (sword), this mirror symbolizes one of the primary virtues of the Japanese Imperial Throne. Specifically, the Yata no Kagami represents wisdom.

The mirror's shape is said to be a representation of balance, integration, and harmony, blending the four cardinal directions and the points in between. This signifies completeness, encompassing the entirety of the world and the universe.

The tale of the Yata no Kagami is intricately tied to the story of the sun goddess, Amaterasu, and her brother, the storm god Susanoo. In Shinto mythology, following an altercation with Susanoo, Amaterasu became distraught and withdrew into the Amano-Iwato, a celestial cave, plunging the world into darkness.

Amaterasu and the Yata no Kagami

Amaterasu, the sun goddess, and Susanoo, the storm god, are siblings with a relationship that can be best described as tempestuous. While Amaterasu is the embodiment of the sun's warmth and nurturing light, Susanoo is the representation of storms, often seen as unpredictable and occasionally destructive.

The tension between them reached its peak when Susanoo, having been banished from the Heavens by his father Izanagi, went on a rampage. In a fit of rage and jealousy, he destroyed Amaterasu's rice fields, hurled a flayed horse into her weaving hall, and even killed one of her attendants. These malicious acts were unbearable for the gentle sun goddess. Heartbroken and overwhelmed, she chose to seclude herself in the Amano-Iwato, a celestial cave, effectively depriving the world of her essential light. A permanent night fell, causing panic and distress among the gods and mortals alike.

Understanding the gravity of the situation, the myriad deities convened at the entrance of the cave to deliberate on the crisis at hand. They realized that without Amaterasu's illumination, life on Earth would be jeopardized. The gods, under the leadership of the deity of wisdom and strategy, Omoikane, hatched a plan to coax Amaterasu out.

The gods forged and polished the Yata no Kagami, a mirror with brilliant radiance, and hung it on a Sakaki tree outside the cave, flanking it with the Yasakani no Magatama, a sacred jewel. Ame-no-Uzume, the goddess of dawn and revelry, devised the main act of the plan. Uprooting a nearby tree, she crafted a makeshift stage. With her garments loosely tied and baring her chest, she commenced a passionate, divine dance, causing uproarious laughter among the gods.

The jubilant noises outside piqued the interest of the secluded goddess. As she slightly opened the cave, the light from the Yata no Kagami reflected her own luminance, drawing her attention. Mistaking it for another radiant deity or perhaps a replacement sun, her curiosity was further fueled. As she emerged more to get a clearer view, Ame-no-Uzume's dance reached its crescendo, and the cheers grew louder.

Using this distraction, the powerful god Tajikarao took the opportunity to pull Amaterasu entirely out, while other gods hastily rolled a celestial boulder, sealing the entrance to the cave. With Amaterasu's emergence, the world was bathed in her light once more, restoring balance and vitality to the realm.

The Yata no Kagami's reflection not only lured Amaterasu from her seclusion but served as a reminder of her own importance and the indispensability of her light. As a symbol of wisdom, the mirror encourages introspection and understanding. It reflects things as they truly are, free from illusion or deceit.

In Japanese spiritual belief, mirrors are often considered to be vessels of truth, reflecting things as they genuinely are, devoid of deception. The Yata no Kagami, being associated with the sun goddess Amaterasu, is believed to carry her virtues, reflecting purity, clarity, and brilliance.

In the context of the Imperial Regalia, the Yata no Kagami also stands for "honesty" or "brightness" and symbolizes the Emperor's wisdom and honesty. Like the other Imperial Regalia, the Yata no Kagami is believed to be housed in one of the Imperial Palaces in Japan, specifically at the Ise Grand Shrine in Mie Prefecture. However, it's not on public display, and its actual existence, like the other treasures, remains a matter of faith.

Further Reading/Sources:

"Kojiki"
"Nihon Shoki" or "Chronicles of Japan"

Final Words

As we conclude this journey through the mosaic of human imagination, pieced together with the fragments of mythical artifacts, we are reminded that these objects are more than mere relics of the past. They are vessels of wisdom, bearers of tales that have transcended time and space. Each artifact encapsulates the essence of cultures, the dreams of civilizations, and the boundless creativity of humanity.

In the realm of myths and legends, these artifacts hold the keys to unlocking our shared heritage—a heritage that speaks of our collective aspirations, fears, and the eternal quest for understanding. They remind us that the human spirit is a mosaic in itself, intricately pieced together with stories, dreams, and the eternal longing for the extraordinary.

However, it is important to acknowledge that myths, legends, and the interpretations around them can vary, and sometimes be deeply personal. If any part of this compendium has caused discomfort or seemed inconsiderate, I sincerely apologize. The aim has always been to celebrate and honor these tales, not to diminish or offend.

Just as the heroes and heroines of old embarked on epic quests to wield these treasures, so have you journeyed through these pages, delving into the enigmatic stories behind each artifact. As you close this book, remember that the magic of these artifacts lives on, not just in their storied pasts, but in the mosaic of your own imagination.

May the tales of these artifacts continue to inspire, illuminate, and find their place in your heart, forever enriching the grand saga of myths that unite us all.

Thank you for embarking on this wondrous odyssey.

Dear Reader,

If you want to know more about me and follow me for new updates on upcoming launches, you may scan the below QR code:

If you want to provide feedback on this book or sign up for email notifications on upcoming launches, you may scan the below QR code:

Also, if you haven't checked out my other book please check it out on Amazon.

Finally, please support the Author and review this book from where it was purchased.

Printed in Great Britain
by Amazon

32374068R00155